CRIMSON CHAOS

STEEL ROSES MOTORCYCLE CLUB
BOOK 1

JENA DOYLE

To my best friend and partner —
42

1

ALBA

Most young girls dream of being a doctor when they grow up. Or a teacher. Something reasonable.

Definitely not a cam girl.

Like many people in sex work, I found myself here by circumstance. Specifically, financial. Which, in my case, said more about the state of the healthcare crisis in America than it did about me as a person. I had once worked full-time at the library. I was a law-abiding citizen.

And yet... none of that saved me when the Big C came knocking on my family's door. It didn't do a lick of good when the cells in my mother's body revolted and mutated, hiding in her pancreas and spreading to her brain before she could do anything about it. With the cancer now in its late stage, my mother had been left bedridden and reliant on expensive medicines insurance simply wouldn't cover.

It drove me fucking nuts. What good was insurance if it didn't help when you needed it?

I'd had to improvise. It started with flashing my tits to lonely people on the internet. And now, my page, "Crimson," garnered thousands of views a day. I wore a kitten mask covering the top half of my face and named myself Aurora Dawn, a play on my real name, Alba, which meant *dawn* in Spanish. All this to say, strangers paid handsomely to watch me masturbate, and I wasn't ashamed of it.

Eventually, I made enough money to quit my day job and perform full-time. But there were limits to what I could do myself. Sure, a clientele for solo girls existed. But most people who watched hetero-presenting porn wanted to see a hot guy railing some much hotter girl. I got comments like:

I bet those lips look great wrapped around a cock.

I wanna see you get fucked.

Can you do a cream pie scene?

Which was why I'd decided to come to this burning dumpster of a party. My friend, Aliza, invited me, but friend was a generous word for our relationship. I hadn't been to one of her parties in ages, but tonight, I was on a mission to find someone I trusted. A partner. A coworker. I made good money on my own, but I could double or triple my income if I had someone to scene with.

I sat on the couch in her parents' sunroom and looked at the mingling bodies while I sipped my tepid beer, weighing my options.

There was Jason Gilbert. Apparently he had a big cock, but he was a bit of a player, and I'd insist on exclusivity while we were filming. Next was Rick Pierson, who was attractive in that boy-next-door sort of way. I'd long suspected he might be gay, even if he wasn't out yet. Hell, I could be wrong.

The couch dipped next to me as a tall guy wearing a leather cut lowered his big body onto it. I narrowed my eyes and pushed my glasses higher up my nose while I tried to recall if I knew him from somewhere.

No. I'd definitely remember those tattoos. They covered his hands and arms, disappearing under his black T-shirt, only to reemerge up by his collarbone, twisting along his neck to his jawline. His brown hair was shaved on the sides and longer on the top, styled back away from his face. He had on dark jeans and black leather boots, but it was the symbol on the cut that got my attention.

KC, it said on one side. *Steel Roses MC* was on the other.

He leaned back on the couch and ran his hands down his thighs, glancing at the party. He seemed uncomfortable... perhaps even more than I was. And for someone as beautiful as him, that struck me as odd.

What did he have to be uncomfortable about? Those cheekbones, those haunting blue eyes, those tattoos, and that smile? I would bet he walked into rooms and women dropped to their knees. I was nearly there myself.

"Hey." He nodded when he caught me staring.

I quickly looked away and smiled, licking my lips before saying, "Hey."

God, I'm a fucking mess. I'd been openly gawking at him, eyeing him like a piece of meat. *What the fuck is wrong with me?*

"I'm Jericho," he said.

"Alba," I replied.

"Are you having a good time?" He gestured around to everyone.

I shrugged. "It's okay."

"Just okay?"

"I haven't seen most of these people in forever." I took another sip of my beer. "They haven't changed at all."

He smiled, seeming to understand what I meant. It wasn't a good thing. They still drank their lives away, partying and acting like idiots. And why shouldn't they? They didn't have a care in the world, the lucky pricks.

"But you have?" he said.

I looked at him, my lips thinning as I pondered what he meant.

"They haven't changed," he explained. "But you have."

"Life comes for us hard and fast," I said.

"Indeed, it does."

"Are you having a good time?"

He shrugged. "Better now that I've met you."

"Ah." I chuckled. "Smooth."

"Was it?" He laughed. "I'm not good at this sort of thing."

"What sort of thing?"

"The whole meeting a pretty girl at a party and striking up a conversation thing."

I fiddled with a string on my cardigan. *Did... did he just call me pretty?* A wicked heat snaked up my chest and into my cheeks. "I doubt that."

"You'd be surprised." He winked at me, and a blush rose up my neck and into my cheeks.

Look, I ran a website where people whacked off to my asshole for a living. I'd been called everything under the sun. Beautiful. Sexy. Big titty Goddess. People would say anything when they're horny.

That was Aurora Dawn taking those compliments. Aurora was the beautiful, sexy, big titty Goddess. Alba was a glasses-wearing nerd who liked *Star Wars* and used to play D&D with her internet friends on the weekends. Alba didn't care about being pretty because she had better shit to worry about than what some stupid man thought of her appearance. But when Jericho did it, something flamed to life inside of me that had long since wilted and shriveled up to die.

He tilted his head toward me and flashed a big smile.

Such a nice smile.

It made him look sweet and innocent, even if the tattoos and leather cut told another tale. They said he was someone who would kill you for saying the wrong thing. Someone who could beat the living hell out of anything in his path.

I bit my bottom lip and pretended not to be interested.

"What do you do for a living, Alba?"

"I'm a librarian." Not technically a lie, if not the complete truth.

"Do you enjoy that?"

"I do," I answered honestly.

"Why?"

I shrugged. "Books are immortalizing."

He narrowed his eyes. "Explain."

"My mom says every time you make something, you put a piece of your soul into it. A whole book? That's a big chunk of soul." I raised my eyebrows. "And the library is filled with them. Words from people who've long since died. Words that can never be *un*written."

"That's..." He whistled and shook his head. "That's profound."

I playfully nudged his shoulder. "Don't mock me."

"I'm not," he said. "I guess I never thought about it like that."

I froze, assessing him. He really wasn't teasing me. He was... *impressed.*

"What about you?" I said. "What do you do all day?"

"I work at my uncle's shop. The Rose Garage on Mount Zion."

"Yeah, I know where it is." Right down the street from my house. I used to walk there when I was a little girl and buy ice cream cones out of the freezer in the back. "Your uncle is Thor?"

He nodded. "Yeah. You know him?"

I told him about living close by. "My house is the last one on the mountain, way up in the sticks."

"Yeah," he said. "I used to wander up there to smoke we—" He chuckled awkwardly, scratching at the back of his head. "Uh, to get away from my uncle."

I laughed and leaned in closer, whispering, "It's okay. I smoke weed up there, too. It's a nice private spot."

"It is," he said. "Great views." He took another drink of water.

"What brings you to Aliza's party?" I asked. "You know someone here?"

Are you dating someone here? The words were on the tip of my tongue, but I held back because what did it matter if he was? He was *wayyyy* out of my league.

"Nah." He pointed to a guy in the next room also wearing a Steel Roses cut. "My brother, Trojan. He's meeting up with a few people."

I knew who Trojan was. Aliza and her friends had been referring to him as the *Drug Man* earlier in the night. All the pieces came together. Trojan and Jericho were Roses, and everyone knew the Roses were criminals. They were into some dark shit. Drugs. Weapons. Territory wars with the DC mafia.

He leaned in closer to whisper, "I'm tagging along for backup."

I nodded, and he narrowed his eyes, as if by getting closer, he was able to see deeper inside. Maybe discover my secrets.

"You sure we've never met before?" he asked. "You look familiar."

"I don't think so," I said. "You're remarkable. I would have remembered you."

He gave me a killer grin, and his cheeks turned a bright rosy pink. "You think I'm remarkable?"

"Your tattoos are amazing," I said. "And you have a nice smile."

"Thanks, Alba." He clutched his chest. "Wow. And to think... you were right up that mountain this whole time."

"Yep," I said. "Maybe we ran into each other when I was little. I haven't been to that garage in a while."

"No." He wagged a long, callused finger at me. "I'd remember someone like you." He leaned in again. This time, he brought his lips to my ear, brushing my blonde hair over my shoulder before saying, "You're remarkable, too."

When I laughed, the sound came from somewhere inside me that needed a release. It had been trapped for so long that the act itself seemed defiant. Was I allowed to enjoy myself like this when my mother was at home in her bed with a nurse watching over her? Was I allowed to be reveling in this man's attention when she was suffering so much?

Remember why you're here, Alba. You're looking for a business partner. Not a boyfriend.

"Now you're just flattering me." I tugged at my sleeves, yanking them down over my hands.

"What makes you say that?"

I gestured around to the people I went to school with. "I've been here for two hours. You're the first person to talk to me. They don't care that I'm here."

"Bah." He waved away my comment. "They're young and stupid."

"Not that much younger than you."

His eyes lit up with surprise. "How old do you think I am?"

I assessed him. Certainly old enough to have gotten all those tattoos. They looked well done, so he must have paid good money for them. No wedding ring, a good sign, but his face still had a youthful-ness that men grew out of when they hit their mid-thirties.

"Twenty-seven," I said.

"Damn," he said. "How the fuck did you know that?"

"Lucky guess." I took another nervous drink of my beer. "How old do you think I am?"

"Twenty-one."

"Close," I said. "Twenty-two."

He shook his head and sighed. "Well, *you're* obviously not young and stupid. Everyone else is."

"Nice save."

"If everyone ignores you, why are you here?" he said. "I mean... why stay?"

I considered lying, maybe saying I needed to get out of the house and meet new people, even though I'd known most of these people my entire life. But I honestly didn't think I'd ever see Jericho again. He was in a motorcycle club. I took care of my dying mother all day. After she passed, I planned to leave Madison County altogether. I promised her I'd use some of her life insurance money to backpack across Europe and see the world. I didn't have time for attachments. I didn't have time for distractions.

By this point in the night, I'd had a few drinks and gotten liberal with my tongue. So when I opened my mouth, out came the truth. "I'm looking for someone to fuck."

Jericho choked on his water, coughing as his face turned red. He leaned forward to set his bottle down on the coffee table so he could pound on his chest.

"Are you okay?" I patted his back.

"Yeah," he wheezed out. "I just... didn't expect you to say that."

"Sorry to surprise you."

"Don't be sorry," he said. "Goddamn. Really? Who are you trying to fuck? Point him out." He paused. "Or her. I don't judge."

"It's not that simple," I said.

"Sounds pretty simple to me."

"No, it's..."

Am I really about to tell him this?

In for a penny...

"I run a website where people pay to watch me masturbate."

He was silent for a moment, darting his eyes back and forth between mine like he was debating whether I told the truth.

"I have videos on other sites, too," I said, talking to fill the gaping chasm between us. "But most of my income is from my own page. I've been doing well by myself, but people want to see me cream pied, so…" I took another awkward sip of my beer, swallowing it down even though it tasted like garbage. I needed something to do with my hands. "Gotta give the fans what they want, right?"

"Oh my God," he said, blinking as he sat up straighter. "Oh. My. Fucking. God."

"What?"

"You're Aurora Dawn." His eyes lit up like he'd just met a Kardashian.

"Uh…" I straightened, panic flushing through me as I glanced around to make sure no one else heard him.

"You are." He grabbed my wrist and yanked up the sleeve of my cardigan, his hand like a vise grip around my bones. But the touch… oh, the touch vibrated through me. I ignored that and focused on his gaze, currently on the tattoo on the inside of my wrist: a scorpion, my astrological sign.

"Lots of girls have a scorpion tattooed on their wrists," I tried.

"Yeah, but not every girl has those pretty doe eyes."

I yanked my arm free. "No one else knows. I'm trying to keep it that way."

"Your secret is safe with me, sunshine." He took another drink of water and shook his head. "Wow. Go to some backwoods party, meet my favorite porn star. Who would have thought?"

"It's not the 1970s," I said. "No one says porn star anymore. I'm a cam girl."

"I'm the luckiest son of a bitch in the world," he said. "Can I get your autograph or something?"

"Okay, now you're making it weird."

He chuckled, and I liked the sound. It had an infectious quality that made me want to laugh just hearing it.

"Wait," he said, something finally occurring to him. "Why are you looking for someone here? Don't you have any number of fuckable porn stars... excuse me, cam boys ... at your disposal?"

I sighed. "They wanna fuck around. I'm looking for someone to be exclusive."

"Oh," he said. "Why?"

"Cream pie, remember?" I smiled. "Why, are you interested?"

He laughed, obviously thinking I was joking, and I wasn't entirely sure that I was. He took another drink of water before saying, "What about your folks? Do they know what you do?"

"I don't know my dad," I said. "Mom suspects, but it's a boundary between us. She hasn't asked, so I haven't told her. Not that I think she'd care."

"Why's that?"

"She's into that free-the-nipple nonsense. She'd probably think it was smart, duping idiots out of their money by showing my vulva."

"Hey." He pretended to be offended. "I'm one of those idiots."

I eyed him up and down. "You don't look like the type of guy who pays for porn."

"I'm not, but I'm curious what makes you think that."

"Like I said... remarkable. You probably have a trail of broken hearts behind you."

"I could say the same about you, and here you sit, alone and looking for someone to fuck."

"And to put it on the internet," I said. "Don't forget that part. If it was just the fucking, I wouldn't be having such a hard time."

I didn't look like much when I was in Alba's skin—glasses, tweed skirt, cardigan. I was every librarian stereotype ever. It didn't help that I actually *was* a librarian. Or I used to be before Mom got sick.

My disguise was intentional, after all. If I'd learned anything from Superman, it only took a pair of glasses to make a person unrecognizable, and like I said, I wasn't ready for everyone to know Aurora Dawn and Alba Wright wore the same skin.

However, with a little makeup, some hairspray, and a cute outfit, Aurora Dawn could have everybody in this room hard and panting in seconds. The confidence of that gave Alba the indifference to carry on with the disguise.

The conversation drifted to other things, and as we talked, I got more comfortable telling him about myself. I circled around to taking a sabbatical to care for my mother, which had led him to telling me about his parents dying when he was little. That was how he'd came to live with his uncle. "Thor's not my blood uncle. He was married to my aunt, but she's gone now, too."

He said the word "gone," and I assumed she also died. But his features dropped like it was painful to talk about, so I didn't ask.

"I still have my sister," he said. "And the MC, of course. My real uncle, my dad's brother, is the president. So I got a couple of cousins and stuff."

After my mom died, I wouldn't have anyone, not even grandparents. Dad left before I was born, and Mom was an only child. She'd never regretted having me, but if she could do it again, she would have enjoyed more of her youth. Having a child changed her priorities. Hence the promise I made. The promise I intended to keep.

I told him about that, too, and for the very first time since Aurora Dawn was born, my two personalities became one. In Jericho, I found a confidant. I figured, fuck it, I'd never see him again. After this party was over, I'd go home empty-handed, and he'd forget about me. I'd drive by his garage every day, remembering this conversation and wishing I'd had the ovaries to ask him out when I had the chance. But I didn't. It was better this way, right?

Hours ticked by like seconds, and pretty soon, it was near midnight. The nurse I'd hired to watch my mother left on the dot, so I couldn't be late.

"Well, Jericho," I said. "It was so nice to meet you. I have to go. The caregiver for my mom gets off soon."

"Oh." His tone was somber, but he nodded and stood while I fiddled with my ride-share app.

"It was really good to meet you," he said. "I hope I run into you again."

He held out his hand for me to shake. Like it was as simple as that. Like I hadn't just bared my whole soul and every fucked-up thing about it to him, and he hadn't just told me about his deep, dark demons.

I shook it, smiling and waving before I turned to leave, deciding to wait for my ride outside. But once I was there, a small spark of outrage lit in my gut.

We'd had a great conversation and connection. I told him about Alba and Aurora, why I was there, and what I wanted. Everything.

Why, are you interested?

God, I was an idiot. Of course, he wasn't interested in having sex on camera. I snorted at his outdated term... *porn star*. But, we had good chemistry, right? He seemed interested in me before he found out who I was, and he kept flirting with me after that.

Why didn't he make a play for my number?

Why didn't he want to see me again?

Why did he let me leave like that?

That tiny spark grew into full-blown fury the more I thought about it.

Goddamn it.

I didn't know if it was the beer or the way we'd been so honest with each other that had me turning around to hunt him down. I found him in the kitchen, twisting the cap off a new bottle of water.

"Hey!" I marched up to him, my hands balled into fists.

"Hey, you're back." His grin almost melted my rage. *Almost.*

"Why didn't you ask for my number?"

He seemed confused at first, his eyebrows furrowing.

"Why'd you let me leave? Why didn't you ask for my number?"

"Whoa, whoa." He held his hands up. "Are you seriously pissed about that?"

"I mean... a little." I crossed my arms, suddenly self-conscious. "I told you my secret identity and everything."

He threw his head back and laughed, the joyous sound ringing through me. "Alba, you told me where you lived."

I took a step back, my frustration evaporating when I understood what he meant.

I'm so ridiculous. "Oh."

"I was going to stop by tomorrow morning on my way to work to make sure you got home safe," he said. "Though it's cute that you got angry because you didn't get enough attention. What? Two million fans not enough for you?"

"Shut up." I scowled, pushing my glasses higher up my face.

"What's your number?" He reached into his pocket and held his phone out for me. I snatched it and sent myself a text message so I'd have his number, too.

"There," he said. "Happy?"

"Very." I turned on my heels to leave, my ride only two minutes away now, but he shot his hand out and wrapped it around my wrist to stop me. This time, the touch made me tremble, especially when he traced his thumb over my tattoo.

"Oh, no you don't." He pressed his chest against my back and his mouth right next to my ear, the hot breath from his words shooting down the front of my sweater. "You got mad at me for letting you walk out of here the first time. I only need to learn my lesson once."

I shivered. Actually shook right there in his arms.

He felt it, too, because he hummed a noise of approval and moved around me, tugging me along behind him as we walked. He put his phone up to his ear and muttered something about leaving. I assumed he was talking to Trojan. When his buddy agreed, Jericho led me out front, and we walked down the street. I vaguely noticed an Uber waiting for me and cursed myself at the fine for that before cancelling it with my free hand.

"Where are we going?" I hissed.

"I better see you home safe myself." We stopped in front of a beautiful obsidian Harley with ruby flames down either side of the tank. "Girls like that shit, right?" He handed me a helmet and lifted a leg over the machine, pulling it upright as he twisted the key in the ignition. "It shows initiative."

I opened my mouth to protest, but he kicked the bike to life and the words died in my mouth. Here was this super-hot biker guy offering to give me a free ride home. Yeah, he was a stranger, but I knew his uncle as well as any young girl knew the guy who ran the corner store at the end of her street. He was a familiar face for someone who didn't have many.

I could trust him, right? He wasn't about to take me to some dark alley to rape and murder me? He *was* a Rose, after all. Those hands had probably choked the life out of a few people. I should have been more scared. Every logical, rational side of me *knew* that.

But I'd spent the better part of three hours telling him all my dark secrets, some of which my mother didn't even know. That eased my hesitation. I put on the helmet and climbed on the bike behind him, wrapping my arms around his stomach so I could hold on for dear life as he drove me home.

2

———————

ALBA

Twenty minutes.

That's all it took for me to fall in love with his motorcycle.

Twenty minutes of my legs around his hips, the wind in my hair, and his firm ass tucked right up against my pelvis. I never listened to anyone who said they bought a bike "because they're fun to ride." Bikes were not fun. They were bulky and heavy and expensive to fix. People bought bikes because they were sexy, and when you had all that power vibrating between your knees, you felt like a fucking God.

Or at least, in Jericho's case, you looked like one.

By the time we turned down Mount Zion Lane, I would have done anything to get him to fuck me right there in front of my childhood home. I ached for him to bend me over and show me how a real man handles a woman. But... none of that happened.

He turned the ignition off and kicked out the stand, tilting the motorcycle as I stood to the side. I took off my helmet and shook out my curly hair, handing it back to him with a grin.

"That was a lot of fun," I said. "Thanks."

"Anytime," he said. "I'm only right down there most days." He pointed down the mountain in the general vicinity of the garage. "We can go for a ride whenever you want."

"Wanna come inside?" I nodded toward the house.

His eyebrows furrowed. "I won't disturb your mom or nothing?"

"No." I found my keys and climbed the wooden stairs to the porch, opening the screen door so I could unlock the handle. "She's on a lot of pain meds these days. She's been asleep since ten." I opened the door to the living room where my mom's hospital bed had been set up to make things easier for her. We'd moved the couches to either side of the room and the television against the wall opposite her, right in front of the door.

Tonight's caregiver, Martha, sat at one end of the couch, crocheting a blanket for her newest grandchild and gasping at something that happened on *The Vampire Diaries.*

"Damon, you tricky shit," she muttered.

"Hi, Martha," I said.

"Hi, Alba," she said. "You ever watch this show?"

I nodded. "Many times."

"I like this Damon," she said. "But Stefan's a whiny jerk, right?"

"I don't know." Jericho shrugged. "If my brother moved in on my girl, I'd be pretty upset, too."

I balked and turned to face him, surprised he knew the story well enough to have an opinion.

"What?" he said. "I have a twin sister. I'm well versed in the Stefan and Damon brother-bonding drama."

"And who's this?" Martha said.

"This is Jericho."

"Oh," she said. "The sun and the moon, huh?"

"What?" I furrowed my eyebrows.

"Jericho means moon in Greek... or Hebrew... or something." She winked and stood, packing her things. "Don't ask me how I know that. It's just one of those *Jeopardy* things."

"*Jeopardy* things?" Jericho shoved his hands in his pockets as he wandered around my tiny living room, raking his eyes over pictures on the wall.

"Yeah, useless knowledge you pick up along the way." She chuckled. "I have a lot of time for Netflix. It's easy to multitask when all you have to do is make sure the morphine keeps dripping."

"It's a bit more complicated than that." I smiled at her.

"Alba, can I talk to you for a minute?" Martha shifted her eyes between Jericho and me before she nodded toward the kitchen.

"Okay." My heart sank into my stomach as I followed her. "What's up?"

"Your mom is getting weaker."

I rubbed a hand over the back of my neck. "I know." I'd known for a while. She could barely hold her phone. She ate less and less every day.

"Sometimes, they feel better right before it happens. They get a second wind. And then..."

I sighed, pushing down the wave of emotion that threatened to hit me. I couldn't deal with that now. Not with Jericho standing out in my living room. "Got it."

"I think her second wind is sliding away." Martha put her hand on my shoulder and narrowed her eyes. "You understand?"

Yeah. Loud and clear. Any day now. Any fucking day.

I hated that, so I locked it up tight in a compartment of my heart I never went to. "Thank you, Martha."

She nodded and slipped on her jacket before grabbing her purse. "Everything's stable. I wrote down the last time I checked her vitals. You should be good until morning."

"Okay, thanks again."

"Uh-huh." She looked between us. "You two behave." She waved before leaving, closing the door behind her. I checked over my mom's fragile form, making sure all was well. I pulled her blanket up higher and turned off the television, dimming the light before returning my attention to Jericho.

He stood in front of the console, looking at pictures from my childhood on a shelf at eye level—Girl Scouts, graduations, swimming leagues. I went to stand next to him, and he narrowed his eyes as he leaned in on one picture in particular. He picked it up and brought it closer to his face.

"Holy shit." He turned it around to face me. It was one from when I was five or six, standing in front of Rose Garage and eating an ice cream cone that had melted down my arm. I stuck my tongue out at my mother and crossed my eyes.

Jericho pointed to two people in the background who I hadn't even realized were there until now.

"That's me," he said. "And my sister."

"What?" I grabbed the photo to bring it closer. "No, it's not."

"Yes, it is," he said. "I still have that shirt. I'll show it to you next time I come over."

I raised an eyebrow. "There's a next time?"

He shrugged and turned to face me. We were standing so close. His body was inches away from mine—all that muscle crowding me, all those tattoos on display.

God, he was so hot.

I licked my lips and looked away, taking a step back to break the overwhelming connection that threatened to choke the resistance out of me.

"You wanna see my room?" I winced internally because my voice shook as I spoke. What was I nervous about? Jericho seemed nice, and it wasn't like he was going to take me up on anything anyway.

"Sure," he said. "Lead the way."

It wasn't a big house. It was just me and my mom, so we didn't need much. A twelve-hundred-square-foot rancher with two bedrooms and a bathroom between them suited us fine until Mom got sick.

When I'd started filming, I converted the basement into my studio. I didn't want to chance my mother overhearing the filthy things my fans said to me when I did a live stream. I'd rented a few books from the library and watched some YouTube videos to turn what had once been an unused cement-floored wasteland into a soundproof room with a bathroom in the corner. (Okay, fine... I couldn't do it all myself, but luckily, I'd made enough money to afford a few professionals.)

My filming supplies took up one side of the space, and my bed sat on the other. I had a wall for my ropes and paddles as well as a chest for my toys. My dresser stood off to the right as soon as I entered, a television on top of it. The rest of the space was eloquently decorated for show. It was the only place I kept as clean as possible.

"Wow." Jericho paused as I crossed the space to my desk at the opposite side. "This is where the magic happens, huh?"

I took a deep breath and turned to face him. "I don't usually bring people home. It's not sexy, you know. Walking in on all this." I gestured to indicate the filming gear and my mother and well... everything.

"I get it." He took a step closer, looking around the bright feminine space right off Pinterest with gray walls and a big, fluffy white comforter. I liked to be warm. I had no styling expertise, but I could recreate a picture well enough.

Jericho sat on my bed and reached for the white teddy bear in the middle of the pillows, sitting it on his lap.

"Thank you again for the ride home."

"You're welcome, Alba." He lifted his eyes to mine and a momentary tension filled the air, one where the urge to ask him to spend the night lingered on my tongue. Even if he didn't want to have sex with me, which I completely understood given the nature of what I did for money, I enjoyed his company. I hadn't realized how alone I felt until he was here. Maybe he read this in my gaze because he pushed himself upright and took a step in my direction. "I have a question."

"Okay," I said.

"The librarian thing, I get." Another step closer, and my heart rate kicked up. "The porn, I get. But this?" He lifted my arm, revealing my tattoo. "Doesn't really go with your vibe, does it?"

I grinned to myself, relishing the memory. "It was a dare."

"Go on." He pursed his lips, perhaps amused at how happy it made me.

"My mother has dozens. One of her legs is an entire sleeve."

"Bad ass," Jericho said.

"We're opposites in a lot of ways," I said. "That's why we're such good friends. She has this hippie free love vibe about her. I'm much more hustle and bustle."

He hummed, nodding. "Your mother dared you to get a tattoo?"

"Well, technically, I lost a bet."

"What was the bet?"

"That I wouldn't get into Thomas Washington's MLIS program. It's very prestigious," I explained. "She said they'd be stupid not to take me, and *when* I got in, I'd have to do something stupid to make up for it."

He laughed and took another step closer. "I think I love your mother."

"She's an awesome lady." My heart ached for the impending doom on the horizon, the agonizing thought of the rest of my life without her. "I was accepted. And when I got the tattoo the next day, I did it in a super obvious spot to spite her."

"Brat," Jericho teased.

"It's hard to cover up a wrist tattoo."

"Don't I know it." He was so close now, his legs on either side of mine, trapping me against the desk. His pelvis connected with my lower stomach, the bulge in his jeans nudging me in directions I had no business going. I looked up at him and took a deep breath, my heart pounding. It echoed so hard between my ears that he must have heard it, must have known how he affected me. He must've had this effect on all the women he stood this close to.

I cleared my throat and tried to look away, but he put his hand on my chin to stop me, splaying his fingers along my jawline and rubbing my lower lip with his thumb.

"I like you, sunshine," he said.

"I like you, too, moonbeam," I said.

He cracked a smile as he chuckled low in his chest. "Don't call me that."

I trembled, certain that any second he would close the distance between us and kiss me.

Just kiss me.

But he didn't. The moment passed and he stepped back. I pushed my glasses up, frustrated by my stupid hormones. If I wasn't so touch deprived, would he still make me react like this? "What should I call you instead?"

He shrugged. "My sister calls me Jer. Thor calls me KC."

"What does KC stand for?"

He laughed, putting his hands in his back pockets. "Maybe I'll tell you some day. After a few drinks."

That made me even more curious, but I dropped it.

"Well, I'm not going to call you KC if I don't know what it means." I searched for my pajamas in my dresser drawers, deciding I wouldn't put the moves on Jericho. He was supposed to be in my life. I already had a picture of him, for Christ's sake. I'd gone out tonight to find a partner, and fate must have been trying to tell me something because I ended up with him. Best not to fuck it up with a one-night stand... at least not yet, anyway.

"Why don't you call me Jericho?"

"You call me sunshine."

"Yeah, because it's your name." He twirled a piece of my hair around his finger, letting it loose like a spring, bouncing back into place. "And all this hair reminds me of sunrise."

Alba. Aurora Dawn. What's one more personality?

"Well," I said, "Alba is sleepy. I'm going to get changed. Make yourself comfortable. There's beer and soda water in the fridge upstairs." I walked to the bathroom, the thought only occurring to me once I was there that Jericho had recognized who I was. He'd seen my videos, which meant he'd seen *all* of me. It was a little silly to go to the bathroom to change.

But Alba respected her modesty. Aurora Dawn had none, and she was off duty tonight.

After I slipped into my oversized hoodie and gym shorts, I found Jericho lying in my bed. He'd taken off his boots and cut, but still had on his T-shirt, jeans, and socks. He was flipping through Netflix on my television when I crawled into bed next to him, slipping under the covers while he settled on *New Girl,* one of my favorites.

"Can I ask a question now?" I curled my body toward him, fluffing the pillow under my head.

"Of course." He turned toward me, and as we lay there facing each other in the dark, I felt freer than I had at the party. The world faded away, leaving just the two of us and this delicate nascent friendship we'd created tonight.

"Why did you join the motorcycle club?"

He sighed and ran a hand through his hair, turning onto his back so he could look away from me. I grabbed his chin, the same way he'd done to me earlier, and forced his gaze back, running my thumb over his bottom lip. It was soft and warm, and he parted his mouth, as if daring me to plunge my finger inside. I almost did.

"The oldest reason in the book," he said. "Revenge. It's a fucked-up story."

"You know all my fucked up." Well... most of it, anyway.

"My folks were killed by the DC mafia. There was a car bomb outside Annapolis seventeen years ago."

"Oh my God," I said, covering my mouth with my hand. "That was your family?"

Of course it was. The Steel Roses MC and the Caputi crime syndicate had one of the biggest rivalries on the East Coast. Might as well say the Capones or the Gottis. "Jericho, I'm so sorry."

"Like I said, real fucked-up shit." He shook his head, running one tattooed hand through his hair. "But it goes back further than that. The former president of the MC, Piston, was in love with the same woman as Benito Caputi. When Gabriella chose Benito, Piston went off in a blind rage and killed one of Benito's brothers."

Jericho sighed and ran a knuckle down the side of my face, determined to finish his tale even if it hurt him. "The bad blood started there, but it escalated two decades after that. Benito used to have a daughter named Alessandra. She disappeared a while ago."

I remembered the story because it took place right around the time I was born. My mother told me she followed it on the news when she was in the hospital giving birth to me.

"What the public doesn't know is Alessandra fell in love with one of our brothers and ran away with him. Benito started hunting down Roses to find her. My folks. My aunt. Crow's old lady." He explained that Crow was the president of the Roses MC, and Benito held him personally responsible for Alessandra's perceived death. My heart broke into a thousand pieces, and I almost started crying right then and there—for him, for Crow, for the Mafia princess who couldn't be free to follow her heart. How fucked up.

"Was Crow her lover?"

Jericho shrugged. "I don't think so. Crow loved his old lady. I doubt he'd cheat on her. But after the bombing, it didn't matter why it started anymore. It didn't matter what really happened to Alessandra. No one ever found Benito's daughter, and she never came back. The war went on."

I grabbed his hand, sensing he needed the support to get through the rest of the story.

"Selene and I went to live with our Aunt Gemma, Crow and my dad's sister." One side of his mouth pulled into a grimace. "She never wanted kids, and all of a sudden, she had two little mouths to feed. But what was she going to do? Leave us in the street?" He shrugged. "Thor came into the picture, but I think it was about keeping us safe. Gemma and me and Selene."

"She didn't love him."

"They loved each other in their own way," he said. "Not the way I wanna love my old lady, but it worked for them."

"At the party, you said she was gone. Did Benito kill her, too?"

He sighed. "Never saw a body. Don't know."

I studied the broken expression in his eyes. For a moment, I saw the little boy he'd been, the one who had lost every caregiver he'd ever had. All except Thor.

"Do you think she's dead?"

"I hope not," he said. "When I see that motherfucker Benito, I'm going to make him tell me where she is and then kill him."

"Jesus."

"Don't tell anyone I told you that, but I mean it. I'll kill him."

"Cross my heart." The thought should have scared me, but it didn't. "Have you ever killed anyone before?"

He didn't answer, just raised an eyebrow. "Have you?"

"Yeah," I lied. "The last guy who gave me a ride home."

He furrowed his brows before realizing I was fucking with him. Then he sank his fingers into my waist, trying to tickle me. I squirmed away, giggling and shoving at his shoulders to get him to stop.

"He's buried under the porch," I said through breathless chuckles. "His name was Comet Beam." That made Jericho laugh harder, digging his fingers into my sides. He climbed on top of me, using his body weight to hold me down, and in the mix of things, I moved my legs to either side of his hips. His cock slotted right up against my clit, a hot shock surging up my body.

I gasped, and a moan slipped from my lips.

It had been so long since I'd been with anyone.

So. Long.

He pressed his forehead against mine, his scent burying in my nose. God, he smelled good, like deodorant and man and motor oil. I wanted him to pin me down and take advantage. Or maybe I wanted to do that to him. I *ached* for him however and wherever he wanted.

He exhaled and rolled off me, leaving me hanging again.

What the fuck? Why didn't he want me?

"We should try to get some sleep," he said. "I have to work in the morning."

"You're staying?"

"Yeah," he said. "If you don't mind. The shop's like... two seconds away."

I nodded. "Sure, moonbeam. Stay as long as you want."

He chuckled to himself, but wrapped an arm under my shoulders and pulled me into his body. I snuggled close to his torso and rested my head on his chest, his strong, steady heartbeat lulling me to sleep.

"ALBA!"

The voice came to me in the depths of my dreams, and I sat upright, looking at the baby monitor on the dresser.

"Alba!"

My mother's weakened shout again. I glanced at the time.

7:30.

Fuck! I was so late. So fucking late.

I tried to get out of bed, but a heavy weight on the blankets trapped me.

Jericho.

Still sound asleep. He'd stayed on top of the covers the entire night.

Like a fucking gentleman.

Part of me panicked. I'd planned on getting him out before my mother woke. I didn't want her asking questions and making jokes. And if she saw *him?* She'd nag until we were naming her grandbabies. She thought I didn't date enough and worried about what would happen after she was gone. She wanted to know someone would be here to take care of me, that I wouldn't be holed up in this house alone.

To be fair, her concerns were valid.

But the other part of me melted at how sweet he'd been. He'd had an opportunity last night. He could have kissed me. He probably could have fucked me, too. He wanted it. I felt how much he wanted it. And he hadn't.

Why?

Maybe I'd woman up one day and ask. But not today.

Right now, I had to get him out. I nudged him in the shoulder and he opened his eyes, stretching his arms up over his head.

"What time is it?" he asked, yawning.

Goddamn it, he was so cute first thing in the morning, all rumpled and sleepy, his hair sticking out in odd directions.

"Seven-thirty," I told him.

"Fuck," he grumbled, rolling to the side. "Lucky I'm so close. I have to be there in twenty minutes."

"Alba!" my mother's voice came again. I went to the intercom and told her I'd be right up.

"You have to go," I said to Jericho.

"Yeah, yeah," he said. "Bet you say that to all the guys you drool on in the middle of the night."

"Gross." I climbed the stairs and opened the door into the living room, greeting my mom with a big smile.

"Morning, sweetheart," she said.

"Morning, Mom." I leaned over to give her a kiss. She'd already inclined the bed so she could sit upright. She shifted her body around, but when Jericho came out of the basement, she froze and stared at him.

"Oh, and who's this?"

"This is my friend, Jericho," I said. "Jericho, this is my mom, Penny."

"Nice to meet you, Penny." He slid his cut on and dropped his boots by the couch, sitting so he could slip them on.

"The pleasure is *all* mine. Trust me." The innuendo in her voice made my cheeks burn.

"Mom!" I half whispered, half hissed.

"What?" she asked. "You think he doesn't know he's beautiful?"

"He is well aware," I said.

"He's sitting right here," Jericho cut in.

"Sorry for my daughter's rudeness," Mom said. "She doesn't know how to act around cute boys."

"Well," Jericho said, "I've never known how to act around cute girls, so we match."

Mom elbowed me in the ribs while I checked her main line and the medicine in her IV drip. She'd need another round before I started for the day, but I was tempted to let the old biddy suffer after the way she teased me.

"Where did you two meet?"

"At a party," I said.

"Well, that's not true, is it?" Jericho walked over to the picture of us, grabbing it and showing it to Mom. "Penny, that's me right there."

"What? No, it's not," Mom said.

"His uncle is Thor, the guy who runs Rose Garage down the street."

"Jesus Christ," Mom said. "What a small world!"

"Yep." I nodded toward the kitchen. "Are you hungry?" *Change the subject, change the subject.* "I'll make some coffee and a bagel to send you on your way."

His bright smile sent my heartbeat all the way down my legs. I had to clear my throat and turn away to banish the thought of following him to work and fucking him on his bike before he went in.

"Sure," he said. "That would be great."

"Vanilla protein mush for me, thanks," Mom added.

I fished her shake out of the fridge and poured it into a glass, watering it down the way she liked before dropping a straw into it and returning to the living room. She took a sip.

"Ahhh." She smacked her lips together. "Morning slop."

"Bagel's coming right up," I said. "How do you take your coffee?"

"Black is fine."

"Hey, same as me," Mom said. "I knew I liked you."

They whispered to each other while I worked in the kitchen, and as I went to put the cream cheese on his bagel, I felt eyes on me from the dining room. I looked up and grinned when I caught him leaning against the breakfast table, staring.

"What?"

He shook his head, pursed his lips, and rubbed at the back of his neck. I handed him breakfast and grinned when he took a bite and hummed appreciatively. "Thank you, sunshine."

Coffee came next. I even gave it to him in one of my favorite to-go mugs that had a recognizable princess-turned-general on the front with text that read, *"Well-Behaved Women Rarely Defeat Empires."* Jericho read it and smiled, taking a big swig of the coffee with a deep sigh. "You're amazing."

"I know. I probably have a spare toothbrush or something if you want to freshen up."

"Nah," he said. "I've got all that at the shop. But thanks."

"Okay." I crossed my arms over my chest, conflicted about his departure. I liked him. His presence soothed me, and he made me laugh. "I'll see you around, then."

"Yeah. I'll text you." He grabbed the rest of the bagel and his coffee, leaning in to give me a kiss on the cheek before turning to leave. "Goodbye, Penny. Nice to meet you."

"Goodbye, Jericho," Mom said.

The door shut behind him. Then her eagle eyes landed on me.

"Don't start," I said.

"Tell. Me. Everything." Her eyes went wide. "Right now."

"Mom!" I balked.

"C'mon! Give me all the details. Warm my cold, nearly dead heart."

"I don't know." I rubbed my hands over my face. "He's sweet and kind and..." I shook myself, coming to my senses. "He belongs to a motorcycle club that sells drugs and kills bad guys and... he's probably a bad guy himself."

"So?" Mom said, sucking back her smoothie. "Bad guys are always better in bed."

"I can't believe I'm having this conversation with you."

"Listen, Alba," she said. "You're only young once. Before you know it, you'll be a tired old woman whose body is killing itself."

I took a deep breath and exhaled.

"That's why I tell you to live out loud. Everyone's going to have an opinion about you one way or the other."

I loved her. I truly did. And I had no idea what I'd do when she wasn't here anymore to give me advice like this.

"Well, he could have fucked me last night and he didn't," I said. "I don't think he's interested."

She raised her eyebrows and pursed her lips. "Trust me... that's not how a man looks at a woman he's not interested in."

I ignored that comment and the way it made my heart flutter, opting instead to focus on getting ready for the day.

My mother thought I worked remotely doing a high-profile job for a museum. I couldn't bear to tell her the truth. I didn't think she'd really care, but there was a part of me that still wanted to hide the fact I went downstairs and talked horny strangers through orgasms. That I exercised in panties and socks I sold to people who watched me masturbate. That in two days I could make what I used to make in a month at the library.

It would make her feel bad, and it was the last thing she needed to worry about. So I dolled myself up, put on my mask, and logged in for my first live stream.

3

JERICHO

I thought about Alba the entire day. Literally the entire fucking day—when I was changing oil, when I was rotating tires, when I was hammering out a dent in some guy's Honda. All I could think about was her tight body under mine — how she'd felt, so hot and soft, and how badly I'd wanted to bury myself deep inside her.

But I held back for the reasons I always did.

Yeah, I had the same impulses as every single guy in his twenties, but much to the chagrin of my fellow penis-owners, hooking up had never been a priority for me. I distracted myself instead. I slaved away at the garage. I worked out. I spent time with my uncle and my sister. I did whatever the MC asked of me, and when I wasn't doing any of that, I tagged along with whichever brother needed backup.

That had led me to Alba and her amazing offer.

"I'm looking for someone to fuck. People want to see me cream pied. Gotta give the fans what they want, right?"

The way she'd casually said it fucking shocked me, and the filthy images that went through my mind afterward made me hard as fuck.

Instantly.

She wanted to be cream pied? Sign me right the fuck up.

Why, are you interested?

She'd been joking when she said it, but that didn't stop me from considering it.

But a deal like that from a girl like her? Dangerous. Too dangerous. Especially for a guy like me.

True, my mother and father had died together, but it wasn't like their relationship was great when they were alive. They'd fought as often as they fucked, and I remember times when they beat the living hell out of each other. And then I watched Thor and Gemma live separate lives in the same house, barely talking or touching.

I reached the age of sixteen without having an example of a healthy, stable relationship. Little surprise that I immediately went into an unhealthy one of my own with Nikki—blonde, beautiful, spontaneous; big laugh, big eyes, big tits.

I'd been in love with her my entire life, and when I hit sixteen and finally looked like a man, she'd been too eager to reciprocate. It started out great. She was my first *real* girlfriend, and it lasted five good years. By the time she turned twenty-one, she'd started looking elsewhere. And for the five years after that, we played a bullshit game of on again, cheat again, off again.

God, the fights were intense. We'd had the cops called on us three times, and at the end, I did a night in the slammer because she'd told them I choked her in a blind rage. (I hadn't seen the bitch in weeks.) But bruises were bruises, and she wanted me miserable.

After that, I'd had enough. I'd never put my fucking hands on a lover, and I wouldn't have people thinking I did. I cut her off, blocked her number, and refused to see her.

The problem was that she'd been an MC hang-around longer than we'd been together. So it's not like I could stop running into her. Six weeks ago, she'd married one of my brothers, Pie, having been knocked up several months back. I struggled to feel anything about the news.

She broke my heart. She broke my pride. She could fuck off.

The opposite of love isn't hate. It's apathy, and all the emotion I'd had for her slipped away as I rotted in that jail cell.

No more. Not again. Life was too short. Why spend it with people who made you miserable?

"Jer!" Selene called from the office. I slid out from under the car and wiped my hands on a rag before slinging it over my shoulder and sitting up.

"What?" I shouted.

"Thor's looking for you."

I stood and grumbled, certain I was about to catch shit for dipping last night. I was supposed to be watching Trojan's back and helping him sell weed to those upper-class, overprivileged assholes. Instead, I sat on a couch and talked to Alba for three hours. Then I'd driven her home and spent the night watching her sleep.

Real obsessive stalker shit, right?

I know. Not a great look.

But I couldn't help myself, and as I walked outside to face the music, I decided I wouldn't even try. If they were pissed, I'd take whatever beating they wanted to dish out.

Legally, Thor was my uncle. But he was only ten years older than me, so he didn't try very hard to be a father figure. Gemma had been the only parent Selene or I knew, and when she disappeared, Thor and the MC were all we had left. I joined up as soon as I could, and Selene would likely be an old lady to one of my brothers before long. It wasn't perfect, but what family was?

"There he is," Trojan said, standing next to Thor. They were friends, even if they looked more like brothers. They both stood about six-three with long dark-blond hair and tattooed sleeves on both arms. Fucking modern-day Vikings, both of them.

"Trojan says you snuck out early," Thor said. The question was implied—*Where did you go?*

"Yeah." I nodded, staying purposely vague.

"You left a man hanging?" Thor wiped his oily fingers off on a rag and raised an eyebrow.

"He was balls deep in some brunette bitch by that point," I said. "The deals were done."

"Who was the girl you left with?" Trojan asked.

"Who says I left with a girl?"

"I saw you," he said.

"Her name's Alba." I pointed toward the mountain. "She lives up the street."

Thor narrowed his eyes. "You mean Penny Wright's little girl?"

"She's not little anymore," I said, intention in my tone and memories of her mesmerizing curves flicking through my mind. "She needed a ride home. Trojan was covered. I figured it was fine."

Trojan raised an eyebrow, seemingly satisfied by the response, and Thor patted him on the shoulder. "All good, brother?"

"All good," Trojan said.

"You coming to the clubhouse tonight?" Thor asked.

"Of course," I answered. Prez had called church. I didn't have a choice.

"Good," Trojan said. "The drop next week is going to be tricky."

"Shit, really?" I ran a hand through my hair, pushing it back from my face.

"Out near Baltimore," Thor said.

"I'll be there." I nodded.

The topic moved on to other club shit, and I added input where I could, but it didn't mean much. Thor was the sergeant at arms. Ex-Navy SEAL. A real fucking badass. But he didn't talk about his time in the military. War messed with people in different ways, and whatever happened to Thor had caused him to leave the service and join an outlaw motorcycle gang. I reckoned it was real fucked up, whatever it was.

Trojan and his brother, Hollywood, had joined a few years ago, earning their patches shortly after. Trojan was also ex-military, so he and Thor bonded quickly. I was closest to Hollywood and my eldest cousin, Bear, but I got along with everyone all right. We were sixty members strong at this point, with more prospects due to patch in any day.

I finished with my brothers and headed into the office to look at my next job while the oil drained out of the car in the garage.

Selene sat at the front desk, reading the romance novel open on the counter in front of her while she idly played with a strand of her dark hair.

I snickered to myself. "Thor paying you to read on the job?"

"Thor pays me to ring out customers." She blew a piece of gum until it popped and pulled it back into her mouth. "You see any customers?"

"You're going to give that man a stroke."

She raised an eyebrow, not looking at me as she flipped the page. "He deserves it."

As someone who graduated medical school on a scholarship and completed a full surgical internship, Selene was a million fucking leagues above this job. She could be at a hospital or some shit, but after a while, she said she was burnt out and needed to take a few months off.

Not that I blamed her.

We were carbon copies of each other, tall and lean with dark hair and bright blue eyes. When we were little, people couldn't tell us apart, and now that we were grown, she liked to say we made a matched set.

Things were weird between Thor and my sister, even before Gemma died. It didn't always used to be like this, but one day something happened and they stopped being as close as they once were. She shut him down when he tried to talk to her, and he gave her muffled grunts instead of complete sentences. Anytime I brought it up with Selene, she told me to mind my own business, which only made me more curious.

What was there to talk about, and why wouldn't she talk about it? But I let it go. They were entitled to their own shit, and it had been a rough couple of years for us all.

"What happened to you last night?" she asked.

"Met a girl." I reached into the plastic bin for the next work order —a Toyota pickup with a rattle in the engine. *Fun.* I liked my patients with a bit of mystery.

"What girl?" Selene's eyebrows furrowed. Another page flip.

"Ummm..." I scratched at the back of my neck with my dirty

fingers while I tried to think of reasons it might be rattling. *Could be the struts. Could be th—*

"Jer." Selene brought my attention back to her. "What girl?"

"Alba," I said.

"Alba who?"

"Oh... uh... Wright, I guess." I didn't get her last name. But Thor knew Penny, and Penny's last name was Wright. Alba's dad wasn't in the picture, so I would assume Penny had given Alba her own last name.

"Don't know her," Selene said, a bit deflated by the anticlimactic answer.

"She's cute." The words came out of my mouth absently as I backed out of the shop door and found the truck in the parking lot. I unlocked the doors so I could get inside and start her up, thankful I'd gotten out of there without a fucking gauntlet round of questioning.

I loved my family.

I really did.

But I wanted to get the fuck out.

Thor had moved in with us when he married Gemma, and now we were living like a fucked-up version of The Brady Bunch, crammed into the tiny house where we grew up. I had a freezing basement room to myself, nowhere *near* as nice as what Alba had done with hers, and Selene still had her bedroom upstairs. Thor kept the primary after Gemma was pronounced legally dead.

I should have moved out years ago. What twenty-seven-year-old man still lived in his childhood home? But it wasn't like I was rolling in dough on a mechanic's wage, especially when my uncle was the shop owner and took a large chunk of the profits. I'd just managed to pay off my truck, bike, and credit card debt, so I hadn't been able to save a lot. Besides, we'd been through so much in the last few years, it never seemed like the right time. They needed me. I needed them.

I listened to the rattle in the truck engine, my mind racing with the possible causes. But my thoughts went back to Alba and what she was doing.

Probably rubbing one out in front of millions of subscribers.

Touching that beautiful pussy and moaning for an audience that would later include me. Did she have on a skirt and those thigh-high socks with the Mary Janes?

Fucking hell.

I got half a chub thinking about it.

Her request went through my head again.

Why, are you interested?

When I'd ended up on top of her in the bed where I'd watched her masturbate so many times, there was desire in her eyes. She wanted me to kiss her. She wanted me to fuck her. And fucking hell, I wanted that, too. I would have done it. I should have done it and gotten it out of my system. But I couldn't.

I needed to keep my dick in my pants for three very important reasons.

First, after Nikki, I'd fucked enough club hang-arounds to know that random sex didn't do it for me. Call me old-fashioned, but I wanted to like the person before I fucked them. Yeah, hooking up was cool. But I was too old for that shit.

Which led to problem number two. I liked Alba.

Really liked her.

Enough to leave her ass alone to protect her. I did a lot of shit for the club, some of which I wasn't proud of. Sometimes the people we loved got hurt because of what we did. Look at Crow—wife, brother, sister, and sister-in-law all gone because of this blood feud with the Caputi family. A feud he didn't even start.

And I couldn't live with myself if Alba took the brunt of my reckless lifestyle.

Hence problem number three. I knew myself.

Even if I said at the beginning the situation was transactional, I was a territorial son of a bitch.

I remembered her stomping into that kitchen with her hands in fists and fire in her eyes, reading me the riot act because I didn't ask for her number. She moved her lips and her hair bounced around her head, but the whole world faded away. And suddenly, the only thing in it was her. She had on a sweater and a knee-length skirt (who wears a sweater to a party?), but she could have been in a muumuu for all I cared.

I wanted to wrap my hand around her throat, push her up against the wall, and tell her *exactly* what I'd been thinking when I met her. All the filthy, rotten things that had gone through my mind.

I wanted to shove my hand in between those thighs and claw at her tights, tearing them until I knew how wet I made her.

I wanted to pull her over my lap and turn her ass red for talking to me like that. Didn't she know who I was? Didn't she know who I ran with?

I'd never experienced a surge of lust that intensely before. She surprised me, and after the life I lived, very few people could do that. So offering myself up and fucking her over and over again while insisting it was professional was thin ice to cross.

Remember problems one and two?

I wasn't down for random hookups, and my feelings for Alba were complicated after only one night. How would I feel after a week or a month of acting out my wildest fantasies with her? On camera? For all the fucking world to see?

Every exhibitionist kink I had in my balls clenched, and I winced as I adjusted myself.

"YOU EVER HAVE a girl put a collar on your neck and drag you around like a dog?" Hollywood asked, clapping Bear on the shoulder. We sat around the bar at the clubhouse, talking before church. A few other members hung out in the background, bullshitting behind us, but I always ended up with these two idiots.

Hollywood was only two years older than me and Bear a year younger. We grew up together and knew everything about each other. Too many things, in my humble fucking opinion, and definitely more about Hollywood than I'd like.

"No," Bear said, taking a sip of his beer. "What the fuck, man?"

My cousin and the eldest of Crow's four children had only ever known the MC. When his old man eventually kicked it, he'd take over as prez himself. He knew it. Everyone else knew it. But some days, I wondered if he struggled with the responsibility. He could be an emo shit when he wanted, introverted and shy. He was fucking smart and had once talked about going to college, maybe being an engineer. But that was years ago, and it had been a while since he'd brought it up.

Hollywood, on the other hand, loved to be loved. That was why he'd gotten his name when he patched in. Beautiful and tan with brown eyes, he attracted women like moths to a fire pit. From what I heard, the men loved him, too. Not that I judged. Who Hollywood fucked was his own fucking business.

"This bitch had me howling at the moon last night." He leaned his head back so he could mimic a wolf's cry. I laughed and took another drink. "I never knew I had that kink, but here we are."

"I wish I could continue not knowing you had that kink," I said.

"Don't be a prude." Hollywood patted my back. "Trojan says you left Aliza's party with some girl last night."

"Yep." I swallowed down another gulp but said nothing else, not even when he raised his eyebrows and looked at Bear.

"And?"

"And nothing."

"Who is she?" Hollywood leaned closer so he could whisper. "Did you finally get laid?"

"Man." I shoved him away while Bear laughed. "Shut the fuck up."

"Hey." Hollywood held his hands up, flashing a shit-eating grin while he backed away. "I'm just trying to look out for my man, KC. How long's it been since you got your namesake wet?"

I took a deep breath and sipped my beer, but didn't answer.

"I rest my case." He turned to Bear, who shook his head and smiled.

KC stood for Killer Cock, a nickname the club had given me after I'd accidentally flashed Nikki's elderly neighbor standing in front of the fridge in the middle of the night. The next morning, an ambulance showed up out front. We later learned she'd died due to complications from a recent surgery, completely unrelated to my dick-slip incident. But once Nikki told Hollywood and the rest of the club found out, the nickname stuck.

It didn't help that I had a big dick, something Hollywood insisted on seeing for himself. For two years, he'd been trying to walk in on me fucking so he could get a glimpse. I'd almost reached the point of taking pity on him and showing him so he'd finally fuck off.

"You gossip like a fucking bored housewife, you know that?" I said. "You think I want my business all over the fucking club?"

"Your business *is* already all over the fucking club." Hollywood winked and grinned. How did I end up with these two? Hollywood and Bear continued to bust each other's balls, but my mind drifted to Alba. I should text her. Maybe tell her I'd like to help her. If it didn't work out, no hard feelings.

But let's be real. On top of all the other reasons I shouldn't do this, the biggest and most obvious was putting sex videos of myself on the internet. Once that shit's there, it's permanent.

Look at me, covered in tattoos, worried about something being permanent. Never stopped me before.

The door to the back room opened, revealing Crow and Thor and the giant meeting table the officers huddled around when church was in session. Crow sat at the head. Well into his fifties, he had salt-and-pepper hair down to the middle of his back that he kept loose around his shoulders.

Despite his towering height and generally growly disposition, I liked my Uncle Crow. I'd never seen him lose his cool on a brother, and once you cracked that angry glower, he was a softie on the inside. Warm and paternal, he'd been a surrogate father to Selene and me when we'd needed one most. He and his kids were the only blood family we had left.

But there was a reason he was the president. For all that he loved his family, he was fucking ruthless when it came to protecting us. I'd seen him rip a man apart with his bare hands, and trust me, standing next to Crow was a helluva lot better than being in his way.

The rest of the crew took their spots. The VP, Aristotle, sat at Crow's right. He was just as tall, intimidating, and gray around the gills, but where Crow wore his age in his face, Aristotle looked ten years younger than he actually was. He had short gray hair and piercing blue eyes—the kind of eyes that matched a soul as cold as ice.

He'd been in the club longer than I'd been alive. He ran the MC's strip club and renovated old houses on the side. He said he'd been born with a photographic memory. He knew everything about anything. His only blind spot was his daughter, Ru, who was like a little sister to me. Last December, she'd started a relationship with Aris's best friend and fellow MC member, Saint. As far as I knew, the shit was still secret. But again, I kept my nose out of other people's business, just like I wanted them to stay the fuck outta mine.

On the other side of Crow sat Thor, who was responsible for keeping the brothers in check. Doc, Slip, and Picasso filled around them, and once we had a quorum, Aris stood and cleared his throat. Even though everyone was still having their own conversations, we quieted down when he spoke.

"Church is in session. Everyone shut the fuck up." Aris sat and tapped his ringed fingers on the wooden table, officially opening things up for discussion.

"Thanks, Aris." Crow interlaced his fingers and leaned forward on the table. "Brothers, we're at a precipice. I need your guidance." A pause. "This is a war that none of us started, but we've been picking up the damage Piston left ever since Benito killed him." Crow met my eyes. "Some of us more than others."

I thought of my parents and my Aunt Gemma, all casualties of a war they'd inherited. I bit back the emotion brewing in my chest and turned to stone to save face.

"We'll never forget what they did to Esquire and his old lady. Or what they did to mine." It had been a decade and his voice still cracked at the mention of her. "We still don't know what happened to my sister, Gemma. But we do know this… There is not enough Caputi blood to pay for their sins. Not until every last one of them is gone from this Earth."

Whoops and claps of approval came from everyone around us, including me. When I found that motherfucker Benito, I'd put a bullet in his head. No questions. No regrets.

"Help me," Crow continued. "We know they're planning a big shipment into the Holabird Docks next weekend. We know they have to come through here to get it."

"How do we know this?" someone asked.

Crow narrowed his eyes. "A little birdie told me."

"This birdie still singing?" someone else chimed in.

Our enforcer, Doc, snorted, crossing his arms over his chest. "Not after I was through with him."

I didn't know Doc's background, and with that scary fucking look in his eye, I didn't ask. In his mid-thirties, he'd shown up with his younger sister a few years ago, and after a quick convo with Crow, he'd been welcomed with open arms. He was our healer. He closed up bullet wounds better than anyone I'd ever seen. But he also knew how to bleed a man dry in seconds using only four deep cuts. I tried to stay off his radar.

"The point is," Crow said, refocusing our attention, "if the intel is good, and I have every reason to think it is, we have the opportunity to steal over half a million dollars in fun and games."

"How many men?" Thor asked.

"We think six or seven," Doc said. "Our birdie wasn't sure."

"Can we spare the crew?" Aris looked at Thor and raised an eyebrow.

Thor nodded, and growls of approval came from the group.

"If it were up to me," Crow continued, "I would have already packed my shit to ride. But it's not up to me. It's up to *us*." He looked around the room.

"We can cut them off at the knees," Picasso said. "They've been slinging their shit through our territory for too long." He shook his head.

"I won't bullshit you." Crow ran his hands through his long hair and sighed. "If we do this, it could be bloody."

"It's already bloody," said Coins, our treasurer. "And it's on their hands."

I couldn't deny it. The Caputis and the Roses had been at each other's throats for decades, much to the chagrin of the local PD. We'd lost more than our fair share of brothers to this violence. And for what?

So here we sat. Planning to steal a massive chunk of arms and drugs from these dickheads.

"Before we vote, let's talk logistics. Can we even do it?" Aris asked.

Slip, our road captain, gave the rundown. He'd been in the club all my life. A former pilot, Slip could drive, fly, or sail anything that moved. And I do mean anything. "By the time we get out of there, they won't know what hit them."

"Thor?"

He crossed his arms over his chest, giving a small grunt before muttering, "Doable."

"It's a tight window," Aris said. "I don't like the odds of the rabbit making it without getting caught."

"That's always the risk, isn't it?" Crow leaned back in his seat and lit a cigarette. "Do we have anyone who could make that run in that amount of time?"

All eyes turned to me. I'd spent a lot of time making my bike faster. A Harley was an old man's machine, big and bulky and notoriously slow. But not mine. Because I'm a fucking mechanical genius.

It was dangerous, but all this shit was dangerous. I could walk out of my house tomorrow and get hit by a bus. Why live in fear of death? The bitch came for everyone in the end. This would fuck over the Caputi cocksuckers, and I'd do anything to bring them down.

"It's tight." I cleared my throat and nodded. "But I can do it."

"Think on it," Crow said. "We'll vote at the end."

We went over other club business, an upcoming charity drive and the annual club cook-off in September. Regular shit. At the end of it, the officers dismissed the prospects so we could vote on the run.

"Well?" Crow looked at me, raising an eyebrow.

"I'll do it," I said. Like there was any other answer.

"All in favor?" Aris said.

"Aye," came the chorus around me.

"Any say nay?"

Silence.

Crow looked around the room and smiled before saying, "We ride at sunset on Sunday."

Some people clapped. Some whooped. I drank my beer and turned to head out, but my uncles called from their spots at the table, stopping me.

"KC," Crow said. "Come here a second."

I took a step closer, my boots echoing on the concrete floor. "What's up?"

He waited until everyone else left before continuing. "This is a big run." Crow stood so he could look me in the eye and put a hand on my shoulder, the same way he used to do when I was a kid. "You sure you're up for this?"

I gazed around the club, spotting Nikki and Pie in a corner up front with her hand on his stomach, that huge fucking diamond gleaming on her ring finger and the baby bump hanging low in her belly. My thoughts went to Alba, and a gooey warmth dripped through my chest. Wouldn't it fucking be something to get her big and round with my kid like that one day—

"KC?" Thor asked, bringing my attention back to my uncles.

"Yeah." I shrugged, taking another long pull on my beer. "No big deal."

"You sure?"

I nodded.

Crow leaned forward. "You know everyone's looking at you to replace Aris when he retires."

I laughed and ran a hand over the back of my neck, glancing up at Thor. "I would have thought you'd be eyeballing me to replace Ole Sarge over there."

Thor gave me the finger. "I'm only ten years older than you, prick."

I chuckled and took another swig. "Yeah, I get it."

"How you feel about that responsibility?" Crow tilted his head to the side and leaned back against the table, crossing his arms over his chest.

Again, I shrugged. "Figure I got a while before I need to worry about it."

"Death comes hard and fast." Crow laughed low and deep. "Bear's lucky to have you."

"You're lucky to have each other," Thor added.

"When the time comes," I said, "if that's what the club wants, I'll do it."

Thor turned to Crow, who clapped my cheek and nodded toward the front. "Go get some tail." Then he leaned in real close. "Stop worrying over that dumb bitch who ain't worth it."

Was that what I was doing? *Worrying?*

No, I didn't think so.

I didn't care that Nikki had moved on. Hell, I didn't even care that it was with another member of the club, my own brother. I missed the intimacy of what we used to have and the trust that came with it.

Of course, if I really thought about it, I never could trust Nikki, and that was what pissed me off. Twelve years down the fucking drain. For what? Goddamn nothing.

I said good night to my uncles and went out front, but no one here held my attention. Hollywood and Bear entertained some girls in a corner, and Doc's sister, Fingers, corralled a few others into dancing over by the jukebox. I could have my pick of any of them. Fingers even stopped to smile and wave at me.

But what would be the point? Even if I had any fucking interest in taking her up on it, my mind would be far away, thinking about a pair of big blue eyes and perfect pouty lips.

I pulled my phone out of my pocket and rolled my finger over Alba's contact, lingering on the text message box.

I should call her. Tell her the truth. Tell her how badly I want her.

Such a stupid thing, right?

I'd just volunteered to lead the merry fucking goose chase out of a tricky situation, knowing everyone trailing me would be armed. Why the fuck should I care about anything else?

The money sounded good. Fucking Alba sounded good. All of it sounded... So. Fucking. Good.

I took another drink of my beer and shook my head, running my hands over my hair.

Maybe I should tell Alba I'll do it. Maybe I should fuck her until I couldn't stand anymore.

I ruminated for five minutes before I made up my mind to get the hell out of there, no matter where the road took me.

4

JERICHO

The urge to go by Alba's house after I left the club damn near overwhelmed my restraint. When I drove past Mount Zion Lane, I almost turned. But I reined it in. I'd only just met her, right? Even if I'd thought about her all day, that didn't mean she had to know.

When I got home, Selene sat on the couch with a blanket around her shoulders, a book open on her lap.

"Hey," she said. "You're home early."

"Yeah. Wanna get to the shop early."

"For what?" She scrunched her nose and looked up.

I cleared my throat and rubbed at the back of my head, ignoring her question in favor of my own. "Hey, can I ask you something? Stays between us?"

"Duh," she said.

"Would you ever do porn?"

"Uh..." She narrowed her eyes, seemingly confused for a moment before muttering, "Like an OnlyFans, or a gang bang orgy?"

"OnlyFans."

"No?" It was an answer, but it sounded like a question, like she was unsure but sticking to it. "Why? Would you?"

I sighed and tried to stay cool, shrugging it off like it was nothing. "No."

She laughed and picked her book up. "Whatever, Jer. Just remember, the internet is forever."

"Yeah, yeah." I turned and headed down the stairwell leading to my room, slumping onto my double-sized mattress. I didn't have a bed frame or much other furniture. Just a dresser and a TV on a nightstand, but I didn't need much. Up until now, I hadn't noticed the things it *didn't* have. Like that big comfortable bed in Alba's basement or the fluffy carpet and bright lights. In comparison, my man cave was barren. Lifeless. Cold.

Was that who I was?

Had I become barren and lifeless and cold?

I didn't think so, but the fucking truth of it was, I hadn't warmed up to anyone in a long time. Yes, I was friendly, but I could count the number of people I considered friends on one hand.

Laying back in my bed, I ran my fingers through my hair and stared up at my ceiling, pretending like the temptation wasn't there.

It would be wrong to grab my laptop and open it to her page, right? Now that I knew who she was. Now that I'd spent a night by her side. It wasn't like I was a porn addict or some shit. I didn't have any *favorite* porn stars.

I'd noticed the tattoo on her wrist the first time I saw her online. Curious and interested in her vibe, I went to her page. I only remembered her because her profile said she was from Virginia, and I wondered if I knew her or what she might look like under the mask. I spent a few moments memorizing her eyes, and then I moved on with my whack session because I had shit to do and wanted to get off.

I never thought I'd meet her. And if I did, I never thought I'd recognize her, not without having seen her behind the mask.

I inched my fingers closer to my laptop on the mattress next to me.

Just for a few minutes...

I shouldn't. It was fucked up, especially because there was a good chance I'd be at her place tomorrow, telling her I wanted to do the shit with her.

But... what if it's research?

If I was going to help her, I needed to know what she was already doing. What worked. What didn't. My pinky brushed against the cool metal, and I lost my reserve. I sat up and opened it, typing in her name before I could stop myself. Her website loaded, the picture of her at the top even more stunning now that I knew how amazing she was as a person.

I lit a cigarette and repositioned myself so I leaned against the wall, my legs outstretched on the mattress in front of me.

Where to start? Where to start?

I filtered by her top-rated videos, clicking on the one with the most views and thumbs-ups. It started with her undressing, running her hands over herself while she said dirty things about what the viewer might want to do to her.

"I've been such a naughty girl." She pouted and blinked those big blue eyes at the camera.

I took a deep breath and pinched the bridge of my nose, ignoring the stab of lust that hit me in the balls. My cock jerked.

Be objective. Be professional.

How can I help her? What makes this video great? What makes the others suck? Focus.

She moved her hands down to her nipples and stomach, rubbing and playing. And then the camera switched angles, cutting to a different view of her touching herself.

God, she was so fucking hot. I tapped ash into the tray and adjusted my cock, now rock fucking hard in my jeans.

This was wrong and fucked up, but heaven help me, I couldn't look away. She sucked me in. I ran my gaze along the curve of her waist, where I could nestle my big fucking hands and hold her down while I fucked the ever-loving life out of her.

I palmed my cock again, sucking back on the cigarette before stabbing it out. She orgasmed in breathless whimpers and full-body spasms, and if she was faking it, she deserved a fucking Oscar. I clicked on the next one and the next one, watching the top ten before I came to a conclusion.

The reasons these were her best had to do with the multiple camera angles and the fact she actually climaxed. The others were from one angle, and though she pretended to come, her heart wasn't in it. If I could tell, everyone else could, too.

I went back to that first video, watching it again and focusing on everything about her—the parted lips, arch in her back, and euphoria in her eyes. Her soft skin, long legs, and pink velvet tongue darting out to lick her mouth.

I couldn't stop it even if I wanted to. I had my cock in my hand and memories of last night flickering through my mind in seconds. How great she'd smelled, like cinnamon and sugar, and how perfectly she fit under me, soft and inviting. She made me laugh, and she surprised me. I wanted her more than I'd ever wanted anything.

I thought about what I should have done when I rolled on top of her and tickled her, slotting myself right up against her pretty little cunt.

That cunt right there.

The one that glistened and puffed when she was wet.

I could have slipped inside her. I could have held her hands above her head and pressed my forehead to hers and pounded her into that mattress. I bet she felt like heaven-wrapped silk. I bet she flooded when she came.

My climax shot through me, and I managed to cover myself in time to keep it from getting all over the place.

Fuck. Me.

I lay there, panting and staring at the ceiling, the sounds of Alba's moans in the background.

What if she finds someone else?

The thought came to me out of nowhere.

What if you log on next week and see her with Hollywood?

That motherfucker wouldn't have even blinked. If he'd been there last night? If he'd been the one to see her, strike up a conversation, and drive her home? He would have already shot the video and had it up online. Hell, he would have already had a porn name, a website, and five places to film.

A hot jab sliced through me, furious and fiery, steeling my jaw and making me ball my hands into fists.

I'd fucking kill him.

I'd fucking kill any man who touches her.

And once I knew that, I had my answer.

Ah, shit.

I wouldn't be able to stay away. Not now.

5

———

ALBA

When he didn't text me the following day, I told myself not to worry. I barely knew the guy, and even if he spent the night in bed next to me, it didn't mean we were suddenly best friends. I did my work, washed and exercised Mom, and cleaned the house.

"I have a proposition," Mom said when I emerged from the basement wearing leggings and an oversized hoodie, my hair in a messy bun on top of my head.

"Okay." I popped leftovers in the microwave.

"Let's move movie night to Wednesday."

I narrowed my eyes. "Why?"

"Because you're a twenty-two-year-old woman. You should go out with your friends on Friday night."

I shook my head. "You're my friend."

"I'm your mother," she said. "It's different."

"I don't want any other friends." I didn't have time for them, anyway. This was my only chance to be lazy this weekend. Tomorrow, I had a ton of appointments and errands to run. Then I'd film for a few hours before editing on Sunday. New videos went live on Monday, and then I had more one-on-ones and live streams.

Who needed friends when I could be making money?

She pursed her lips, refocusing on the television when I came into the living room. I plopped down on the couch and blew on my poor excuse for enchiladas before taking a bite. It was decent, but definitely not gourmet like the box said.

We got three episodes into *Mad Men* before she fell asleep, and I grabbed my laptop. I had some business stuff to take care of, reconciling my Excel spreadsheets and checking on my income streams from the various sites. Sometime around eleven, my phone buzzed.

Jericho: You up?

No "hey, how are ya?" No "sorry it's been two days since I texted." Just... *you up?*

I thought about leaving him on read. It would serve him right. But I enjoyed his company. And two days was customary, right? As not to appear desperate? So I wrote back.

Alba: Yeah, what's up?

Jericho: Can I come by?

Fuucckk... I was in leggings and a hoodie. I'd just scarfed down about five gallons of popcorn. My hair was a mess. I was a mess. *Shit.*

Alba: Sure. When?

There were footsteps on the porch outside, followed by two quick, quiet knocks on the door. I jumped and sprang off the couch.

No... Was he already here?

I ran my hands over my hair, checking the peephole to confirm it was, indeed, Jericho.

Fucking hell.

I'd had no opportunity to prepare myself, but fuck it. It was eleven at night, and he hadn't given me very much warning. I opened the door and smiled.

"Hey, that was fast," I said.

"I was in the neighborhood." He nodded down the street and toward the garage.

"Right." *This late?* What a long day.

"Can I come in?"

"Sure." I took a step back and gestured inside. He shoved his hands in his pockets and smiled, brushing past me to step into the living room. I got a whiff of his manly scent again, and it took me back to two days ago when I was under him in my bed. He'd been so warm and hard and strong. I closed the door and cleared my throat, self-conscious in my disarray. Taking a step closer to him, I pushed my glasses up higher and forced a smile on my face.

"What's up?"

"Um..." Jericho ran a hand over the back of his neck and looked at my mom. "You mind if we talk downstairs?"

Uh-oh. Yikes.

"Okay." I tried to keep calm, but my heart beat loudly as we walked to my room. This could only be about one thing. Why else would he want to go downstairs with me? Out of sight of my mother?

Okay, be cool. After the night we had, I suspected this could be a possibility. I'd been honest with him. This was the next logical progression. He'd gone home, given it some thought, and decided he wanted to take me up on my mostly-not-serious offer.

What would I do? What would I say?

Part of me would jump for fucking joy, throw him on my bed, and climb him like a tree. But the rational part of me would turn him down, and that side would win. I liked him too much. I wanted a friendship with him too much. Business would get in the way of that.

We went into my room, closing the door behind us before I turned to face him.

He still had his hands in his pockets and leaned against my desk, crossing one leg over the other. "I've been thinking."

"A terrible idea, really." I took a deep breath and headed to the bed, sitting down and crossing one leg under my body.

He smiled before saying, "You can make more money on your own." He crossed his arms over his chest. "You don't need a penis."

"Go on." I was intrigued. The fact he had shown up in the middle of the night with this said he'd been thinking about it since he left. He'd been thinking about *me* since he left.

"You have ten videos with over a million likes. In those ten, you change the camera angle. You play with different lighting. They look more professional."

"I know," I said. "They took three hours to film. Another two to edit."

He nodded. "I said you didn't need a penis, not that you didn't need help."

My eyebrows furrowed. "What are you proposing?"

He took a deep breath and stood, running both hands through his hair and linking his fingers around the back of his neck, his tattooed arms hanging down his massive chest. "I'll film."

"What?"

"You perform, and I'll film."

I couldn't believe this. My mouth hung open, and my heart damn near skipped out of my chest. "Why?"

Now he was confused. "Why what?"

"Why would you help me?"

"Oh, I'll insist on a cut," he said. "I don't know, ten percent or something. You decide what you think is fair."

"That still doesn't explain—"

"I like you, Alba. I can help you, so I will." He shrugged, and standing there like that, under my recessed lighting, he looked more menacing than he actually was. Like a Greek God. Like any second he might bend me over and break me in half. "It seems like easy money. And I am *not* going to mind the show."

"Jericho." I stood and crossed over to him. "You don't have to do this."

"I know. But I want to. And if it turns out you were right and you do need a penis, I probably know a guy or two who could help you with that."

"Two?" I raised an eyebrow, a small smile on my face.

"Whatever you're into," he said. "But baby steps, okay? You on board?"

The impulsive side of me screamed from the depths of my subconscious. *Yes, yes, yes.* But a practical voice was more skeptical. He said he wanted to help me, but mostly, people only cared about themselves. He asked for a cut, so I had to assume his motivation was financial. And whatever it was, maybe it was none of my business. The biggest risk was that I broke ties with him and never saw him again.

No, the biggest risk is you fall in love with him and never want him to leave.

I ignored that because I didn't intend to hang around here much longer, certainly not long enough to fall in love. In the meantime, I couldn't deny I needed the help, and he'd made more than a generous offer.

"I accept." I held out my hand for him to shake.

He did, flashing me a charming smile. "I have some shit to do for the garage tomorrow. I should be done by the time your mom goes to sleep. Can I come over then?"

I nodded. "Sure."

"Okay." Straightening, he turned to leave but paused at the door to return to me. He ran a pinky down one side of my face and brushed a few stray hairs back behind my ear. "One more thing."

My pulse kicked up in my throat, and I swallowed, my mouth dry and scratchy. "Yeah?"

"Those ten videos have the most views because you made yourself come. You're faking it in the others."

Had I been that obvious?

"Do us both a favor and don't touch yourself tonight. Don't touch yourself tomorrow. Save it for me, okay? Can you do that?"

A hot lance sizzled through me, right to my clit. I nodded and muttered a strained, "Yes."

"Good girl." He gave me a kiss on the forehead. "Get some sleep. It's late, and we've got a long night tomorrow."

He cupped my cheek and left me standing there, panties soaked, turned on by his command, and bewildered by my immediate agreement to it.

BUTTERFLIES FLITTED around my stomach for the rest of the night. I tried to sleep, but I tossed and turned, imagining what would happen the next day.

Sure, I'd had lots of boyfriends in my short twenty-two years. I'd fucked around, and my number was much higher than it probably should have been for my age. The national average was seven partners in the course of a lifetime, but I'd already well surpassed that before Mom got sick.

If I'd been raised by any other person, I might have been ashamed of that. But my mother believed in a sex-positive environment and taught me virginity was a social construct. What I did paid for her well-being, so I had long since let go of any shame society wanted to put at my feet for that.

I cleaned and cooked, preparing for the week ahead. After Mom fell asleep, I dolled myself up in Aurora's lingerie. I put in her contacts and did her makeup, creating the smoked-up sex kitten everyone loved. I did her hair, pulling it back so it was half up in pigtails on the back of my head. By the time Jericho texted he was here, I had completely assumed Aurora's disguise.

He let himself in and came downstairs, pausing at the door to rake his sky-blue eyes over me from head to toe. I'd put on a robe, but I wore very little underneath.

"Hey." I nervously twisted my fingers together.

"Hey." He closed the door behind him and cleared his throat. Fuck, he looked as amazing as ever. Jeans and a T-shirt and the cut, all those tattoos on his arms, and his dark hair brushed back away from his face.

"How was your day?"

He waved off my question. "Fine. Typical stuff."

I nodded, and silence fell between us.

This is awkward.

"Before we begin," I started, "we should talk about boundaries."

"Okay."

"Like I said, no one else knows about this. Not my mom. Not my friends. I'd like to keep it that way."

"I'm not telling anyone."

"My safe word is crimson," I said. "If I feel uncomfortable at any time, I'll say it. You stop what you're doing. You leave the room until I'm ready to talk about it. Is that cool?"

"Sure," he said with a smile. "Totally cool."

I loved that sexy smirk. It lit up his whole face.

"I'll pay you fifteen percent," I said. "If you help me make more money, we'll talk about twenty or thirty."

He pursed his lips and nodded. "Entirely too generous, sunshine."

I smiled at the nickname and continued. "I've never done this before. You know, performed while someone else is filming me."

"Well, I've never filmed anyone masturbating before, so we're both gonna pop our cherries tonight."

Another awkward pause.

"Is there anything you want to add?" I asked. "Any boundaries you want to keep?"

He took a deep breath and let it out slowly. "This is professional. If it doesn't work out, it doesn't work out. No hard feelings."

"Agreed." I waited to see if he would add anything else, and when he didn't, I touched the belt on my robe and hesitated. "So... should we do this or..."

He narrowed his eyes, now more serious. "That depends. Did you do what I asked?"

"Of course," I said. "Though it was a bit high-handed of you to assume I would."

"Then why did you?"

I tipped my chin higher and let my robe fall to the ground as I said, "Because it turned me on."

His smile widened, clearly pleased with himself, before taking a deep breath and trailing his eyes over me again. I'd worn a sexy scarlet bra with a matching thong. The garter belt at my waist connected to my thigh-high tights. I looked amazing.

He cleared his throat and glanced away, going to the camera on the tripod.

"Do you know your way around that thing?" I climbed on the bed and crawled to the center, going up on my knees when I was there.

"Yeah." He bent over it, taking it off the stand and fiddling around with the buttons. "Took some AV classes at community college. I have one like it."

I paused, raising an eyebrow. "You took classes at community college?"

"Not just a dumb gearhead after all," he whispered with a small laugh.

"I never thought you were just a dumb gearhead."

"No?" He came closer and held the camera up between us, the red light indicating he'd started recording. "Tell me. What did you think when you first met me?"

"That you weren't someone to fuck with."

"Well, you were right about that. What else?"

"That I liked your tattoos."

"Hmm," he said. "What did you like about them?"

"What is this? *Dateline*?" I ran my hands up my thighs, my fingers poised on the snaps connected to my tights. "I'm paying you to film me. This is my show, remember?"

He licked his lips and grinned. "Well, go on then. Give me a show."

Not *them*. Not *the world*.

Give *him* a show.

I snapped my gaze to his, and the atmosphere shifted. What had once been friendly, albeit a little awkward, was now charged with a potent tension that stretched between the two of us. When I'd done this before, it had just been me, and though I recorded myself, it felt the same as any other time I'd masturbated.

With him here? Everything seemed different. My fingers burned hotter as I traced them up my legs to my waist, cupping my boobs before going to my neck. I tilted my head to the side so my hair fell on my chest, and I sat back on my haunches, spreading my legs so Jericho could get a good shot in between them. I moved one hand under my underwear, fingering my clit.

I said the stuff I normally did. "I've been so horny all day. I couldn't wait to get home and finger my pussy for you."

He looked from the screen to me and back again, drawing my attention. I used to pretend like the camera was some mystery man, but now I had someone to play with, someone to react to. We may end up putting this on the internet, but this performance had started being for him when he commanded me not to touch myself last night.

Like it or not, he was in this now.

"You told me to wait." I unhooked the snaps on my thigh highs, refusing to break eye contact. "You told me to save it up for you." He hung his mouth open, and the growing bulge in his jeans showed me how much he enjoyed this. So did I.

My skin buzzed with electricity and my veins flooded with adrenaline and dopamine, all the feel-good chemicals. I leaned back and slid my panties down, biting my bottom lip as I flung them at him. He caught them with his free hand and grinned, so I kept going.

"How many times did you jack off thinking about me?" I raised an eyebrow and tilted my head, curling my tongue around my canine as I teased him, knowing he was trying to be quiet because this was *my* show. And theoretically, I was saying these filthy, naughty things to the viewer. I put my hand between my legs and arched my back, balancing my legs on the balls of my feet, spread open and wide for him.

He zeroed in on me rubbing at my clit, and I moaned, making him grab at his cock.

"How bad do you want this?" I asked. "How hard do I make you?"

Desire soaked my brain, making me mutter stuff I hadn't planned on saying. When I did a scene, I viewed it more as playing a role. I put on Aurora's skin, thought of a stereotype, and bought into it. But having him here? It bordered on too close to being real. The lines between pretend and reality had blurred, and I wasn't sure I could reel it back in.

I wasn't sure I wanted to.

I reached under my pillow, where I'd stashed the vibrators I wanted to use—a clit suction toy and a big, buzzing dildo. I called this one Fat Jack because it was huge and girthy and the fans like to see me get wet and take it all the way inside. It had to have been what... twelve? Thirteen inches?

Either way, I was going to get myself so ready I'd have no problem squatting on it before the end, bringing myself to a big climax.

I turned on the clit suction toy and brought it to my sensitive nub, hissing in a breath as soon as it touched. I was already soaked. Having Jericho in the room made things a million percent more erotic.

This is a performance, my logical brain screamed from the depths of my subconscious. *Not sex. Get your mind in the game.*

Refocusing on the job, I pulled my tits out of my bra and pinched a nipple, rolling my hips into the toy. I moaned and squirmed to get my legs open wider.

"Is this what you wanted to see?" I said. "Is this why you wanted me to wait for you? To save it for you? Is this the fantasy you craved?"

He couldn't help it now. Jericho cleared his throat and gripped his cock harder, and that made me burn so fucking hot. My blood was on fire. I could feel it building. I didn't need the dildo.

I stuck two fingers inside of me just as I crested. Euphoria surged through my molecules, launching me sky high and freezing time in the same glorious moment. Fireworks. Absolute fireworks. I came with the thunderous applause of every cell in my body.

And when reality set in again, I collapsed on the bed, panting and smiling and laughing softly.

Wow. What a ride.

I turned to look at Jericho, only to find him gaping like he'd never seen a girl before. I smiled and sat up, and he put the camera down on the tripod before shoving his hands into his back pockets.

"I think we got it," he said, his voice hoarse and crackly. He nodded and took a few steps back toward the door.

"Where are you going?" I furrowed my eyebrows. "If we can get them done that fast, we should do at least two or three. We can make more money."

He swallowed and took a deep breath. "Sure. Yeah. Uh... okay."

"What's wrong?"

He chuckled softly to himself and shook his head. "Watching you... filming you... it's making me hard as a fucking rock. I'm about to come in my pants like a teenager."

"Yeah?" I raised an eyebrow and leaned back, balancing my weight on one hand behind me. "Then get over here and come on my tits like a man."

6

JERICHO

*F**ucking hell.***

Someone had taken a sandblaster to my vocal cords. My cock jolted when she commanded me like that. I mean... who would refuse such an offer?

I took a step forward.

What if this worked out? What if this was good? Too good. So fucking good...

Another step.

"Come on, Jer," she said. "You watched me come. It's the least you can do."

Oh, this girl was going to be the death of me. My heart thudded against my ribs as I went, and once I stood in front of her, those big eyes blinking up at me from behind her mask, nothing in the world could have stopped me.

She unbuttoned my pants, tucking her perfect lower lip under her front teeth as she went to the zipper next, sliding it down one metal tooth at a time. Then she leaned back, her hands spread behind her, and raised an eyebrow.

"Well?" she said. "Go on."

I cleared my throat, and with a shaky hand, reached inside to pull out my dick. I locked eyes with her, waiting to see the fear and panic I'd seen in Nikki's the first time I'd done this to her. Instead, Alba's grin widened, and she looked back up at me.

"You have a beautiful cock, Jericho," she said. "I can't wait to see what you look like when you come."

Just when I wrapped my hand around the tip, she gasped and said, "Wait." Alba rolled over and grabbed the lube, tossing it to me with an excited nod. I squirted some on my hand and went back to it. "That's better, huh?"

So much better. With this tenuous trust between us and the thrill in her eyes, I wouldn't last long. I'd known it before I even started. But that was the point. She wanted to get this awkwardness over with because there was no doubt in my mind I'd fucking get hard every time we did this.

I scanned the length of her again, focusing on her pussy and how badly I ached to fuck her. Standing this close, the scent of her arousal hit me square in the face, tangy and sweet and damn near irresistible. I could drop to my knees right here, wrap those legs around my head, and sink my tongue inside her.

She must have read this in my expression because she tsked and said, "See something you want?"

"Lots of things."

"Hmm." Then she reached up and stuck her fingers in my mouth, the taste of her sweet cunt lingering on her skin.

Dear. Fucking. God.

I came so fucking hard that I groaned and fell forward, putting my free hand on her shoulder to hold myself upright. She stuck her tongue out, like she meant to catch it, and my balls clenched harder. It hit me in the back of the knees and behind the eyes, making me light-headed for a second. I hissed in a breath, and Alba laughed but in a good way that made me feel like I'd given her exactly what she wanted.

"There it is," she said. "Oh my God, that was so fucking hot."

I looked down, and she wiped my come off her tits to lick it, giving me a low moan of approval.

"Fucking hell." I fell into the bed next to her. With my hands still trembling, I wiped them off on a towel and ran them back through my hair, blowing out a long, slow breath and trying to get my fucking head screwed on straight. She unraveled me. She turned me to fucking putty.

How the hell had I lived this long without her? More importantly, how would I ever go on without her?

"Jericho." She curled into the space next to me, resting her head on my chest the way she'd done the first night I'd spent here. "I think you and I are going to work together just fine."

I laughed, rubbing my hands down my face. "Yeah. No shit."

After we cleaned ourselves up, she rolled a blunt, and we went outside to smoke. We sat on the wooden picnic table in her backyard that overlooked the valley below, and after what happened, the buzz and fresh air revitalized me.

The sky was clear tonight, the stars shining brightly. If I squinted hard enough, I could see the Milky Way. But the whole fucking universe paled in comparison to how beautiful Alba looked in her post-orgasmic glow. She'd washed the makeup off her face and put on her leggings, hoodie, and glasses, but I thought it made her cuter even if she didn't.

"Thank you for helping me." She handed me the blunt.

"You're welcome." I took it and inhaled.

"Can I confess something?" She turned her body to face me, not waiting for my agreement before she continued. "I've never orgasmed that hard before. I liked having you watch me."

My heart beat faster, and I took a puff just to give myself something to do besides react.

"Yeah, me too." I handed it back to her.

"Really?" Her eyes lit up. "I was afraid I stepped over a line when I told you to come on my tits."

"No." I shook my head. "I liked that, too."

"You and I are about to get *real* comfortable with each other."

My cheeks burned, and I thanked fucking God it was night so maybe she wouldn't notice my blush.

"What's that look?" she said.

"What look?"

"That one." She rubbed the crease on my forehead. "You're worried."

"I'm not worried."

She raised an eyebrow, clearly not believing me.

"Okay, I'm a little worried," I confessed.

"Why? I won't put you online," she said. "I'll edit you out."

"That's... that's not it."

"Then what?"

I paused for a moment, pulling on the blunt before handing it back to her. "I'm not a good guy, Alba."

She rolled her eyes and took it, wrapping her lips around it again. "You think I don't know that?"

I whipped my attention to her.

"You were selling drugs at a party. You're in a biker gang."

I ran a hand over my hair and down the back of my neck, chuckling softly at her insinuation. "It's not a gang."

She narrowed her eyes and handed the blunt back. "Don't worry. Once my mom..." She cleared her throat, blinked, and looked away. "After it happens, I'm not going to hang around."

Now, I was confused. "What do you mean?"

She shrugged. "I'll get some life insurance money. I'm going to sell everything and travel around the world."

I paused as I smoked the blunt, remembering she'd told me that the night I met her.

"You don't have to worry about me for very long."

I winced, a strange tug on my heart aching in my chest.

Another reason not to do this. Another reason to tell her no. Don't get attached.

"This is quick money, and then we both move on with our lives."

She smiled, shifting her hawk-like gaze up and down, trying to figure me out. "You're still uncomfortable with that."

There was no reason to lie, so I took another hit of the blunt, passed it to her, and let the smoke out before sighing. "Yeah, maybe I am."

"Why?"

I opened my mouth to tell her the truth, that I was terrified I might fall in love with her, that I might *already* be in love with her, and fucking her on camera would make shit more complicated.

But...

I didn't say that. I'd only known her two days. Who the hell felt this way about someone after knowing them for less than a week? I wasn't a fucking sap, and I didn't want to scare her off.

Instead, I said, "I don't want someone to recognize me and hunt you down. Drag you into things that wouldn't be good for you."

Again, she seemed unperturbed. "That's fine, Jer. I won't push you into anything you're uncomfortable with." She took another long inhale and handed the tiny roach to me. "For the record, I haven't been with anyone else for a long time. I'm clean." She gestured to her mouth, reminding me of her taste still lingering in the back of mine.

"Oh," I said. "It's been a long time for me, too."

She laughed like I'd cracked a joke, but when she realized I wasn't chuckling with her, she stopped and her features dropped. "Wait. What?"

"What?"

"Okay, on the count of three, define a *long time*."

I shrugged in agreement.

"One... two... three..." And then she blurted out, "Six weeks." At the same time, I said, "Nine months."

Her jaw hung open and she sunk her fingers into my forearm. I froze, realizing my mistake as soon as the words came out of my mouth. I'd been honest. So had she. And now I sounded like the fucking loser who couldn't get laid.

My cheeks burned harder. I hated weed's ability to drop my inhibitions.

Why the fuck did I tell the truth?

"Nine months?" she repeated, louder than I wanted her to.

"Shhh." I put a hand over her lips and stabbed the blunt out with the other. "I don't need the whole fucking town to know."

"How is that possible?"

Why the hell was I telling her this? It couldn't have been the fucking weed. Was she this easy to talk to? Or did we no longer have any secrets from each other? I'd seen her asshole up close and personal. She'd licked my jizz off her tits. Where were the lines anymore?

"Are you gay?" she asked.

"No," I hissed.

She laughed and bit her bottom lip, pushing her glasses higher on her nose. "Then why?"

I cleared my throat, figuring I might as well be honest. So I told her about my old man, Thor and Gemma, and Nikki and the last twelve years. The fights. The breakups. "She's pregnant with another guy's baby. My brother, Pie."

"She got with another MC member?" Alba widened her eyes, clearly outraged.

I nodded. "Married and all that shit."

"That bitch," Alba said.

I chuckled and shook my head. "It's fine. I didn't love her as much as I thought I did."

She didn't say anything for a while, so long that I didn't know what to do with myself. I finally reached inside my pockets and found my smokes, pinching one between my teeth to light it. I offered her one, but she declined.

We sat there until I couldn't stand it any longer. "Okay, fucking say something."

"Is she the only girl you've ever—"

"No," I said. "There were a few after her."

"Only a few," she said.

"I don't like people I don't know," I said. "I've got trust issues."

She laughed and held up her hands. "No judgment here. I've got daddy issues."

"What about you?" I asked. "How many notches are on your bedpost?"

"Oh. We don't need to get into all that."

Her refusal to answer made me even more curious. "Come on. Don't be shy."

"Like..." She pursed her lips. "Twenty-five? Thirty?" She shook her head. "I lost count somewhere around there."

"Wow," I said, raising my eyebrows and drawing out my tone, more surprised than appalled. "That's a lot."

"Hey." She nudged me in the shoulder. "We said no slut shaming."

"No," I said. "I woulda lost count around like fifteen. You remembered past twenty?"

She held my gaze for a moment, probably deciding whether I was fucking with her, and when she realized I was, she laughed again and pushed to her feet, climbing off the picnic table. She stepped in between my knees and wrapped her arms around my neck, pulling me into a hug. Her incredible smell assaulted my senses, and I had to resist the urge to bury my nose in her hair for more.

"Thank you for telling me," she said. "Thank you for trusting me."

"Same." I put my hands on her waist, and fucking hell, I was right. They looked incredible wrapped around her body.

"But Jericho, I swear to you," she said, cupping my face, "say the word and it's just us. I won't touch anyone else until it's over."

"I know," I said. "I think I trust you."

"Good." She nodded toward the house. "Now put that out. I want to go inside and watch our video."

I laughed, the sound coming from deep inside me, from a place that made my spirit lighter.

7

———

JERICHO

After we went back to her room, we lay in her bed and watched the footage. I hadn't stopped recording when I sat the camera down, so it caught the two of us after she'd kept me from leaving. My head was out of view, but everything from my shoulders down could be seen. The way Alba looked at me had my cock's attention, and I almost dragged her on top of me to make good on her offer.

But I didn't.

"Jericho," she said. "I have to tell ya, this footage of you is making me super wet."

"Yeah?" I asked.

She nodded, pursing her lips. "What do you say we post the whole thing and split it fifty-fifty?"

I took a deep breath and let it out on a sigh. "I don't know."

"Think about it," she said. "What you said is right. Having someone else film makes it easier. But there's a bigger market for couples than there is for solo girls."

I knew that.

"You don't have to tell me tonight," she said. "The stuff with me is enough to upload. But the two of us would make more money."

I knew that, too. But once I did this, there was no *undoing* it. Footage of me jacking off on Aurora Dawn's chest and her licking it up afterward would be online forever. Fifty-fifty was a lot. She'd gone over her last few months' income with me, and if we could double or triple that? Hell, I'd be out of Thor's basement in weeks.

"Do it," I said.

"Really?" Her eyes widened.

"Yeah," I said. "Edit it tomorrow. Make it look nice. Put it online."

"Okay," she said, sitting up and turning to face me. "If you're going to do this, you need to do it right. You need a stage name. You need a website. How about... Damon Dark? Or Billy Blue? Because of the eyes?"

"Kaleb Cox," I muttered. For my biker name. KC.

She gasped. "Wow. You had that ready to go."

I didn't say anything because she didn't need to know I'd spent the last two days thinking about it.

"I love it." She typed something into her notepad and went back to the video.

Was I actually doing this? If any of the guys at the club found out... if *Hollywood* found out... I'd never live it down. Might as well pack my shit up and join the Caputi cocksuckers because my brothers would rag on me every chance they could. At least I'd had enough foresight to take my fucking cut off before we started filming, so other than my tattoos, there weren't any identifying features.

"Jer, this is good." She pointed to the part where I fell forward onto her, my groans of ecstasy making her even more excited. "This is really good. Trust me."

"I trust you, Alba," I told her. "I just—I didn't come here with the intention of being a porn star by the end of the night."

"Cam guy," she corrected.

"Whatever."

She clapped and threw her arms around my neck, kissing me on the cheek. "Thank you."

The adoration and gratitude in her eyes damn near melted my pathetic fucking heart.

"I'm not making this a regular thing," I said. "I don't intend to jack off on your tits every single time."

"Of course not," she said. "There's my mouth and my ass and my pussy—"

"For fuck's sake." My cock gave a half-hearted jerk at the filthy way she talked.

"If we're going to do this, we need more boundaries," she said. "Where do you like to be touched? How do you like your dick sucked?"

Shock raced through me, slicing me down the middle, and my focus cut to her. She always fucking surprised me.

"Uh—the usual way, I guess." I tried not to shift in my seat, even though the visual of her big doe eyes staring up at me from between my legs made me run hot.

She giggled, rewound the video, and started it from the beginning again. "No, I mean like... Do you like to throat fuck, or do you want me to suck on the tip while I jack you off? Do you like your balls played with?" She talked absently while she fiddled with the editing software, clicking a few buttons to toy with the lighting. "Do you like a finger in the ass?" She gasped and looked at me. "Do you like to be pegged?"

"Fuck, sunshine," I said. "Slow down."

She pushed her glasses higher up on her nose. "You don't have to do anything you don't want to."

"This isn't fucking prom night," I said, which made her return her attention to the laptop. "Let's just... take this one step at a time, okay?"

She nodded and said, "Okay. Whatever you're comfortable with."

We watched the rest of the scene, and when I collapsed on the bed next to her, something about the expression on my face stunned me. I looked... *relieved.* Happy. The way I smiled when Alba rolled into me and put her head on my chest sent a warm sticky ache down my spine to my gut.

We looked good together, and this felt good, too. *Real* good.

The expression in my eyes said she hung the stars in the sky. It was there for a moment and then gone, but I saw it. I should have been more concerned about that. I should have put more distance between Alba and me because of it. But I ignored it because this was too right and too perfect to stop. Like I was always supposed to be here. Like I was always supposed to meet her.

She closed the laptop with an approving hum and set it on her nightstand, scooting farther under the duvet before rolling over to face me.

"You don't have to sleep on top of the covers, you know," she said. "I think my mom has an old bundling kit from the 1700s that we can put you in if you're worried about my virtue in the middle of the night."

"Hilarious." I lay down so I could face her.

"Let's play a game," she said. "It's called twenty questions. You ask a question, and I have to say the first thing on my mind. No thinking about it. Then we switch. Okay?"

This seemed dangerous even though I agreed to it, but I'd never deny Alba anything she wanted.

"I'll go first," she said. "What's your favorite movie?"

"*Die Hard*," I said. "Yours?"

"*Pretty Woman*," she said. "That part where they have sex on the piano? Full-body chills."

I laughed.

"Okay, you ask me something."

"What's your... favorite pizza topping?"

"Pepperoni and olives," she said.

I clutched my chest. "My girl."

I paused while I waited for her question. She curled her bottom lip between her teeth, a mischievous look in her eye. "How many times have you jacked off thinking about me, Jericho?"

I cleared my throat and squirmed my hips because my cock wanted to answer instead. "I shouldn't tell you that."

"Why?"

"Because it'll ruin our friendship."

The sound of her soft laughter had my cheeks burning. "How

about this? I'll tell you how many times I've masturbated thinking about you if you tell me how many times you've done it to me."

I shook my head. My girl was a fucking tease and knew it.

"Countless times," I said. "Countless."

"Did you go home and do it yesterday?"

I sighed. "Yeah."

"And today?" she asked. "Before you came here?"

"Yeah."

She swallowed, and I caught the muscles working in her throat... a throat I ached to bite and lick.

Silence. She looked at my lips, the glow of the television illuminating the desire burning behind them.

It would be so easy to connect my mouth to hers, to claim that tongue and those breasts and that gorgeous cunt. I could have her wet and ready under me in seconds. The wanting had never been an issue. It was all the other shit that complicated this.

"You didn't answer your part of the question," I said to distract myself. If I didn't, I would do it. If I didn't, my heart would beat right out of my chest, and I would twist my fingers in her hair and I'd—

"Every single time since I met you," she said.

My dick jerked again, and I reminded him to take several fucking seats. There were millions of reasons why this was a bad idea on a professional level, billions more on a personal level. But when she blushed and smiled, I could have forgotten them all.

"Two days ago," she said. "And when you filmed me."

This time, I swallowed and turned on my back, gripping my straining cock under my jeans.

"I think," she went on, "if we're going to do this, we should fuck before we film." Another giggle came from her. "Nine months is a long time, so my expectations are low."

I looked back at her, openmouthed. "Fuck you."

"Aw." She pretended to pout, which I knew was meant to mock me, but ended up being more lovable than anything else. "It's okay. We'll get you back up to speed in no time."

I narrowed my eyes. "Nine months or not, I could still rock your world."

"Oh yeah?" She raised an eyebrow and pursed her lips. "Prove it."

I took a deep breath in through my nose and let it out slowly.

Ohhhh... She didn't know who the fuck she was messing with. Visions of my hand around her throat went through my mind, my teeth devouring her mouth, my cock splitting her in two. Her screams on my tongue, my nails in her skin, my—

Jesus Christ.

The proposition hung between us. One second. Two seconds.

And then I pounced, rolling on top of her and scrambling for her hands, which flew at me in a poor attempt to defend herself. She laughed while I growled, and when I finally got her wrists in one fist, I pinned them above her head and slid the other hand down her arm to her rib cage, pausing millimeters from her breast.

Her heart pounded against my palm, and I leaned over her torso, my hips in between her legs and my cock right up against her clit. Except I was on top of the covers, and she was still under them. She squirmed against me, but the more she moved, the tighter I squeezed, until she finally relented and huffed in frustration.

I chuckled, dark and low in my torso, and dragged my hand over her chest, up her sternum to her throat. I gave into my baser desires. letting the feral side of me have a little slack on the leash. Her pulse fluttered under my palm, and my heart kicked at how much power I had over her. Right here. In my hand.

Alba stiffened, those big blue eyes meeting mine.

"You cannot imagine how badly I want to fuck this throat." I leaned down and pressed my lips tenderly to her windpipe. "How I want you to gag around me. And when you do, I'll tell you if I want a finger in my ass." I stared down at her, my focus catching on the way her lips curled into that devilish smile. "And you'll do it. Won't you? Because you're my good girl. Right?"

She bit her bottom lip and nodded. "Yes."

"That's what I thought." I rolled my pelvis against her, dragging my cock against her clit, and she rewarded me with a moan. I did it again. And again. Her head lulled to the side and she sank her teeth into her bicep as she matched me thrust for thrust. Her nails dug into my hand still holding her captive, but I didn't care. Nothing could stop this.

I was fascinated by her. The way her hair stuck to her forehead, the way her nose sloped down the front of her face, the way she smelled like flowers and weed and *girl*. Jesus Christ, I had to stop or I would blow my load right here like it really was prom night.

"Fuck me, Jericho," she whimpered. "Please. I'm on birth control. We're both clean. Please, just do it." Alba turned her head, bringing her lips close to mine, so close I tasted her breath.

I reared back and froze.

"No kissing." I glanced between her startled eyes. "That's how this stays professional. So when you leave... when club business calls... this ends. Agreed?"

If she didn't, I would have to stop.

"Okay." She nodded. "I won't kiss you." There was a pause before she added, "Until you kiss me first."

It seemed agreeable at the time because it was my fucking rule and I wouldn't cross it. Kissing was personal, *really* personal. And I thought if I kept at least one hard limit, the line between colleague and girlfriend would stay bright fucking neon in my mind.

I nodded and sat up so I could push my jeans off my legs. She kicked the covers down, tugging her pants with them. And then I was between her thighs again, holding myself up with one shaking arm by her ribs and positioning my straining cock at her entrance with the other.

"You're sure?" I asked, giving her one last chance to back out.

She grabbed my hips and yanked me into her. I tumbled forward, barely catching myself before I collapsed. And fucking sweet Jesus, her pussy was so tight and so fucking warm and wet, and fuck...

She might have been right.

I didn't think I was gonna last—

"Fuck me, Jericho," she said, cupping my face and bringing my focus back to her eyes. "You said something about rocking my world?"

I pulled out enough to surge back in at a different angle, pushing my entire cock inside of her. And she didn't even blink. Every other girl I'd been with had grimaced through the first few minutes. Even Nikki.

But Alba?

She bucked and arched into me, moaning and clawing at my shirt, urging me to go faster and harder. Even though this was vanilla-ass missionary, it was some of the hottest sex I'd ever had.

Sunshine was right to suggest this because ten pumps later, my balls clenched and my orgasm hit me right between the eyes. I emptied myself inside that tight little cunt like a fucking virgin.

Sweet. Fucking. Jesus.

I saw stars.

When I came back to my senses, Alba laughed and wrapped her arms around my neck, tugging me down on top of her while I panted and tried to get my fucking shit together.

"It's okay, Jericho," she said, pressing tender kisses to my forehead and eyebrows. "That was just for you."

8

———

ALBA

We talked into the night, asking questions and teasing each other until we laughed so hard we couldn't breathe. I didn't ask about the no-kissing thing, and he didn't bring it up again. But I stuck by it, even when he wanted to fuck me again this morning. He woke me at five a.m. with his fingers skating up my inner thighs and filthy whispers in my ear.

"Roll over," he said. "Let me take you before I have to go to work."

He did, slow and sensual, with one hand on my clit and the other wrapped around my body to hold me close. I tried to remind myself this was for the website. This was so we could get used to each other and the chemistry between us.

Alba and Jericho didn't fuck.

Aurora and Kaleb did for money.

That's it.

That's all.

End of story.

Alba and Jericho didn't even kiss.

So when he came hard inside me, his teeth deep in my shoulder, marking me and spurring my own climax, I told myself not to over-think it. And when we showered together, giggling and rubbing soap over each other's bodies, it meant nothing. Just two colleagues getting ready for their main job.

He had a run for the MC, and I had a full day of editing.

We wouldn't see each other until tomorrow, and that was okay. I'd upload what we had and we'd both make more money in a week than we ever did before. He'd charmed my mother the same way he had the first time, making her blush and roll her eyes with barely any effort.

"I'll come over as soon as I can," he said.

"Of course." I handed him coffee and a bagel. "Be careful."

"Always." He kissed my cheek, winked, and left. But this time, I went to the front door to watch him climb on his bike and drive away.

"Look at you," Mom said.

"What?" I turned to face her, my cheeks burning and my eyes wide like I was hiding a secret.

"You're blushing."

"No, I'm not." I went back to the kitchen to make my own coffee.

"Yes, you are." Mom slurped her vanilla protein mush. "Are you two a thing now?"

"No," I snapped, perhaps a little too quickly. I cleared my throat and tried again. "No. We're friends."

Mom laughed at me like I was an idiot because I was. I thought of the way he'd come last night, how beautiful and powerful he looked, how much it had turned me on to see him like that. Fucking Jericho was life changing, and I thanked whatever fates were looking out for me that we'd run into each other at that party.

"Well, perhaps you and your *just friend* would like to go out next Friday instead of having movie night with me?"

I narrowed my eyes and peered around the corner at her. "What?"

"I've arranged to have my own supervision," she said. "You can go on a date with Mr. Biker Blue Eyes."

I rubbed at the space between my eyebrows, sighing at how much that was going to cost. "Mom, we can't afford—"

"Let me worry about that," she said.

That made me even more suspicious. "Who is this person? Do

they know about your medicines? Do they know how to administer them?"

"Stop." Mom reached out to grab my hand. "Can you pretend for a moment that I'm the mother and you're the daughter and you've got twenty-two-year-old things to worry about?"

I took a deep breath and let it out through my nose. "I don't like this."

"I know," Mom answered. "But I still have a few brain cells left. And a few friends, apparently."

I swallowed down my guilt at trying to parent my parent. Maybe she was right. Maybe I needed to take a break. "Do I get to meet this mystery person?"

"Maybe." She narrowed her eyes. "If I'm ready to introduce you."

"Okay." I dropped the argument and picked up the remote. "What do you want to watch?"

I put on her soap operas and grabbed my laptop and headphones. I had a long day of editing ahead of me. Not that I particularly minded staring at Jericho for hours on end, but I wasn't good at this part. It took me longer than I thought it should, and I had no artistic vision.

After that, I set up a page for Kaleb Cox and put some filler on his profile until I could discuss the specifics with Jericho. I gave the video a snazzy title, "Stranger Comes On My Tits," and pressed upload.

Then I waited.

This was the part I hated the most, the anticipation of the inevitable reaction. I mean, it was a sex video, not a summer blockbuster, but still. I wanted to please my fans. I wanted them to know I genuinely cared about the quality of their whack, and I'd heard their concerns loud and clear.

They'd wanted a penis. I brought them a penis.

And an impressive one at that.

Jericho's cock was incredible, and resisting the urge to drag my tongue along it last night had taken an act of God. I deserved martyrdom.

Aurora Dawn, patron saint of big penises and horny nerd girls who liked sucking them.

I took off my headphones and closed the laptop before checking on Mom. She'd fallen asleep, so I went outside to catch a quick buzz.

Was I making a mistake with Jericho? I liked him a lot. But I needed this business to keep going, no matter what. He'd made it very clear this was a professional relationship. No strings attached.

Fuck it.

I didn't know if I planned to do this once I didn't have a reason for it anymore, and life was too short to worry about what might happen one day.

Sufficient unto the day is evil thereof.

I never considered myself religious, but the bible had a few nuggets of wisdom hidden in all that toxic misogyny. What would Jesus Christ think of me helping my mother at the expense of my chastity? He got down with the prostitutes and lowlifes, didn't he? The thought made me snicker.

By the time I came back inside and checked, the video had already been viewed two thousand times with a ninety-eight percent approval rating. Comments like "Fuck yeah, lucky guy" and "God, that was fucking hot" appeared under it. Warmth spread through me, and I dug out my phone to take a picture and text it to Jericho.

Alba: You're a hit, Kaleb.

I grinned to myself and ignored the pang that hit me square in the chest.

You better lock that down, Alba. There is no room for emotions here.

9

———

JERICHO

"Selene says you haven't been sleeping at home." Hollywood leaned up against his bike. We were at the rendezvous point, the same meetup spot we always hit on our Sunday runs. There was over half a million in guns and marijuana in the storage container behind us.

The buyer was supposed to meet us here five minutes ago. If he didn't show in the next ten, Hollywood and I would have to hunt him down, and I really didn't want to do that.

I raised an eyebrow and tilted my head to the other side, inhaling on my cigarette but refusing to comment on Hollywood's implied question.

"You haven't been at the clubhouse, either," he added.

I cleared my throat and took another long inhale. My phone buzzed in my pocket so I pulled it out to check.

Alba: *You're a hit, Kaleb.*

I laughed at the screenshot.

Look at all those horny little pervs appreciating my namesake.

"That her?" Hollywood nodded to my phone.

I clicked it off and put it in my back pocket, taking another long drag.

"C'mon, man, give me something."

"You don't have enough drama going on in your own life, so you gotta snoop around in mine?"

"I'm bored," he whined, throwing his head back like an impudent child. "This Sunday run eats up too much of my weekend."

"Get a hobby. Try a podcast," I said.

He scowled but shut the fuck up when bikes pulled into the lot. These were our extended brothers from out west, the Ohio chapter of the Steel Roses. It was good to see them, and we did the deal the same as always. They backed their truck in. They loaded up. We took the money and stuffed it into our saddlebags. We headed home. End of story.

Except this time, we got about halfway there before I noticed strange headlights behind me, an Aston Martin DB11. In this part of town, it stuck out like a sore thumb. At first, I'd been intrigued. But they'd been there for a while, and when we took the off-ramp to head into our turf in Madison, they continued to follow me.

We stopped at a light, and I pulled up alongside Hollywood to flash three fingers at him, a signal between us that I thought we had a tail. He nodded, indicating he saw and agreed.

We split up.

The tail stayed on me, which made me more fucking concerned since I had the bulk of the money. I turned on a road that weaved through the woods and up the side of a mountain. I gunned it on the straightaways while the Aston struggled to keep up, especially when I handled the steep turns with ease. I'd grown up on these roads. I knew them like the back of my hand.

Plus, I was on two wheels and they had four.

With my heart racing and exhilaration surging through me, I cut left, taking another hidden road that jutted out of nowhere.

The tail handled it well, apparently no longer giving a shit about being anonymous. Finally, I got on a road where I could let loose, really hit the turns and open the old girl up.

Five minutes on the windy street and my stalker was so far behind that I couldn't see them. I took a path that led me to a peak where I watched them from higher ground. They circled back on the roads, convinced I had taken a turn I hadn't. Eventually they gave up and turned around to head home. Part of me thought about following *them*, but I had to get to the clubhouse to tell Slip and Thor about it.

When I finally made it back, Hollywood had beaten me by twenty minutes.

"You lose them?" he asked when I climbed off the bike.

I nodded and took off my helmet.

"You know who it was?" Slip crossed his arms over his chest, his hawk eyes focusing in on me as I shook my head.

"They kept up with me for a long fucking time," I said. "I'm almost impressed."

Slip nodded as Thor and Crow came out of the clubhouse to get my version of events. We walked inside while I repeated the details, the sounds of music and partying a familiar comfort to my nerves. We headed to the back so they could sit around the table while I rehashed the story.

"Could be the Caputi fuckers," Thor said.

"Could be the PD." Crow rubbed his fingers over his forehead.

"Not in an Aston." Slip looked at me. "Keep your eyes open. Let us know if it happens again."

I nodded. "Saint and Aris make it back okay?"

They had another run with the New England chapter earlier today.

"They're on their way home now," Thor said.

That eased the stone in my stomach. If it was just me, that was one thing. I was smart. I knew these roads. I could lose anyone if I wanted to. But I didn't like the idea of anyone fucking with my brothers.

We talked for a few more minutes before Crow dismissed me and I went to the bar. Bear and Hollywood entertained themselves in the corner, random girls on their laps. A few guys from a visiting chapter sat in another corner, the club girls doing their best to show them a good time.

I debated hanging around for a while, but I'd meant what I said to Alba. I didn't intend to fuck around while I was working with her, so what was the point? She'd texted me to say how much money we'd already made and how much more we could still make.

I wanted to go to her, and I was all fucked up in the head about it.

It had only been two nights. I shouldn't be thinking about her the way I was. I shouldn't get this stupid fucking flutter in my chest whenever I thought about sliding in between those creamy thighs. I shouldn't feel like my skin was on fire any time I remembered how she tasted and smelled, how I desperately wanted to spear my fingers through her pussy and swallow down her moans.

What the fuck had she done to me?

"I don't fucking care, Thor," a girl said in a hushed tone to my right. I glanced up to see Thor and Selene standing at the far end of a darkened corridor together, as if hiding from the rest of the world. She had her arms crossed over her chest and he leaned up against the other wall, mirroring her posture.

"That's a lie," he said. "I'm your uncle. That's how everyone sees it."

She gave a sad laugh. "You were never my uncle. Not really."

What the fuck...

I wasn't supposed to be hearing this. Things had been fucked up between them for a long time, longer than I could remember. When Gemma was around, they were friendly. We were kids and Thor was in his twenties. But after Gemma left and Selene started bringing guys home, things got complicated.

Really fucking complicated from the sound of it.

Was I... supposed to deck my uncle for whatever this was?

Or was I supposed to stay out of it?

I cleared my throat, and both of them lifted their eyes. Thor straightened like his ass was on fire and stalked toward me, lowering his arms and nodding as he passed. That left me alone with my sister.

She raised an eyebrow. "Yeah?"

I wanted to ask. Every protective instinct I had wanted to berate her. But... did I really want to know? What if they were fucking? Would that change how I saw Thor? Would that change how I saw my sister? Ignorance was bliss sometimes.

"You okay?" I said instead. A better question, leaving room for open-ended interpretation on her part.

"Yeah." She shrugged. "Why?"

I frowned. We didn't lie to each other, not about the important shit. So either this wasn't important, or it was really fucking important and she didn't know how to tell me, not yet. I trusted my sister to say something if it got bad, so I dropped it. For now.

"No reason, I guess."

She nodded at the keys in my hand. "Where are you headed?"

"Home."

Now was her turn to be confused. "You're not planning to make Fingers's night?"

I laughed. "Nah, not into robbing the cradle."

Selene's cheeks flamed, and she looked away, rubbing the back of her neck. I acted like I didn't know why she'd be embarrassed about me saying that.

"See you at home?"

She shrugged. "Don't know. Maybe I'll get lucky. One of the New England guys is super hot." She waved at him from across the room, and when I followed her gaze, he winked and grinned.

Clapping her shoulder, I shook my head and took a step toward the door. "Good luck. Be careful."

"Always am."

Another lie, but whatever. I had my own bad decisions to make.

I'D BEEN ABOUT to climb on my bike when someone called my name from behind. My spine stiffened at the voice, a small groan of annoyance echoing from the back of my throat.

"Jer," she said again.

I turned to face her, taking a deep breath. I'd gotten over Nikki. I didn't feel a damn thing for the lying, cheating bitch anymore, but that didn't mean I enjoyed talking to her.

"Hey, Nikki," I said. "How's it going?"

She sighed as she waddled closer, her six-month pregnant belly protruding from under a T-shirt that had once fit her perfectly.

"Oh, it's going." She eyed me up and down, a small smile on her lips. "How are you?"

"Fine." I crossed my arms over my chest and leaned back against my bike. "What's up?"

She shrugged. "Just wanted to see how you were doing. We haven't talked since—" Since I did a weekend in lockup because of her. "Well, it's been a while."

"Over a year. How's married life?"

She grinned and rubbed her hands over her stomach. "Honestly, it's great."

It should have stung, but it didn't because my thoughts went to last night and how great I'd felt in Alba's arms. I cleared my throat and shoved my hands in my pockets. "What do you want, Nikki?"

"Hollywood says you're seeing someone?"

"Hollywood doesn't know what the fuck he's talking about."

Nikki shrugged. "Who is she?"

I narrowed my eyes, apprehension slithering up my spine.

Why the fuck did she care?

It was on the tip of my tongue.

"I just—I hope she makes you happy. That's all."

I appreciated the sentiment, even if I'd rather swim through shit than talk to Nikki again. "Have a nice night, Nik."

I swung my leg over my bike and stuck the key in the ignition as she took two steps back and frowned. There was guilt in her eyes, regret over the fact we'd tried so hard for so long and it still hadn't worked out. Mostly because of her.

She turned to head back inside, and I kicked my bike into first and took off. I didn't even have a destination in mind. Alba's house. Mine. Nowhere at all. I just couldn't stay there.

Inevitably, I ended up there anyway, at the top of the mountain on Mount Zion Lane, smoking a blunt while I stared at the view. Even in the dark, the outline of the trees gave way to the valley below. Technically, Aris owned all this land, even the garage and the sheds out behind it. But that was to protect the MC. Out in those sheds stood whatever the Roses needed to hide that week. Drugs. Arms. Money. At any given moment, they could be empty or full.

I told myself that coming here had nothing to do with Alba. Nothing to do with her at all.

I just liked this smoking spot.

That's all, right?

Eventually, the light from Alba's front door caught my attention, and I resisted smiling as my librarian cam girl came closer, bundled up in a knit blanket, her hair in a messy bun on top of her head and her glasses perched low on her nose.

"What are you doing out here, you creeper?"

"Well, I'm creeping." I passed the blunt to her, which she took, inhaling. "Isn't it obvious?"

She chuckled and nodded back toward the house. "Wanna come in?"

I should have told her no. I should have broken this off and gotten as far away from her as I could. Tonight I'd been chased by God knows who and tomorrow, it could be worse. I could be alive this second, dead the next, and if she got involved with me? Her life would be linked to mine and to the MC forever. I thought of Alba pregnant with some other dude's baby, all because I'd sworn her off and she had nowhere else to go.

But then my thoughts went to an image of Alba pregnant with *my* baby, a *Property of KC* tattoo on the inside of her wrist, one I kissed every fucking night after I fucked my old lady to sleep. Something hot and wicked went through me, and I wrapped my arms around her waist, pulling her in close and ghosting my lips over her nose and forehead.

Stay professional, I reminded myself when I wanted to go for her mouth. *This is going to end soon. This isn't forever.*

She'd said it. I'd said it.

I should go home. Get some space.

But that's not what I told Alba. Out loud, I said, "Yeah, sunshine. Take me inside."

10

———

ALBA

The next morning, I woke up with Jericho wrapped around me, one arm over my stomach and his leg tucked between mine. I looked at the time—6:45. I had half an hour until my alarm went off, and the sleepy side of me wanted to close my eyes and forget consciousness was a thing.

But then I registered the hard body behind me, evidence of his maleness poking me in the butt.

I rocked into him, and he groaned, stretched, and held me tighter.

We hadn't fucked last night when I'd brought him in. I could tell something was off with him, so I took him downstairs, tucked him under the covers, and wrapped myself around him until the tension eased.

But this morning?

Well, I lived to be a tease.

I rolled my ass against him again and he moaned, nibbling at my shoulder and digging his fingers into the crotch of my panties so he could pull the fabric to the side. His cock pressed at my entrance, and I arched into him, granting silent permission he hadn't asked for. I gasped when he surged home, all the way in, all at once.

Jericho was big, and I wasn't prepared, but he moved his callused fingers to my clit and the friction opened me like a lotus, bared completely to him. It was slow and lazy, born out of this intimacy between us where we swore there was none. I came first, clawing at his arm wrapped around my chest, euphoria exploding in my veins.

His orgasm hit next, and he dug his teeth into my skin, marking me. Maybe I'd turned into some kind of sicko because I hoped it'd be permanent. I hoped everyone saw them and knew he'd put them there.

When we were a sated pile of mush, I climbed out of bed to hit the shower. Jericho wordlessly followed me, blinking into the bathroom light with that adorable, sleepy look on his face.

"Morning," he grumbled.

"Morning." I turned on the water and stepped inside, closing the glass door when he came in behind me. I backed up until my knees hit the cool tile bench, adjusting the second showerhead so I had some water, too. "What are your plans for the day?"

He shrugged. "Work. There's a pickup that needs a new engine. Maybe some new struts, too."

"Fun."

"What about you?"

I grabbed the washcloth and sudsed it, circling it over my arms and breasts and down my stomach. "Um... I have some client calls. Maybe I'll film a scene later."

"You better wait for me to get home to film." He wrapped his arms around me, nibbling my earlobe and sending chills down that whole side of my body. "Wait... client calls?"

"I meet with fans one-on-one," I said absently, like it meant nothing. Because it did mean nothing to me. It didn't matter whether the fans watched my live feed or my edited videos. Camming was camming. But Jericho's arms tensed around me, and he let out a low growl, almost like a warning.

"What's that noise?" I raised an eyebrow.

"I don't like it."

"That's too bad. It's a big part of my income." I pursed my lips and tried to pull away, but he held me tighter.

"How big?"

I laughed and pressed my lips to the center of his chest, trying to seduce him into letting go. "You can't afford me, Mr. Mechanic Man."

"Maybe Jericho can't afford you, but Kaleb can."

"Oh, not yet," I said, giving him another kiss. This time I went lower, above his heart. He loosened his hold and paused, staring down his body at me flicking my tongue over the divots in his stomach. Inching lower. Teasing choice bits. His cock jerked against me, making me chuckle.

"I thought we were exclusive," he said.

"No one's touching me," I said. "They don't even know who I am. They're just getting a private show." Another kiss. Another lick. A hint of teeth just above his cock. It kicked harder.

Jer took a deep breath and let it out through his nose. "It does make me hot to know I'm the only one who gets to touch you."

"See?" I coasted the tip of my tongue over his cockhead. He groaned and put his hands in my hair, tugging me up.

"Don't think you can seduce me into being okay with this." He grabbed my chin and forced me to look back at him. "How much would you have to make to stop doing the private sessions?"

"We'd have to film a lot more. Like... a lot more. Some of my clients tip me a grand at a time."

He nodded and leaned down to kiss my forehead. "Challenge accepted."

I laughed until I realized he wasn't kidding. "Oh. You mean that."

"Yeah." He shrugged like it was normal. "We can film in the morning before I go to work and when I get back at the end of the day."

I grimaced, my pussy practically revolting at the thought. "That's a lot of fucking."

"Listen, I'm a territorial shit." He took a step closer. "You said we were exclusive. That means no one else. Now, I know you've got bills to pay, so if there's a way I can have my cake and eat it out, then..."

I rolled my eyes at his pun.

"It bugs me, you talking to other people the way I want you

talking to me. Even if it's just online." He ran his hands over my shoulders and up my neck to cup my jaw. "I don't share. Ever."

I understood, and if the shoe were on the other foot, I wouldn't like it either. I wouldn't say I was falling in love with Jericho, but there was a part of me, still small and innocent, that considered him mine. Already and forever.

"You should know, you're like... a thousand times better for me than any of them. And you're here. Right here. In front of me." I kissed his chest again. His neck. His collarbone. "There's no way I'd leave you for them."

"Doesn't matter," he said. "You're mine. End it. Tonight."

I looked between his eyes, willing to compromise, but wanting to be sure this plan would work. "You make up my income first, then I'll end it."

He growled his protest, but didn't argue any further. Just flipped me around and bent me over the bench so he could fuck me again before work.

I SPENT most of the day taking care of Mom, and once she was settled in, I texted Jericho, who gave me very specific instructions for later.

Jericho: Don't come on any of the calls today. Save it for me. Only me.

Which I agreed to because a) it was super fucking hot when he talked like that, and b) it was easy to fake it with these people. The real work was about them. Making them miserable or happy, depending on what they were into. At the end of the day, they paid to come. It didn't matter whether I did.

By the time Jericho got home, I'd made enough money to afford the medical payment and next week's grocery bill, and I still had time to put the chicken in the oven.

"Wow, four times in one week," Mom said when he came in the front door, dirty and filthy from the shop. He had a duffel bag in one hand and his cut in the other. "Aren't we lucky?" Mom looked at me in the kitchen, but I ignored her in favor of my greasy mechanic.

Jesus Christ.

I didn't know T-shirts covered in motor oil and ripped-up dirty jeans could be a kink, but there I stood, lusting after my cam colleague and blushing in front of my mother.

"Are you saying you're sick of me, Penny?" Jericho smiled and winked.

"I'd never get sick of you, Jericho," Mom said. "But I am wondering if you're gonna start paying rent. A week's a guest. A month's a roommate."

"Mom!" I hissed.

"What?" She shrugged at me. "We could use the help."

"He is helping," I said.

"How?" She furrowed her brows at me.

"Never mind." I returned my attention to Jer. "Are you hungry? I'm making chicken with rice and broccoli."

"Sounds great," he said. "I'll take a shower and be right up."

I smiled and bit my bottom lip, watching him walk through the living room to the door leading downstairs.

Again, I felt Mom's glare on me. "What?"

"What's he doing here?" she said. "Are you two dating?"

"We're working together," I said before I could stop it. "On a project."

"What project?"

I rubbed the space between my brows. "You said you wouldn't ask how I paid for things."

She narrowed her eyes. "That's when I thought you were paying for them *by yourself.* Are you sleeping with him for money?"

"What?" I acted shocked, but she wasn't too far from the truth. "No!"

"Operating a phone sex line is one thing, but I draw the line at prostitution."

"Is that what you think I do?" I asked. "Operate a phone sex line?"

"Well?" She crossed her arms over her chest. "You won't tell me what it really is, so I assume it's something you don't want me to know. I hear you down there talking to people sometimes."

I took a deep breath and pulled the chicken out of the oven. "It's not 1994. No one calls phone sex lines anymore. Everyone looks at OnlyFans."

"What's that?" Mom grabbed her phone and started typing, but I couldn't get to her fast enough to stop it.

"Oh," she said. "Oh, damn. Girls are doing this these days?"

I cleared my throat and nodded to the basement. "*We're* doing this these days."

"You're doing this... together?"

My cheeks burned, and I shook my head. "I was doing it on my own, but I met Jericho at a party and then... well... we're doing pretty good so far. Please don't judge me."

"Judge you?" She laughed and shook her head. "Honey, I commend you. I wish this shit was around when I was your age. God, you know what I used to do when I was in my twenties? Restock videos at Blockbuster. Jesus Christ. OnlyFans. Wow."

I laughed, a great weight easing off my chest. "I'm happy I told you. I'm sorry I kept it from you this long."

She smiled. "You can always tell me anything, baby."

"I love you, Mom."

"Love you, too."

I hugged her, and overcome with the notion this might be the last time I confessed anything to her, tears welled in the corners of my eyes and spilled down my cheeks. Sobs choked out of my throat, and Mom held me tighter with her weak arms.

Then my stomach growled, and she laughed, letting me go.

"I like him, you know." She nodded toward the basement. "He looks at you the right way."

"Oh yeah?" I wiped under my eyes. "What way's that?"

"Like he's afraid he'll break you, but he's damn determined to protect you from everything else that ever could."

I cleared my throat and tried to smile through the ache that caused.

"It's the way your daddy looked at me." She dabbed at her eye and forced a smile on her face, grabbing my hand with a squeeze. "But I want you to promise me something."

I narrowed my gaze. "Okay, Mom. Anything."

"Don't you dare fall in love with him."

My heart clenched, and my stomach dropped somewhere around my knees.

It might already be too late for that.

I pushed that thought away and forced a grin.

"Don't be ridiculous," I said, rolling my eyes. "I've only known him a week."

She mumbled a low *uh-huh*. "I've dated lots of bad boys in my day, Alba. That life?" She shook her head. "It's dangerous. Bloody. And if they don't end up dead by the time they're forty, it's the pen." Something flickered behind her eyes, an expression I could only guess at. "He'll never choose you over the club. He's sworn his life to them, and they'll always come first. Before everything."

I opened my mouth to ask how she could possibly know that, but the basement door opened and Jericho walked through it, freshly showered and dressed in clean clothes with that smile on his face.

"You want me to set the table?" He looked between my mom and me before heading into the dining room to do it anyway.

I wanted to circle back to her comment about how she knew what life in an MC would be like. She'd grown up in the suburbs. My grandparents died some time ago, and my sperm donor's parents didn't know I existed. My dad had been a business owner-turned-alcoholic who lost it all shortly after conceiving me. None of that involved bad boys or outlaws or sexy men on bikes.

But I chose not to bring it up again. Instead, I focused on getting supper together. It had been months since we'd eaten in the dining room like a proper family, but Jericho sat across from me and I angled Mom at the head. We turned the TV off and talked about our days.

"I finally figured out the pickup." Jericho took a bite of the chicken and sighed, nodding like it was amazing. "Delicious, sunshine. Jesus."

"Thank you."

He filled us in on the things he'd done at work, and I told him Mom knew our dirty little secret but didn't care. And somewhere around me refilling everyone's drinks, Mom piped up with, "Hey, Jericho, guess what?"

"What's that, Penny?"

"I found someone to babysit me for free on Friday night."

"Really?" He smiled, glancing up while I poured water from the pitcher into his glass.

"Yep," she said. "An old friend I haven't seen in a while."

"Is it an old friend or, you know, an *old friend?*" Jericho winked, making her laugh and shake her head.

"Maybe both."

"All right, Penny." Jericho nodded at her. "Get it."

"I was thinking maybe you could take Alba on a date. Get her out of the house."

I gasped and straightened, setting the pitcher down so I could reprimand my mother at her own table. "Mom! I don't need your help—"

"Of course," Jericho interrupted. "I'd be honored."

I sighed. "I'm sure you've got a million better things to do on a Friday night than take me anywhere."

"Yeah?" He pursed his lips, stabbed a broccoli floret, and bit into it before saying, "Like what?"

"All your biker club stuff." I scooped some rice into my mouth. "Don't you have like... bad guys to beat up or whatever?"

He snorted out a laugh, my cheeks burning when adoration flitted behind his eyes. And I knew then what my mother meant by liking the way he looked at me.

"I only do that on Sundays." Jericho tilted his head to the side and smiled. "Fridays are for taking out pretty girls."

"Then it's settled," Mom cut in. "Don't come home before midnight. No, one. I need the extra hour to recoup."

"Jesus Christ." I laughed and covered my face with my hands.

"Deal." Jericho grinned and took a drink of water, the muscles in his tattooed throat working when he swallowed.

God, he was so gorgeous. And funny and smart and sweet. I didn't know how I'd lucked out and found him.

I'm not a good guy, Alba.

He'd told me that our second night together after he came on my tits and I licked it off my fingers. But I didn't believe that, not anymore. Jericho might end up being the best thing that ever happened to me, and that terrified me most of all.

He'll never choose you over the club.

My mother's warning rattled through me, and I reminded myself I still planned to leave. I still planned to get out of here as soon as I could. Jericho had no place in that plan, and I needed to remember that.

11

———

JERICHO

I stared down at the piece of paper in front of me and pursed my lips. "What the fuck is this?"

"It's a kink checklist." Alba smiled widely, nudging it farther across the bed. "You mark things you'd be into, things you'd try, and things that are a hard limit."

It had three long columns of stuff I'd never heard of before with two boxes next to each: giving or receiving. I was supposed to mark Y for yes, M for maybe, and N for no. She'd already done hers and now waited anxiously for me to fill out mine.

"Can't we just fuck and figure it out?"

"Production value," she said. "Remember? I have to know what you like and don't like."

I rubbed at the back of my neck, setting the list to the side so I could use my weight to crowd her and make her lean back on the bed. She wrapped her legs around my hips but reached for the paper, pretending not to pay any attention to me.

"Facials? I think we've established that's a yes to giving." She scribbled something on the paper while I kissed my way down her neck. "What about you? Want me to squirt on your face?"

"That's a possibility?" I perked up my head, my eyebrows raised.

She shrugged. "If you play your cards right."

"Damn." I grinned like an idiot and climbed back up her torso, relaxing on the bed next to her. "You're fucking filthy. I love it."

She narrowed her eyes and rolled over, putting a hand under her head to support its weight on her elbow. "What do you want me to do to you?"

I considered. "No one's ever asked me that before."

"I want you to fuck me on your bike."

The visual that went through my mind stunned me. I'd done some wild shit, but my cheeks burned when I thought about bending her over the seat and holding her down while I fucked the life out of her.

Probably best not to film that one, though.

"And somewhere beautiful." She smiled, seemingly lost in her fantasy as she pushed her glasses higher on her face. "I like to be fucked in public, and I like when other people watch." She told me a whole fucking laundry list of things she wanted to do, places and ways she wanted me to take her.

"If you want my ass, you have to plug me first. I insist."

I'd never fucked anyone in the ass. Nikki never wanted to, and my cock was too big for anyone else to even attempt. (I know it takes some arrogance to say that, but it's true.)

"Have you ever done anal play?" She rolled into me, putting her chin on my pec and looking up at me with those big blue eyes. I brushed my thumb over her lips. Such a dirty fucking mouth on such an innocent-looking girl.

"Nope," I said.

"Would you want to?"

I laughed, saying the first thing that came to my mind. "If you get three shots in me, I'll do anything you ask."

"Three shots?" That made her smile. "Only three?"

"Any more and I'm a mess. Any less, and I'm not drunk enough."

"I'll keep that in mind." She draped one leg over my hips and sat on my pelvis, reaching for the list again. I put my hands on her thighs which were so soft and hypnotizing, I ached to have them pressing into my ears while I face-fucked her pussy. "Okay, throat fucking, yes. Threesomes?"

"No." I'd be firm on that.

She pursed her lips and marked it down, but there was amusement in her eyes.

"Roleplay?" Her brows rose up her face.

"Sure." I nodded and bucked my hips, making her lurch forward. "You wanna dress up in a schoolgirl outfit? Do a stint in detention with Professor Kaleb?"

"Only if you dress up like a Salvatore and keep me locked up all day since you can't go out in the sun."

I narrowed my eyes, considering. "Which Salvatore?"

"Either one."

"Wrong," I teased. "The only answer is Damon."

She giggled and shook her head, going back to the list. But I'd had enough. I grabbed it and tossed it to the side, pulling her forward so she lay across my torso. I brushed her hair out of her face and smiled.

"How about this? I'll show up tomorrow, ready to film. I'll tell you what to do, and you'll listen."

"I'm the professional here."

"Yeah?" I leaned closer. "Well, I'm the one with the dick. And I'm going to put it wherever I want."

She gasped, her mouth hanging open.

"Consensually, of course." I grinned, relishing in the mock outrage on her face, and I rolled us so she was under me. Working my way down her body again, I unbuttoned her jeans and tugged down the zipper so I could get my hands under the waistline. Sitting back, I yanked them off her.

"If you keep your shirt on, your tattoos won't be as noticeable." She ran a foot up my thigh, digging her toes into my crotch and running her arch over my cock. Goddamn me, she was so fucking sexy. I could spend eons in this bed with her. But we had a plan tonight, and that was to plan tomorrow night.

"Okay." I shook my head, reminding my cock to wait for his

fucking turn. "I'll go down on you first. Then you'll blow me. We'll rearrange the camera, and I'll fuck you."

"Yeah." She nodded. "There's room for improvisation. Go with your gut." She edged her foot closer to my balls. "Or your… intuition." She tilted her head to the side. "Either way, get the camera."

"Right now?"

"Yeah, Kaleb. I want you to eat my pussy until I come. And if you do it real good, I'll show you my hidden talent."

"Hidden talent, huh?" I inched off the bed and grabbed the camera, firing it up before angling it on the tripod.

"Yeah, it drives all the boys wild."

Swallowing down a slice of possessive jealousy, I handed a mask to her before retrieving my own. She tugged off her shirt, and I took my spot between her legs, yanking them closer as I lay down.

I bit her inner thighs, coasting my way toward my goal. Then I dove in. Licking her. Teasing her. Kissing her. She moaned, pinching her nipples, and I grabbed her hips so I could get closer. Jesus, I could have been down there for years. Decades. Who the hell knew? Because once I started fucking her with my fingers, time didn't matter anymore.

She said something about squirting on my face, so when she got close and tightened her fingers in my hair, she murmured, "Harder, harder," and I rubbed her clit as fast as I could with the palm of my hand.

Alba came with a loud groan and an arch of her back, her legs shaking while she tried to push me away. But I wouldn't let her. I stayed on her, lapping at everything she had to offer. She laughed and moaned, and the way she panted made me feel like a Goddamned king. Nikki had never been that free with me. She'd never orgasmed like that before.

"Fucking hell, Kaleb." She sat up and ran a hand down the side of my face, smiling in that hazy post-climax way.

"You like that, sunshine?"

"Yes," she said.

I kissed her knee, sitting back on my heels so I could take in every inch of this moment and the way she looked, spread out for me like this.

"Can I have your cock now? Please?" She pouted.

I normally didn't get into the whole master and submissive dynamic. Sometimes I wanted her to hold me down and take what she wanted. But having her ask me for my dick, which I would give to her at any time and on any day, sent a rush of power straight to my balls.

"Yeah, you can. Get on your knees."

Alba grinned and twisted us around so she could climb off the bed and walk to the camera, leaving me to sit there, stroking my cock and trying to keep my head in the game.

"Okay, that was really good." She gave me a smile. "Let's have you stand for the blow job."

Right. We were shooting a fucking porno here.

"Or would you rather sit?"

I tried to keep my brain in charge. I tried to talk like I had some Goddamned sense in my head, but when I opened my mouth, the only thing that came out was, "I don't care where you suck my dick. Just get back over here and do it."

She laughed and knelt between my knees, her arms on my thighs, her eyes peering up at me while she wrapped her pretty fingers around my cock.

"How long's it been since someone sucked you dry, Kaleb?"

I didn't get a chance to answer before she licked the tip and all words left my brain completely. She circled her warm tongue around the head and took me in her mouth, all the way back, sliding down her throat. It constricted around me.

I clenched my hands in her hair. Sparks of lust and euphoria shot down my legs, and I made noises I'd never heard come out of a man before.

"Fucking sweet Jesus!"

She chuckled, and the vibrations rang through me. She did it again and again, marking another thing off our list. Alba fucked me with her face. All I had to do was sit there and watch it and try not to blow my load in two fucking seconds.

"God, you're so good at that. Look at you. Such a good little slut for me." I muttered a bunch of shit people say when they're in the heat of the moment and the hormones take over and all reason fades away. Alba worked me right over the edge.

"I'm about to come." That's all the warning I gave before she sucked me all the way back, gulping down every last drop.

I couldn't fucking think.

I couldn't fucking breathe.

I ran my shaking hands over my face and laughed as Alba stood and wiped at her mouth.

"Aw, moonbeam. Looks like I rocked your world."

All I could do was breathe and give her the finger.

"Ever been chained to a bed and birched?" Hollywood clapped me on the shoulder and took a big swig of water. He and Bear were helping out at the shop today, and while I normally enjoyed their company, I couldn't get my fucking mind off the videos Alba and I had filmed yesterday.

Smut that likely found its way to the internet by now.

After she sucked me off, I needed a few minutes to get my bearings before she climbed on my face and rode me until she worked out six weeks of pent-up energy. Until the nine months between her and Nikki turned into fucking nothing.

"Birched?" Bear scooted out from under an old Honda and narrowed his eyes. "Jesus fucking Christ, Hollywood. What the fuck are you into?"

"It's this girl I've been seeing." Hollywood wiped his hands on a rag, going back to the truck up on the lift. He had the wheels off, just about to check the brakes. "She likes some wild shit."

Objectively.

Alba had tied me to her bed last night and used my tongue like a dildo for the whole internet to see. Did that count? Probably. But I wasn't about to tell Hollywood and Bear. These two assholes would spread it around the club in seconds.

"I'm gonna do the world a favor and tell you to stop sharing in general." Bear shook his head and sighed.

"What about you?" Hollywood raised an eyebrow at my cousin. "I saw you go home with that brunette the other night."

"There's no brunette. Stay out of my personal life." Bear slid back under the car, effectively ending the conversation.

But all that did was make Hollywood turn his attention to me. "KC?"

"Hollywood."

"How's your—"

"No fucking way."

That shut him up, and he stood to walk over to the office, mumbling as he passed, "Y'all are a bunch of prudes."

That's not how I felt, not when I spent all fucking day thinking about her. Dreaming about her. Fantasizing about what I planned to do tonight. I'd make her dress up in that schoolgirl outfit she'd promised. I'd make her confess every rotten thing she'd ever thought about me.

Wondering what she was doing right now, I dug out my phone and texted.

She replied quickly with a shot of her covered in a face mask, making a kissy face.

I couldn't have adored her more if I tried. I sent back naughty instructions about what I wanted her to do when I got home, but she only sent me a teasing cleavage shot in response, followed by a winky emoji.

The brat.

I would have to take it out on her ass.

"Who ya smiling at, KC?"

I glanced up to find Ru standing in front of me, her arms wrapped around a stack of textbooks. Aris's daughter and a fellow MC princess, she and Selene were like sisters. Unfortunately for me, that made her an adopted little sister. A few months ago, she'd gotten into a car accident with Saint, and I'd rescued them approximately half a second after they hooked up. Hollywood and I were the only ones who knew what happened, and to this day, they still hadn't gone public. But that shit was none of my business, so I never brought it up again.

"No one." I clicked my phone off. "Selene's in the office."

She narrowed her blue eyes and brushed her curly brown hair behind her ears. When she made that face, she reminded me so much of her father, like she saw down to my soul without me having to do anything. She reminded me of someone else, too, but I couldn't figure out who.

"Is that the girl you went home with the other night?" She raised her eyebrow. "Alba?"

"Jesus, you all gossip like fucking children."

Ru laughed, and Hollywood came back into the garage, throwing an arm over her shoulders as he looked down at her books. "Whatcha got for me?"

She grinned and turned to face him. "Economics and marketing homework." She held her books out. "Want some?"

"Ew." He scrunched his nose and backed away. "Fuck off with that."

"Selene's going to help me with the econ. She's really good at math." She gave him a saucy smile and backed into the office, shutting the door behind her.

Hollywood nodded at her retreating form. "Hey, when'd Ru get to be so fucking smart, huh?"

"Ru's always been smart," Bear said from under the car, wrenching something tighter. "I think the real question is... when'd you get to be so fucking stupid, huh?"

"Fuck off before I drop that Honda on your ugly fucking face." Hollywood came closer and threatened to kick the jack, making Bear rush out from under the car and jump to his feet.

"You fucking asshole." Bear punched out at Hollywood, who

dodged it and shoved his fist away, giving him a quick tap on the cheek. Bear's face turned beet fucking red, and he launched himself at Hollywood, pushing him out of the garage doors and into the parking lot. Bear growled and Hollywood laughed. It reminded me of being a kid and doing the same thing with them.

"Hey, whoa, whoa, watch where the fuck you're going!" Trojan shoved at his brother as they passed, nodding when he came into the garage. "Hey, lady killer."

"What's up?"

He shook his head. "Same old shit."

Trojan had inherited the calmer side of their genetics. Hollywood lived for the flash and the glamor. Trojan had once been in the army. Special ops. He'd seen shit. He'd done things he wouldn't talk about. Level-headed didn't begin to describe the dude.

I liked him. He had always been a good friend to Thor, a good brother to the rest of us, and a good ole man to his wife, Marissa.

"Your uncle around?"

I shook my head. "Haven't seen him."

He and Selene had gotten into a fight or something, and whenever that happened, he made himself scarce for a few days.

"Check the clubhouse. Sometimes he holes up there."

Trojan nodded, eyeing me with skepticism. "You ready for Sunday?"

He meant the meetup at the docks and the rabbit chase out of there. Honestly, it was a big fucking deal. And if I dwelled on it, I might talk myself out of it. So I didn't.

I grinned and nodded, pretending to be nonchalant. "Yeah, man. Born ready."

"All right, kid." When he turned to leave, he pointed at Bear chasing Hollywood across the field out behind the place. "Hey, keep an eye on my bonehead brother, yeah? He's a fucking idiot sometimes, but we love him."

I chuckled. "You got it."

Funny how little details could stick out in a moment. Like the way Trojan's boots made clouds of dust on the gravel as he walked away.

Or the glint in his smile as he waved goodbye to his brother several yards in the distance. Or the shimmer coming off his cut as he mounted his bike and rode off.

My phone vibrated again, drawing my attention down to a half-naked Alba, one arm wrapped over her chest, covering her nipples, and the other hand between her spread legs, hiding her pussy.

Jericho: Move your hands.

Alba: Oh, that'll cost you.

Jericho: Name your price.

Alba: Three words: Hot. Werewolf. Roleplay.

I laughed, knowing she was only mostly serious. *Fuck yeah.*

Jericho: You got it, sunshine. Show me your goods.

The pictures came rolling in. What the fuck had I done to deserve her? And what would I do without her? Once this was over and she came to her Goddamned senses, ending this idiotic affair with me, I'd be so fucked.

Maybe that's the moment I knew. Even though I'd met her less than a week ago. Even though I couldn't admit it to myself or anyone else. But deep down, I knew.

Alba was it for me.

12

ALBA

"I have to go," I told my client, closing my legs while he wiped himself off.

"I saw your new videos," he said. "You've got a man now?"

I smiled, putting my bra and underwear back on. "Yeah. He's sweet."

"As sweet as me?"

"No one's as sweet as you."

He forwarded me another $200.

"You're a darling." He laughed. "Well, look, I'd be willing to pay double for both of you."

"What?" I narrowed my eyes.

"Yeah, if he does what I tell him, and you do what I tell you." John shrugged. "Could be fun."

I tried to imagine Jericho going for that, and the thought made me giggle. "I'll ask."

"Good. Thank you for the fun. See you in a few days."

I ended the chat and sat back, considering John's offer. Jericho had been pretty clear about not sharing me with anyone else. Did a live session as Aurora and Kaleb count as a threesome? That might be cutting it too close. Maybe we could open it up to my entire fan base, even if John wouldn't get our sole focus.

I got off the bed and put my laptop on the dresser, smiling at the sight of Jericho making my mom laugh on the monitor. He waved goodbye to her and headed toward the basement, the door opening before his boots thundered down the stairs. He slowed when he made eye contact with me, dragging his gaze down my outfit and back up again.

I was still in my lingerie from the call with John.

He'd specifically told me to be naked, on my knees, thigh-high stockings in place, and ready for his scene.

"You're early." I raised an eyebrow and put my hands on my hips.

Jer narrowed his blue eyes and closed the distance between us, grabbing me around the waist and pulling my pelvis close to his. "I couldn't wait to get here. Not after the way you teased me all day."

I disentangled myself from his arms and went to the dresser, digging around for the white linen tights. "Well, I still have to change."

"You have client calls earlier?"

I nodded, biting my bottom lip as naughty ideas brewed in my heart. "John wants to watch both of us."

That got his attention, and Jer's eyes grew wide.

"He said he'd pay double."

He pursed his lips. "What's he paying now?"

I shrugged. "At least two hundred an hour. But I walked away with nearly a grand tonight."

"A grand?" Jer's eyes bulged. "You think my dick's worth a grand?"

I smiled, going back to him to grab his ass and give it a big squeeze. "Baby, your dick's worth much more than that to me."

He laughed and ran a finger down the center of my nose. "Take off the bra and panties. Put on the tights." He smacked my butt, jostling the plug I'd put in there earlier, and moved to the camera, checking the settings to make sure everything was the way he wanted it. I stripped down, stuffing my legs into the thigh highs before bouncing over to the bed.

Digging my fingers into the soft comforter, I waited for him to get ready. He took off his cut, putting it at the far end of the room so it'd be completely out of the frame, but he left his long-sleeved shirt on, my idea to keep his tattoos hidden. The MC had enemies, and Jer didn't want to put me in danger if anyone recognized him, which I respected.

Then he turned to face me, the heat in his gaze simmering my blood.

"Aurora." His deep voice rattled through me, pushing me into the right headspace for what was about to happen. We'd spent most of the day preparing. He knew my limits. He knew what I wanted out of this scene. So now? There was nothing more to do than do it.

"Kaleb."

He wrapped his mask around his face, tied it at the back, and came closer, stopping at the edge of the bed.

I grinned, re-adjusting my lace covering and pushing up on my knees so we were eye level.

"Did you do what I told you?" He kissed my forehead. My temple. My cheek. My neck. Everywhere but my lips. "You were a good girl?"

Again, I nodded. "I was so good for you. Everyone else can try to make me come, but only you know how to do it right, Kaleb."

"That's what I like to hear." He pushed me until I lay on my back and adjusted me so we were at the best angle for the audience, his hands on either side of my hips to hold himself over my body.

"Do you want me to lick your pussy?"

I nodded, biting my bottom lip.

"Tell me."

God, he was so fucking hot when he talked to me like that. "Lick me, please. I've been so desperate for you."

He smiled and disappeared down my body, trailing a line across the center of my stomach and teasing closer to the skin that had throbbed for him all day. He pressed his strong fingers into my knees, holding me open for him and spreading me farther so the camera got a good view. I nearly arched off the bed when his tongue speared through me.

I might live for a thousand years and the sensation of Jericho between my legs would never cease to make me weak. He read me like a book, waiting for my reactions and rubbing his hands over the insides of my thighs and up my body. He circled one around my throat, creating the illusion of holding me down while he ate me out. He fingered me and scratched my legs and worked me like he owned me.

And Jesus Christ, when I came, my entire body exploded. Hard. I fisted my hands in his hair. He slipped two fingers inside me, pumping me, the euphoria of this moment yanking me under its spell.

"Jesus fucking Christ. Fuck yeah, Aurora."

The release decimated me. Every muscle in my body clenched, and I curled into a ball, but Jericho kept going, kept working me until I was too sensitive and had to push him away.

Maybe it was the buildup of the whole day or the flickers of emotion crushing my chest, but this climax took me over in a way I'd never experienced before. It pulled me apart and put me back together, and when the world finally righted itself, my head was woozy and the world had gone hazy.

"Stop." The word sounded breathless and scratchy, like someone had sandblasted my vocal cords. "Stop. Stop." I opened my eyes and glanced down at my body where he stood at the edge of the bed, wiping at his mouth, his forearms and chest completely drenched.

I took a deep breath and let it out on a sigh, my cunt pulsing in arousal at the sight.

"That"—he pointed to me and the wet blankets under me—"was the hottest thing I've ever fucking seen. You squirted fucking every-where." He took a step back toward the camera. "I hope we got that." Jericho grabbed at his dick over his jeans while he messed with the screen. "Jesus, it looks even better on camera."

"Kaleb," I lay down, a heady urge overwhelming my nerves. "I need you."

He flicked his attention back to me and grinned. "Yeah? What do you need?"

"Will you fuck me?"

He smirked and stood between my legs again, running his hands down my thighs and up to my hips before circling my waist. "Is that all? A good fucking?"

Who didn't?

When I nodded, he unbuttoned his pants, sliding the zipper down before shucking them to his ankles and stepping out of them.

"Get your mouth over here. I need something, too."

He went back for the camera while I turned around and laid my head off the bed. I knew this was coming. I knew what he wanted, and after what he'd just done to me, I couldn't wait to return the favor. Jericho filmed himself fucking my throat in his POV, something he loved after I'd done it to him last night.

My secret talent? I had no gag reflex.

I breathed in through my nose and gathered all my spit in my mouth, making it extra sloppy and wet for the audience. The goal of any good face fuck was to be disgusting by the end. Makeup all over my face. Mascara running down my cheeks. He wanted me destroyed, so he took his time. Slow. Commanding. And I moaned and dribbled and squealed. Because it made a good video.

He stopped and pulled out, flipping me around so I could sit up.

"Oh, look at you. You messy little slut." He wiped his hand over my face, smearing it in, and I smiled at the way my cheeks burned. "Are you ready?"

"Yes, please." I rolled over onto my hands and knees, anticipating the next part and knowing I had planned for it all day. He'd known, too. He'd wanted to do this.

But when his eyes landed on the pink jewel just above my pussy, he froze. He gripped the tip of his dick and swallowed. "Aurora... are you sure?"

His hesitation made me pause, but I hummed appreciatively, trying to reassure him. He thought he was too big. He thought he'd hurt me. But that was a bunch of stupid shit Nikki put in his head. I'd done anal lots of times, and I couldn't wait to come impaled on that monster.

"My safe word's crimson." I wiggled my butt, inviting him back. "I'll tell you if I need to stop."

He took another step closer, clearing his throat as he regained Kaleb's cocky swagger. Positioning us so we were in the shot, he lined himself up at my pussy and inched inside. I wilted into the pose with my head between my arms. My grin grew wider as he rubbed his hands up my back and down again before latching onto my hips.

Once he was inside, I moaned and rocked against him.

God, he felt so big, filling me completely. Not just with his cock, but with his affection and adoration and filthy fucking mouth.

Jer never wasted any time. He fucked me hard, pulling out only to surge back in rough and deep. He spanked me and pinned me down by the head, owning me in front of the whole fucking internet.

It was when he stopped that the excitement swelled inside me.

Time for the grand finale.

Different strokes for different folks, okay? Some people didn't like anal. Some people tolerated it. But me? Just another pleasure center, baby.

When he inched out the plug, angling it up and down to maneuver it without hurting me, I clenched my hands into fists and I bit my bottom lip, arching my butt up higher to tell him I was desperate for it.

The cool lube hit my ass next, and he smeared it around, pushing some inside and twisting his fingers as he pulled them out, giving me a teaser of what was to come.

"I can't believe you're going to let me do this, you nasty girl."

I groaned, teasing the tip of his dick with my butt. "I think I'll die if you don't."

"We don't want that, do we?"

The only bad part was the stretch when he first squeezed himself inside, and it took me a few seconds to get used to him. He pushed in, pulled out, pushed in, pulled out. Pushed farther this time, finally surging past that second ring of muscle. When he put his hands on my hips and tilted just right, my entire world came apart.

I knew true ecstasy. I was experiencing it for all the world to see.

"Fuck, that feels so good." Jer moved us so he sat on the edge of the bed and my feet were perched on his knees. From this angle, the camera could see him fiddle with my clit and fuck me extra deep.

It took five minutes.

Maybe less.

My pleasure and euphoria ramped up to a level I'd never experienced with anyone else. Was it him? Was it being filmed? Was it all of it? I didn't know. But when my climax pulled me under this time, I squirted again, all over the floor, consuming me and my sense with it.

After that, I became his flimsy rag doll. My legs couldn't hold me up anymore, so he had to put me back on the bed and wrap his arms around my waist while he finished. He groaned and pulled out and came all over my back while I lay there, grinning like an idiot in my new level of serotonin-soaked bliss.

It hit me while I teetered on the brink of subspace. Somewhere along the line, this had stopped being about making money and started being about him. Us. I *liked* fucking Jericho, perhaps too much.

I never wanted to fuck anyone else ever again. I never wanted to film with anyone else. I never wanted anyone else inside me. For me, it was Jericho, and that was a big, stupid problem.

13

JERICHO

I made Alba a promise, and I stuck to it. Every day, I came home to her and Penny. I washed myself up and helped her with dinner. Afterward? I fucked her all night. We made as many videos as we could.

We did shit that I'm ashamed to admit was me, but it was the best fucking sex I'd ever had. Nothing was off the table. And I do mean nothing.

Aurora and Kaleb brought out each other's perversions, and once the dice had been thrown, there was no stopping the roll. I woke up every day desperate to be inside her. I thought about her the entire time at work. I came home anxious to set up the camera and tug her on top of me.

A week into this arrangement and I had become as addicted to her as I was to my smokes and coffee. Selene texted me when I didn't come home again on Thursday.

Selene: So, you living with this girl now?

I didn't answer because I didn't know what to tell her. Alba and I were making a fuck lot of money, and in less than a week, we'd more than doubled what she'd previously been doing. We were close to replacing her income from the live sessions, so she cancelled them.

In their place, *we* did live sessions. Turned out, people wanted to watch me do fucked-up things just as much as they wanted to watch Alba.

By Friday, I didn't know what I'd do when she left. I'd meant what I told her. I wasn't a good guy. I had blood on my hands and more to come. I would only endanger her by being in her life, and eventually, I was going to need to make a choice—either bring her in fully and make her my old lady, or cut her loose.

Both would protect her, but this half-in, half-out bullshit wouldn't, and I knew that from the start.

"Not too much," Penny said. Alba leaned over her bed and brushed makeup across her cheeks.

"It's not." Alba pursed her lips and tilted her head to the side. "I think that's it."

Penny held up the mirror and nodded. "Jericho, what do you think?"

The makeup had given some color back to her face and intensified her eyes. "Looking super hot."

"Yeah?" Penny shot me a playful wink. "I might even get lucky, huh?"

Alba gasped, but I threw my head back and laughed.

"You're all set." Alba packed up her makeup and headed toward the basement. "Give me twenty minutes, and I'll be ready."

"I'll be waiting." I didn't have anything super fancy planned, just a picnic along the river and maybe a ride to an overlook with a pretty view. Alba's days were filled with providing for her mother. When she wasn't physically nursing her, she filmed. And when she wasn't filming, she did chores and cleaned up. Doing all of it by herself gave her no time to relax.

So that's what I wanted, to relax, even for just a little while.

"I worry about her," Penny said, drawing my attention back to the present. "After this is over. After I kick off."

I cleared my throat. "She's strong. She'll get through it."

"Will you promise me something?"

I raised an eyebrow. "I don't know if I'm the right person to be making promises."

"You've got a good heart. Whatever bad you think you've done, I'm sure it was because you didn't have any other choice."

That hit me right in the gut. How the hell could she know that?

"I know what the MC life is like. I don't want that for Alba, but she's an adult. She'll make her own choices. Just promise me. When I go, take care of her, will you? Watch out for her."

I wanted to grab her hand and tell her I was doing that right now. That I'd probably be doing it for the rest of my life, even if Alba didn't want me to. But I didn't say any of that. I gave her a nod and a soothing smile. "Sure, Penny. I can do that."

We spoke more about my family and the MC. Penny was easy to talk to, and she had a sense of humor like a whip — sharp, biting, and hilarious. But when Alba came upstairs, I shot to my feet and the rest of the world fell away.

She had on a sheer black top with snakes embroidered over her ribs and breasts. She'd paired it with her cardigan, cut-off shorts, black tights, and boots. Her hair hung in wild curls around her head, and she wore her glasses.

The perfect mix of Aurora and Alba.

Jesus Christ.

We weren't going to make it out of this house. I had to drag her back downstairs and slide those shorts down her legs and—

"You look amazing," Penny said. "Total smokeshow. Jericho's a lucky man."

Understatement. "Yeah. We should go."

"Wait," Alba said. "When's this mystery babysitter getting here?"

"Any second," Penny said. "Jericho's right. You need to go before you cockblock me."

I chuckled, but Alba rolled her eyes and grabbed her purse. "Fine. Love you."

"Love you." She gave Penny a kiss on the forehead and followed me out of the house and toward my bike. I turned, roaming my eyes over her wild curves and long legs, imagining her boots digging into my back while I fucked the hell out of her.

Yep, that was happening later. No matter what.

I handed her the helmet and grinned, letting my expression scream all the dirty thoughts in my head.

"Now, now." She put on the helmet and raised an eyebrow while she strapped it around her chin. "I may fuck on the first date, but I am still a lady. You need to wine and dine me."

"Yes, ma'am." I climbed on my bike started it, ignoring the flutter in my balls when she got on behind me. The only thing keeping my heart from pounding right out of my torso was her arms wrapped around my chest.

I drove us out to the river to a spot where I liked to go to when things were rough with Gemma and Thor. The sound of the water soothed me. It made me feel small and humble at a time when so much was outside my control.

When I shut off the bike, she climbed to the side and took off the helmet, glancing around with those big eyes that drove me feral.

"This is beautiful," she said.

"Yeah," I agreed, but I didn't mean the scenery.

"How'd you know this was here?"

I shrugged. "Got lost one day. Found it by accident." I grabbed our meal out of the saddlebag, vegetables and fruits and cheeses. Something light but filling. Because she'd need her energy for what I had planned tonight.

She'd said something about fucking me on my bike, and I couldn't wait to bend her over it. With the way she looked, I didn't think I'd be able to hold out very long.

"You come here a lot?" She cracked open the waters I'd brought and poured them into the red Solo cups while I set out the food containers.

"Used to."

"When?"

"When things were bad."

She nodded, understanding without me needing to elaborate, and took a bite of an apple before looking around and narrowing her eyes again. "Why'd you bring me here?"

"Because you need a break." What was the point of denying it? We didn't have time for lies between us. Only truth.

She made a sad, laughing noise and shook her head. "No room for breaks. Can't afford it."

"Maybe you couldn't before," I said, taking a bite of a carrot. "But you can now."

"What are you going to do with your half?" She ate more fruit, the juice from a strawberry dribbling down her chin. My eyes caught on it, and I wanted to lick it off her.

"Buy my own place," I said, watching her wipe it away with a napkin. "Maybe start my own garage if I can save enough."

She raised her eyebrows. "You'd leave your uncle?"

I sighed. "He doesn't pay me enough to deserve me."

Alba laughed, and God, how I loved to make that sound pour out of her. "Do you want kids?"

"Fuck yeah." The thought of getting her pregnant went through my mind. Me, coming home every day to miniature versions of her. It made something tighten in my chest, and I had to take a deep breath to loosen it. "What about you?"

"I thought I'd have a family to share it with. But now?" She shook her head. "I don't know if I want them if my mom isn't there to see me raise them."

"Blood isn't the only family out there."

She gave me a half-hearted grin that didn't reach her eyes before she took a bite of cheese and glanced away.

Conversation flowed between us. She teased me and laughed when I did it back to her. It felt natural in a way it never had with Nikki. I'd always walked on eggshells around her, like I couldn't say or do anything without upsetting her. Now that I spent this time with Alba, I realized it was because Nikki and I never knew how to communicate with each other. Alba and I could be honest and blunt. It didn't hurt or escalate.

After we finished eating, I packed up our mess, put it into the saddlebag, and nodded back toward the bike.

"Get on," I told her. "I've got one more surprise."

TEN MINUTES up the road took us to an overlook with a view of everything in Madison County. We could see the downtown district and the river cutting through it. The sky was clear tonight, the stars shimmering overhead like they knew we needed a romantic backdrop, and they were eager to participate.

"Wow." Alba's mouth hung open when I pulled off the road, shutting down the bike and kicking out the stand. She climbed off and took a few steps forward, grinning like she'd never seen the moon before. "Thank you for bringing me here. Thank you for tonight."

"Of course." I wrapped my arms around her from behind, her head fitting perfectly under my chin and her ass right up against my cock. She smelled so fucking good, and I ducked my head closer to her neck so I could inhale her deep and remember this night. Remember how this felt. "Now, I think you said something about wanting to come on my bike under the full moon."

She gasped and stiffened in my hold. But that perfect round ass rolled into me like her body reacted without her logical brain telling it to, which filled me with a sick sense of power over her. Like a fucking king.

Fuck yeah. My girl wanted me as much as I wanted her.

"Right here?" She whispered it so low that I could barely hear her.

"Yeah." I leaned down to bite her earlobe, and she shivered. "Right here. Wanna fuck my face in front of all of Madison?"

Another tremble echoed in her body, and I had her.

She turned in my grip, wrapping her arms around my neck so she could push up on her toes and whisper, "Only if you fuck mine afterward and let me put it online."

How in the fucking world could I say no to that?

"Get your phone out."

She did, and I leaned her up against the bike, grabbing two masks from my saddlebag. I wrapped one around my face and gave the other to her. Her hands shook so hard she couldn't get the strings knotted, so I helped her, trying not to let the fact that she was trembling get to my head.

I tugged at the button of her shorts, yanking them down to her ankles and kneeling like a reverent sinner in front of my goddess. She held up the phone in front of her face while I clawed at her tights, splitting them open right at the sweet spot.

"Hey," she said. "You owe me $7.99."

"Bill me."

Alba gasped and I howled with laughter, staring up at her while I jerked open the buttons on her bodysuit. She didn't have on anything under that, which made me fucking hard as a rock thinking about her pussy pressed up against the leather seat for the entire ride here.

What a filthy girl.

She moaned when I licked her. I sucked her the way she liked, fucking her hard with my fingers while her legs were spread wide open. It didn't take much to make her come. With some passionate scratching and a fist around her throat, she orgasmed like the world was ending. Which was how I felt when she handed the phone to me, switched us around, and dropped to her knees, her shorts still around her ankles.

Alba could suck dick like no one I'd ever known. Fuck me, I'd have daydreams about it until I died. Long after this was over. Long after we called it quits. I would close my eyes at night and visualize her lips wrapped around my base, the tip of my cock firmly planted down her throat.

Fucking hell. I watched through the phone as she took what she wanted from me, and when I came, my knees trembled and I nearly fell over. Groaning, I emptied myself inside her hot, wet mouth, and she held it all so she could stick her tongue out at the camera afterward like a dirty fucking slut.

My dirty fucking slut.

Then she swallowed it down and grinned.

I was so fucked because the skip in my chest and my sharp inhale had nothing to do with fucking her mouth, and everything to do with my stupid fucking heart.

14

JERICHO

I meant to take her home. It was getting late, and I wanted to fuck her in bed before the night ended. But two miles from the overlook, a familiar set of headlights popped up in my rearview. The same ones from the run, the ones that had chased me through the mountains outside Madison.

How'd they find me again?

Who the fuck were they?

I didn't have much time to worry about it because I had Alba on the back of the bike. Getting her to safety was my first priority, but I couldn't take her home and risk this stalker figuring out where she lived. Likewise, I wouldn't take her to my place for the same reason. Selene was there alone most of the time.

So I took the long way to the one place I knew was protected twenty-four-seven.

The clubhouse.

Now, it wasn't one of my date night ideas to take my new *whatever this was* to meet my entire family, but until I shook this asshole, I didn't have a better idea, and I didn't want to scare her.

When we turned into the gate, she tightened her arms around me.

"Where are we?" she asked.

"Tell ya in a minute." I punched in the code so the first round of metal doors pulled open. The DB11 went by us as the doors closed. Then I drove us to the next gate and punched in a code for the second. And finally, the third gate opened once the one behind us shut.

SRMC had never been one to take security lightly, and Thor would be caught dead before anyone infiltrated our compound.

"Is that KC?" a familiar voice shouted as I parked the bike next to the others.

"Hollywood," I said. "What the fuck are you doing here on a Friday night?" I took off my helmet and helped Alba off the bike. "Shouldn't you be out breaking hearts?"

He clutched his chest. "Got too many to break right here at home." He looked at my girl and widened his eyes, mischief and mayhem flickering behind them. "And who is this?"

"This is Alba." I wrapped an arm over her shoulder, pulling her in close when she stuck a hand out for Hollywood to shake.

"Nice to meet you," she said.

"Likewise." Hollywood's grin stretched from ear to ear. "How do you two know each other?"

"She's off-limits," I said. At the same time, Alba said, "We're friends."

Friends?

Friends?

She'd just had my cock down her throat, her voice still scratchy from the way I roughed up her esophagus. "Friends" was the *least* of what we were.

"Well, which is it?" Hollywood said. "Because if you throw her to the wolves not knowing yourself, they're gonna eat her alive."

"Not if I eat them first," Alba said with a wink.

My lips twisted into a smile, and I bit my bottom lip. My girl was fucking sharp. I didn't have to worry about her holding her own.

Hollywood's eyes lit up like a kid on Christmas morning. "What are *you* doing with KC?"

Alba pushed her glasses up higher, a blush and a grin on her face.

"Never mind." Hollywood threw his hands up. "They call him KC for a reason, right? Now, tell me. Is it as big as I hear? Everyone else in the club has seen it except for me."

"Dude, what the fuck?" I shoved at his shoulder and moved around him.

"Bigger," Alba murmured as we passed.

Hollywood gasped and laughed, trailing after us as I guided Alba toward the open garage door. I loved the clubhouse. It reeked like old beer, sex, and cigarettes, but it smelled like home.

"Stop goading him," I teased, talking over the sound of AC/DC blaring into the night. Switch and Saint huddled around the pool table while Ru, Selene, and Nikki sat at the bar. Thor, Trojan, and Slip were on the couches at the fair end, Slip's old lady, Scribe, on his lap. Some hang-arounds and club girls milled about, entertaining the New England chapter of SR that had come through town a few days ago. Judging by the hoops and hollers in the far corner, the Madison chapter was showing them a *very* good time.

All eyes snapped up when we walked in, and not because of my dumb ass. No, they were looking at *her*. Beautiful, radiant her. All wondering what the fuck she was doing with stupid fucking me.

I hadn't brought anyone to the clubhouse since Nikki, and short one or two hang-arounds, I hadn't been rumored to hook up with anyone. Now even Nikki clutched her pregnant belly as she stared at Alba. Selene stood and came closer, raising an eyebrow and holding her arms out wide.

"You must be the infamous Alba," Selene said. "I'm the sister."

"Of course," Alba said. "I could have guessed that."

"When we were little, no one could tell us apart." Selene raked her eyes over Alba, judgment mixing with concern. Then they came to me. "Why'd you bring her here?"

"I need to talk to Thor."

Selene hummed and took another sip of her beer, nodding toward our uncle at the other end. "They've been talking shop all fucking night."

I nodded and squeezed Alba's hand, leaning in to ask, "Will you be all right for a few minutes?"

She nodded and smiled, and I gave my sister one last warning look before heading toward the MC sergeant and road captain with news of my stalker.

15

———

ALBA

I'd never been more thankful to wear Aurora's skin than I was that night. Yeah, I hadn't put my contacts in, but even with the glasses, I was confident in my bodysuit and cut-offs. My tights were ripped from where Jericho had fucked me earlier, and with the taste of him still in the back of my mouth, I shook hands with his ex and pretended like she wasn't a million percent prettier than me. Even six months pregnant.

"Nikki," she said, rubbing a hand over her enormous belly. Was Jericho *sure* the baby wasn't his? Because the way she looked at me wasn't the way someone looked at the new girl of an ex they'd gotten over.

"And this is Ru," Selene said, pointing to another girl around the same age as us. "The VP's daughter."

So many people. So many names. Luckily, the members of the club had theirs on their cuts, so it was easier to remember for me. But this girl? Ru? She reminded me of someone else, and I couldn't put my finger on it. Something about her eyes, her nose, and her curly brown hair.

"How'd you meet KC?" Ru asked, taking a swig of her beer.

"At a party." I took a drink of mine after Selene set it down in front of me, swallowing the bitterness and telling myself it had nothing to do with Nikki's stare.

"Oh, right," Nikki said. "You're the girl he abandoned Trojan for."

"He didn't *abandon* Trojan," Selene said. "Trojan was fine on his own."

"Must have been some prime pussy," Nikki said.

I cleared my throat, wondering what I should do. I didn't buy into the whole territorial feminine rage thing. She owned a piece of Jericho I'd never have, and I recognized that. We both had people who loved us *before*, and if Nikki could respect my new place in his life, I'd respect her old. It didn't have to be like this.

"Looks like the knockoff version of me," she said.

Apparently, Nikki didn't feel the same way.

"Or maybe you were just the prequel version of me," I said. "You know, the shorter, shittier lead-up to the main event?"

Selene and Ru gasped, but Nikki glared at me, almost like she was trying to figure out if I'd really said that to her.

"Besides, why do you care?" I sipped my drink. "Didn't you like... fuck the entire club or something?" Nikki's mouth fell open. "Not that I'm slut shaming you, but maybe you should have broken up with your boyfriend before you did."

Ru burst out laughing, and Selene's grin widened.

"What are you ladies giggling at?" another guy said, coming up to stand next to Ru. He threw an arm over her shoulders and tipped his beer over his lips. His name tag read Saint.

"Nikki's trying to intimidate KC's new girl, and New Girl is showing us why KC's a fan of that mouth," Ru said. "Alba, this is Saint, my dad's annoying best friend. Saint, this is KC's new girl, Alba."

Saint smiled. "KC's new girl, huh?" Then he looked at Nikki, who snapped her jaw shut. She pushed to her feet and waddled away in the slow rhythmic pace of someone in the last few months of pregnancy.

"Aw, c'mon," Selene said. "You can dish it out, but you can't take it?"

Nikki gave her the finger over her shoulder and slumped down on the couch next to a tall, bearded guy with a bald head. *Pie.* Her husband. The brother she'd cheated on Jericho with.

"Don't mind her," Selene said, rolling her eyes. "The pregnancy hormones made her skin thin as shit. Once upon a time, she might have kissed you for talking to her like that."

I snorted. "Really?"

"Yeah, or punched you in the face. Either would have been entertaining." Selene shrugged like getting punched in the face was no big deal, and then she topped off my beer with the tap. She crossed her arms over the bar and leaned toward me, narrowing her eyes like she was peeling me back layer by layer. "So what do you do, Alba?"

I tried not to squirm at her scrutiny, knowing I couldn't be honest. Jericho and I had agreed to keep it a secret, and the MC was the last place he wanted anyone finding out about our videos.

"I'm a librarian."

Saint laughed and Ru elbowed him in the gut, whispering a hushed, "Stop it."

Selene narrowed her eyes even more. "A librarian?"

"Yeah. I mean"—I shifted uncomfortably, taking another sip of beer—"my mom's been sick, so I haven't worked in a while. But back when I did." I cleared my throat, looking between the three of them. "I ran the program for teenagers."

"What's wrong with your mom?" Selene straightened, her gaze turning more serious. "If you don't mind me asking. If it's too personal—"

"Selene used to be a surgeon," Ru added.

Selene rolled her eyes and shook her head. "I never finished my residency."

"You graduated medical school. That's all that counts."

Saint leaned down to whisper something in Ru's ear that made her giggle and stare up at him with adoration in her eyes. She'd introduced him as her father's annoying friend, and he definitely was too old for her, but the way they looked at each other hinted at something deeper and more intimate.

"So?" Selene brought my attention back to her.

"Cancer," I said. "Terminal."

"Oh, damn." She winced. "Sorry to hear that."

"Thank you."

She smiled and clinked her beer with mine. "Cheers to parents gone too soon."

Ignoring the rising tide of sadness, I blinked back tears and saluted with her. And that made me love his sister, right then and there.

"I've got to go to the bathroom," Ru said, pushing to her feet. "Nice meeting you, Alba." Then she headed toward the back of the club.

Saint looked between us and took a drink of his beer before nodding and backing away. He lingered for a moment, but then casually made his way after Ru.

"Are they..." I didn't finish, deciding it was none of my business.

Selene sighed and shook her head, her eyes filling with a desperation, or maybe pity. "You sure you wanna get involved with a Rose?"

I furrowed my eyebrows. *What is that supposed to mean?*

"We're all a bunch of fucked-up monsters." She gave me a sad smile before turning to walk away, leaving me alone at the bar.

A bunch of fucked-up monsters.

I looked around. Jericho sat with a few other leather-clad tattooed dudes across the garage. To the right, a group of girls danced with other guys. Some older. Some younger. Behind me, women whispered sweet nothings into the ears of men wearing the Steel Roses colors. The entire place was made for catering to their hedonistic fantasies. Everything about it stank of iniquity, a house of Sodom, and I loved it.

Deciding I had to pee, I made my way to the bathroom and did my business, checking my makeup in the mirror after I washed my hands. Despite Jericho being so rough with me earlier, I still looked hot. I smiled and turned to head back into the hall, but someone coming down the corridor blocked my way.

"Hi there, gorgeous." A man about twenty years older winked and tossed back a shot, holding out an arm to block my path. "Do I know you?"

"No." I gave him a small smile and tried to duck around his body.

"Are you sure?" He narrowed his dark eyes, and I looked at the SRMC-BOS patch on his cut. A brother from another chapter. Boston, I guessed. His name tag read Brutus.

"Aurora," I lied. I didn't like the way this guy looked at me, so I tried to get around him again.

"Aurora," he repeated, grabbing my wrist to stop me. "That's a pretty name. You from around here?"

My heart kicked in my chest, and the man's piercing stare terrified me. It was as if he didn't see me as a person. He only saw me as a toy, something he could use. Is that how he viewed the other women here? Is that how they viewed themselves? Selene and Ru seemed like self-assured powerhouses. Hell, Nikki and I had a disagreement, but even I could admit, she seemed tough.

"Yep," I said, trying to yank my arm away. "I have to go—"

"I remember you. You look like someone. Do you know Alessandra Cap—"

"Get off me," I said again, this time louder, yanking harder.

"What's your problem? I'm just trying to talk." The man tugged me close, hissing in my face, and I struggled against him until he finally loosened his hold and I stumbled back, landing hard on my palms and butt.

Jericho pushed the guy against the wall with one hand, pounding into his face with the other.

"Get off me means get your fucking hands off her," Jericho shouted. "You understand?"

"KC!" Thor shouted, yanking him off my assailant. "KC, enough! He got the point."

Jericho took a few steps back, and the guy sank to the floor, blood dripping down his chin from his broken nose. A few of his brothers came to help him, but I focused my attention on Jericho, who ran crimson hands through his hair before grabbing my arm and tugging me to my feet.

"Are you okay?" He ran his eyes over the length of me, checking for damage.

I hissed in a breath as a sharp pain echoed up my arm, and I held up my hand, where a piece of wood stuck out of my palm. I'd gotten a splinter from the floor, and Jesus Christ, as much as it hurt, it looked a million times worse.

"C'mon," Jer said. "I can fix that." He grabbed my good hand and stalked to the back, leading me along behind him.

I sat on a bed in a room at the far end of the clubhouse while Jericho nursed and dressed the wound. Once the wood was out, the cut wasn't that bad, even if it hurt like hell. He wrapped a bandage around it and pressed a kiss to the center of my palm before winking and rising to clean up.

"Wait," I said. He paused and turned to me. "Come here."

He sat back down, and I grabbed the peroxide, pouring it on a piece of gauze before rubbing it over his knuckles. He winced and hissed, but let me take care of him.

"You didn't have to do that," I whispered.

"Do what?"

"Pounce on that guy like that."

"Yeah, I did." He shook his head and looked at the ground, giving me a coy smile. "If I didn't, everyone in that room would have thought it was okay to handle you like that. Now, they know it's not."

I acted like that didn't thrill me to death.

"No one touches any woman who says let go." His hand jerked when I went over a particularly sensitive area. "Especially not someone that's m—"

My fingers froze and I straightened, snapping my gaze to his. That bordered a little too close on something we weren't supposed to feel for each other. This wasn't permanent. This was only until my mother died. Only until I got the hell out of here. Only until I couldn't run anymore. But I had to admit hearing him call me his made my heart pound in my chest. I wanted to be his. I had wanted that maybe since I met him.

Don't fall in love with him, came my mother's voice. *He'll never choose you over the club.*

He must've sensed my hesitation because he made an awkward laughing noise and rubbed at the back of his head. "Someone I'm fucking. We're exclusive. Remember?"

"Right," I said, going back to cleaning him up.

"I won't stand for anyone hurting you." He pulled out of my grip and cupped my jaw, tilting my head up so I had to look at him. "Ever. You fucking get me? No one hurts you. Not me. Not anyone."

"I know." And I did. I believed that might have been one of the most honest things he'd ever said to me.

"Now it's time for your punishment."

"My what?"

"Oh, you didn't think I'd let that friends comment go, did you?"

I moved my eyes back and forth between his. "Friends?"

"When Hollywood asked what we were and you said… *friends.*"

"We are friends."

"Uh-huh." He stood, walking over to the door so he could flip the lock closed. The sound reverberated through the room, kicking my heart into overdrive. I knew this look in his eye. This wasn't Jericho. Not anymore. Kaleb had been let out of the cage, and he was here to play.

Fine. He wanted to do this where everyone could hear us? *Let's play.*

He turned to face me, his hands linked together at the small of his back. "I still have the taste of your cunt in the back of my mouth. Is that something friends do?"

I swallowed, likewise relishing the taste of him lingering on my tongue, and I leaned back on my good hand, staring up at my devious God of chaos, waiting to see what he would make of this impudent human girl.

"Your lipstick is still on my cock." He took another step closer. "Is that something friends do?"

My pulse echoed in my clit, and my pussy throbbed. God, I wanted to touch myself. But I knew if I did, it would piss him off. I'd never seen him this commanding, and it both exhilarated and terrified me. I needed to tread carefully. I danced with his devil tonight.

"I know how it feels when your ass comes around my dick." He put his hands on either side of my hips, leaning down to bring his face millimeters from mine. I tasted his breath, which smelled like me and beer and cigarettes. And *him.* So deliciously him.

God, I wanted to kiss him.

I wanted to tunnel my fingers into his hair and devour that mouth until it melted for me. I stared at his lips, licking my own and drawing his attention down to them.

"Tell me we're friends again," he snarled. It held more bite than I'd ever heard him use with me. Was it the jealousy of seeing another man put his hands on me? Or was it because he'd told himself this was professional, and after only a week, it felt so far removed from that? Like Jericho and I had been made for each other. Literally.

"Say it."

My throat felt dry and hoarse as I muttered, "We're friends."

"Do friends fuck each other's faces?" He fisted my hair and unzipped his jeans, yanking my head toward his cock. Instinctually, I put it in my mouth, sucking it how he liked to get him hard as a rock. "Do friends take their fucking like good little sluts?"

He pulled me away from him, the sting in my hair matched by the anticipation burning in my gut. I turned around and bent over the twin-sized bed, the smell of dust and old sweat hitting me in the face. But I didn't focus on that because Jericho wrenched my shorts down to my ankles and unclipped my bodysuit. He wasted no time preparing me, and honestly, I didn't need it. I'd been wet since he went down on me at the overlook.

He pressed one hand into my shoulder blades and the other to the side of my head, pinning me down while he slipped all the way inside me.

The first thrust always hurt. He was so big, and I was so tight. Until I got used to him, I took pleasure in the agony. It tumbled together in my head, the pain and euphoria.

"Do you get so fucking wet for your other friends?" He growled next to my ear, his massive body covering me as he nipped at my shoulder and neck. It sent shivers down that whole side of my body, and I curled my fists into the blankets, struggling to maintain my balance against his punishing thrusts. In. Out. In. Out. So fucking deep. So fucking hard.

And it hit just the right spots every time.

I tried to put one hand between my legs to massage my clit, but he grabbed my wrist and twisted my arm behind my back.

"Oh no, friends don't get to touch. This pussy is mine, and I told you I didn't share. Not with my... *friends.*"

He slowed his pace, bringing me back down to torture me.

I kicked my feet out, frustration raging from my throat in an angry growl. "What do you want from me?"

"What do I want?" He paused, slowly dragging himself out of me, inch by agonizing inch. "God, what the fuck do I want? So many things."

"Why aren't we friends, Jericho?" I murmured. "Do you want more?"

"Yes," he snarled, sinking his fingers into my wrists so hard that his nails would leave imprints. I didn't care. "I want all of you. All the time. Every day. Every night."

Yes. Yes. Yes.

God, I wanted that, too. A great terrible knowing toppled on the brink of shattering over my head. I knew what it was, but I didn't want to face it yet.

Not yet. It'll be too much.

My heart pounded against my ribs. Every nerve in my body had come to life, reminding me to live in the present with him.

"You have it." I rolled my pelvis against him, moving him inside me and making him hiss in a breath through his teeth. "You have me, Jericho."

He pressed his forehead against the back of my head and fucked me hard again, so rough that our thighs slapped together in a loud, punishing rhythm. I almost didn't hear him mutter, "But I want you forever."

It broke something inside me, something I hadn't even known I'd built around my heart. There was a part of me, a part of *both* Alba and Aurora, that wanted to keep him forever, too. I came with tears on my cheeks, and when he finished deep inside me, I expected him to step away and wipe me down with a towel like he always did.

Instead, he knelt to the ground behind me and kissed the insides of my thighs.

"I didn't mean to scare you." Another kiss right on my abused clit. I jumped and fell forward, but he wrapped his arms around my thighs to hold me upright. "I won't ever hurt you." He flicked his tongue over my swollen flesh, angry and fiery from his cock. But the soothing heat of his mouth made me spread my legs wider for him. I moaned.

He seized on the opportunity, sucking my clit and working his fingers inside me. I came again, and this time, I couldn't hold myself upright. By the end of it, I was slumped in his lap on the ground, my head back against his shoulder and his arms wrapped around me from behind.

"Now that was a fucking sex scene," Jericho said.

I gave a half-hearted chuckle before rubbing my hands over my face. My nerves vibrated with the knowledge echoing in my bones. I was pretty sure I was in love with Jericho, that I'd been in love with him all this time and only now started to realize it. And that was such a terrible idea.

16

JERICHO

I couldn't describe the urge that came over me at seeing that motherfucker put his hands on Alba. He shouldn't be putting his hands on *anyone* telling him to get off, but her?

It was like a switch flipped in my head.

One second, I was sitting there talking to Thor and Slip about my tail.

The next, I had the guy's throat in my fist, pounding my other into his face. I knew what was going on. I knew when I dragged her to the back room like a fucking caveman.

I loved her. It had only been a week, but I loved her. Call me obsessive or fucking psycho. I didn't give a shit.

One week in and I wanted to marry her. I wanted to put a ring on her finger and sink my teeth in her neck every night to make sure every fucking asshole on this planet knew I would come for him if he so much as looked at her the wrong way.

After that, I didn't know what to do. I couldn't leave her, not anymore, which meant I had to bring her in.

But I saw the look on her face when I slipped and spilled my fucking guts, when I almost told her she was mine. She panicked. She froze up, and if I hadn't changed the subject super fucking fast, she would have bolted like a scared rabbit.

She still might.

Penny had told us to come home around one, so at midnight, I extracted myself from Alba's sleepy embrace and dressed. I wanted to raid the fridge for food and water before driving back to her house. Once I got to the kitchen, I found Thor sitting at the island, scooping a spoonful of Cinnamon Toast Crunch into his mouth. At thirty-seven, the childish cereal was at odds with this fully grown outlaw.

But honestly... the shit looked good as fuck. I poured myself a bowl and sat next to him. We ate in silence for a few moments before he cleared his throat and pursed his lips.

"It's serious between you and the Wright girl."

Not a question, so I didn't answer. Just kept eating my sugar-filled goodness.

"Do you think your tail saw her with you?"

My memories flickered over the drive back to the compound. There were moments when they were right up on us. "It's possible."

He nodded once in that cold, stoic way of his. "Then you have to protect her."

I didn't disagree.

"You know what I mean?"

I snapped my attention to him.

"I'm sending Castor up there this morning," he continued. Castor was Crow's second eldest son, one of the twins, and Bear's younger brother. "I want an eight-point security system around her house. We'll keep an eye on her, but this is your fault. You need to fix it."

"I'm not allowed to fuck now?"

"You should have known you had a tail before you got back to Madison."

True... but also... *fucking ouch*. What crawled up his ass and died?

Then I remembered Selene had been here a few hours ago, and she wasn't here now. She might have gone home alone, or maybe she was in the back with someone else. Either would piss him off. Everything about her pissed him off these days.

"You know the rules. She's in or she's out," Thor continued. "No half assing the MC."

"I know."

He hummed a noise that sounded like acknowledgement. "You're easily recognizable. You know that, too. Right? With the tattoos and the haircut and the six feet three inches of kick fucking ass."

I narrowed my eyes as I struggled to understand what he was telling me. My mind immediately went to the videos we put on the internet. Yeah, I wore a mask and so did she. Most of the time, she had on a wig and I had on my long-sleeved shirt. But he'd made his point, and I picked up what he laid down.

"If they saw you with her, they'll use her against you," Thor said. "Watch her."

I cleared my throat and rubbed at the back of my head, realizing I couldn't keep my secret anymore. I needed Castor's help in more ways than Thor knew.

"I will." I took a deep breath and finished my cereal in silence.

"You ready for the run?" Thor stood and came closer, dropping his bowl in the sink for a prospect to clean.

"Yeah, I think so. Been memorizing the route. I'm pretty sure I can do it in fifteen minutes."

"Pretty sure? You better be real Goddamned sure."

"I'm sure." I nodded. "It'll be fine." I wanted to tell him I had a good feeling about it, but I didn't. Something bugged me about the tail that I couldn't shake. It set the whole thing in a different weird light. But what choice did I have?

I was the quickest one in the crew, so I had to go.

"I have to tell you a secret," I said to Castor in front of Alba's house.

We'd gone home around one-thirty. Eight hours later, Castor

texted that he wanted to stop by before going to the clubhouse. Thor's orders.

Now that he was here, I had to ask something else of him.

Castor narrowed his eyes at my confession. "Okay."

Then he got even more suspicious. Sure, he was a prince of the MC. Crow's second child, my cousin by blood and almost brother by choice, once he was done prospecting. But the dude had been a computer nerd his entire life. If there was anyone I could trust with this, it was him.

"Alba runs this website." I told him the whole truth and ignored the twist in his lips as he struggled not to crack up.

"Jesus Christ. Really taking that KC thing to a whole new level, huh?" Castor laughed and clapped me on the shoulder. I punched his arm to bring him back to reality.

"Can you upgrade her security or not?"

"Of course." He shook his head. I walked inside Alba's house, smiling at Penny and introducing them before taking Castor downstairs to Alba's setup.

Alba looked up from her spot at her desk and smiled. "Hi, Castor. Thanks for coming."

"No sweat. After the way you put Nikki in her place, I'm yours forever, Alba."

I raised my eyebrows. "What? You talked to Nikki?"

"Don't worry about it." Alba wrapped her arms around my waist and kissed my jaw.

Castor refocused on me, pointing a tattooed finger in my direction. "You owe me."

Of fucking course. "What do you want?"

He turned to the laptop and started typing. "I'll think about it. Now let me get to work."

We did. Alba went upstairs to tend to her mother, and I went outside to upgrade the cameras around the house. At first, Alba had balked at the expense.

"The cameras we have are fine," she said.

They were at least twenty-years old, and they didn't have Bluetooth or any of that shit. I convinced her it was for the club's safety as well as hers, which wasn't exactly a lie, if not the total truth.

Until I knew who the tail was, I didn't trust they wouldn't follow me back here. I couldn't be here all the time, as much as I wanted to be.

When Castor finished, he found me out front, installing the new video doorbell.

"I've got you set up to run through a VPN in Russia. From there, you're covered by so many different servers, no one could find you if they wanted to." Castor snorted. "Fuck, *I* couldn't find you if I wanted to. And that's saying something because I can find anyone."

"Thanks, man," I said, just as Alba came outside and held up a plate of sandwiches.

"Lunchtime?"

I thought I couldn't love her anymore. Gemma used to say the way to a person's heart wasn't with jewelry or gifts. It was food. And God fucking damn it, she was right. I didn't know a turkey sandwich could make me fall in love with someone, but I'd never wanted anyone more than when I watched her little mouth curl around the food she'd prepared for us.

And it all felt so... domesticated.

Penny teased Alba and I teased Castor. They both shot it back and my heart lifted. I loved Alba, but I still had my hesitations about making this official. It was safer for everyone if I pretended she never existed.

Maybe if I'd just walked away at the start. Maybe if I'd let her get her ride home that night at the party instead of taking her myself. But some part of me must have known as soon as I saw the picture of me and Selene on her shelf.

My place was here.

My place was with Alba, and her place was with me.

I spent the next week with her. It was easy for me to stay there and get up for the shop every day. The shortened commute gave me an extra thirty minutes to fuck Alba in the morning, and God, that lightened my mood so much before having to be around Thor and Selene all day.

"I'd like to make an amendment to our deal," I told Alba on Friday morning. We were in the shower together, her arms around my waist and her chin on my sternum. I'd planned on taking her on our second date tonight, one that preferably didn't end with losing a tail at the clubhouse.

"Oh?"

"Yeah. I've been spending a lot of time here."

"I noticed," she said. "Mom noticed, too."

"Is it a problem?"

She shook her head. "No, I love having you around."

"I love being around." The *you* went unsaid, but the way she looked at me told me she'd heard it anyway.

"What are you suggesting?"

"I could help you with bills. I could rent the room upstairs."

"Jer." She shook her head again and took a deep breath, stepping away from me and rubbing her hands over her face. "I'm not sticking around after..."

"I know." I cleared my throat, acting like that didn't stab me in the chest. "I'm not asking you to. When you leave, I'll keep the place."

She narrowed her eyes. "What? Why?"

"I like it. It's close to the shop, and Thor and Selene aren't here."

She pursed her lips. "You're serious."

"I am." I'd rather she be here when I moved in, but I couldn't stop her if she wanted to go. "I'm not asking you to change your plans. I'm just asking to be a part of them."

Alba crossed her arms over her chest and glanced down between us. "I know she looks okay now, but things are going to get messier." She cleared her throat like she was biting back a sob, and my heart broke for her. "With my mom."

"I know." I wrapped my arms around her and pulled her into a hug, our bodies touching all the way from my neck down to our knees. "I'll be here for it. I swear."

"Don't do that." She wiped at her eyes and broke away from me. "Don't make promises you don't know if you can keep."

"What?"

"What about when she's shitting herself and throwing up blood? No one wants to stick around for that."

"Sunshine." I grabbed her face and tilted her chin up so she had to look at me. "You think I'm afraid of a little shit and blood?"

This wouldn't even be half as messy as some of the fucked-up things I'd seen. I'd beaten men to death with my hands. I'd watched the light drain from their eyes, knowing I was the one who stole it from them. I wasn't afraid of death. I'd stared the bitch down a time or two.

"No, I guess you're not, are you?"

I shook my head and almost kissed her right then in the shower. That would be the final line between us. I would kiss her and confess my feelings and pray she reciprocated. But I couldn't do that unless I knew she was in this, too. And she hadn't agreed to stay with me.

Instead, I pulled her closer, leaning in to nibble on her earlobe. She melted, putting her arms going around my neck and tunneling her fingers up the back of my soaking wet hair. Once my cock joined the conversation, jolting against her pelvis in a blatant request, she lifted one of her knees to my hip and twisted her pelvis so I slid smoothly inside her. And good fucking God, how amazing she always felt, so wet and tight and accommodating.

She moaned and ground against me, the sensation echoing up my spine, and I thrust deeper inside her, having to be connected in every single fucking way.

I grabbed her hands and held them above her head, our palms sliding skin to skin.

Most of the time, I made sure she came first. I made sure my girl was sated and fucking loose before I even thought about finishing. But this time? It hit a whole new fucking level.

This time, we came together, like some phony rom-com type shit.

But I swear, the fucking heavens parted in my soul. Our bond snapped fucking taut like a guitar string, vibrating all the way through me.

Nothing I'd ever done had come close to this.

And holding her in the aftermath? It nearly broke me.

"Move in," she finally said. "You can stay when I go."

I wanted to argue and say, "How about you just stay?" or "How about I go when you go?" But I leaned down and kissed her neck instead, moving to her cheek and her temple and memorizing the way her soft skin felt under my lips.

17

———

ALBA

I made a mistake when I said Jericho could move in because my feelings for him were growing more complicated by the day. Soon, I feared I wouldn't want to leave once Mom was gone. I worried I wouldn't be able to run away from all of this. I'd trampled in his quicksand, and now I couldn't get out. Struggling only made it worse.

"Hold out your hands like this." Jericho wrapped his arms around mine, his hard body pressed up behind me. I had his nine millimeter in my hand, earmuffs on my head, and a target twenty yards in front of me. "Take a deep breath." I did. "Pull the trigger as you let it out."

Bam!

Bam!

Bam!

The kick shocked me, and my shoulders jerked back against Jericho, his stable weight keeping me safe and secure.

I'd never shot a gun before, so having him here with me made it less nerve-racking. The power in his presence and the strength in wielding a weapon like this turned me on in a big way. Honestly, everything about him turned me on.

Which led me back to problem number one.

I felt something for Jericho that I shouldn't, and that scared me.

I should end this now before it hurts too much.

How could I tell him that if it went on much longer, I would never be able to break it off when the time came? He didn't want me tied with the MC, and I didn't intend to stay when I had nothing holding me here. I couldn't live in the place where she raised me, see all the things we used to do together, and know I'd never be able to do them with her again. Despite my feelings for Jericho, that would hurt the most.

I *had* to go.

"I love the way your ass hits when you shoot," he murmured, grabbing my butt and giving it a hard squeeze. I practically turned to goo.

When would it stop? This wanting, this yearning for him?

"Gives me lots of gunplay ideas." He held me tighter. "Want me to fuck you with my nine?" My cheeks burned imagining it, and when I didn't immediately say no, he threw his head back to laugh. "Just when I think you can't fucking surprise me anymore."

After the range, Jericho drove me around on his bike, which was another thing I'd miss when I left. Because who didn't love five-hundred pounds of vibrating combustion between their legs?

Jericho fucked me hard and rough that night. Marking me. Biting me. Scratching and paddling me. I did the same to him, and when we collapsed in the bed next to each other, gasping and panting down our high, we talked.

"Why do they call you KC?" I finally asked.

He sighed and shook his head. "It stands for Killer Cock."

My eyebrows went halfway up my head, and I laughed hysterically as he told me the story.

"It's actually kind of sad," he said. "She was a nice lady."

"Jesus, Jer," I said, wiping tears from my eyes. "That's horrible." But I couldn't stop chuckling.

He told me about the run he had to do the next day and how it terrified and exhilarated him at the same time. The Steel Roses and the Caputi family were enemies, and they had a lot of bad blood between them. Benito Caputi had killed his parents, his aunt, and his grandparents.

"A lot of our people have gone down protecting this town from those pieces of shit." He shook his head. "They're not good people. And Benito? He's the worst one. He's decapitated Roses, dismembered them, and sent us their parts."

My stomach rolled. "Really?"

"He's been on a rampage against us since the eighties."

"Forty years?" I raised my eyebrows. "How old is this guy?"

Jericho shrugged. "In his sixties, I guess. He's been the head of the DC mob scene longer than I've been alive. Longer than Crow." He sighed. "I shouldn't be telling you any of this."

"Why *are* you?"

"I had a tail the other day," he said. "They followed us on our date. They were following me on my run last weekend."

My heart pounded as an alarm rattled through my brain. *A tail?* "Was it him?"

He didn't answer. Instead, he said, "You need to be prepared." He grabbed my hand and brought my knuckles to his lips, giving each one a tender kiss. "That's why I took you shooting tonight. You brought me into your world, but Alba, I brought you into mine, too. I warned you I wasn't a good guy."

I nodded, understanding what he wasn't saying. I'd been seen with him, and now, I might have a target on my back because of it.

"We can stop this... if you want."

Startled, I met his gaze. "What?"

He furrowed his eyebrows and clenched his jaw. I didn't want that. I didn't want that at all, and the suggestion made my eyes burn.

Christ, how would I ever be able to leave him when the time came?

"I'm asking a lot of you," he said. "I'll ask more before it's over." He shifted closer to me, lowering his voice like he was afraid to speak the next words out loud. "But if you tell me to go, I'll go. I'll never contact you again. You'll be safe."

Never contact me again? No, I didn't like that, either. Not one fucking bit. Of course, what did I think would happen at the end of this? Wasn't he suggesting the very thing I planned to do once Mom was gone?

"Why would I want you to do that? You said you'd protect me."

"I can't be here all the time."

"We've got the security set up. The garage is two seconds away." I wrapped his hands tighter in mine.

He smiled, resolution and adoration radiating out of his baby blues. It seemed like he could see right down into my soul. Who knew, maybe he could. I'd like to think whatever he saw there matched what existed inside him.

"It'll be okay, moonbeam," I added, hoping my optimism relaxed him.

The nickname made him laugh, and he rolled so he was on top of me and in between my legs again. I couldn't stop fucking him. I was addicted, and I didn't care anymore.

The next morning, a knock at the door interrupted our breakfast.

Castor and Ru stood on the other side, a look of annoyance on his face and a big, excited grin on hers. "Hi, sorry to swing by so early."

I remembered Ru from the party. The VP's daughter, the one who looked so familiar.

"What's up?" I invited them inside and both took a look at my mother before following me into the dining room.

"Mom, you remember Castor. This is Ru." I gestured to my companions. "This is my mom, Penny."

"Nice to meet you," Mom said, but when she looked at Ru, something flicked behind her eyes, like she'd seen a ghost. There and gone so quick, I convinced myself that I'd imagined it and sat them at the dining room table. Jericho came in from the kitchen, naked from the waist up with sweatpants on and an apron around his waist.

"Morning, gorgeous," Castor said.

"Morning, beautiful." Jericho laughed. "What do you two want?"

"I have a business proposition for you." Ru held out a binder with laminated pages and clearly marked dividers along the side.

"What is this?" I took it and flipped through it, my eyebrows furrowing at a business plan for a website. For *my* website.

"Castor told me what you were doing," she said.

I gasped and looked at her accomplice.

"No," Castor said. "She conned it out of me. I didn't tell her anything."

"Nuance." Ru waved him away. "Look, I won't spill your secret. Unlike some people, I can keep my mouth shut. I can help you." She nodded to the binder. "I'm in marketing, but I also do video editing and Photoshop on the side."

I looked at Jericho, who pursed his lips, raised his eyebrows, and went back to making French toast. Ru ran through her idea. She'd edit the videos and diversify our income streams in exchange for a small cut of the profit.

"I can increase your speed and turnaround time by fifty percent, freeing you up for more content creation." Ru straightened and cleared her throat. "Plus, I can use the experience as an internship, and I won't have to apply to some stupid marketing firm."

"Jesus, Ru." Jericho shook his head and came to stand behind me, looking over my shoulder at some of her estimates.

"You put a lot of thought into this." I couldn't believe the figures she'd put together. This was more than I needed, more than I wanted. But... who was I to look a gift horse in the mouth?

"Fuck the patriarchy," she said, holding up her fist in an epic Gloria Steinem power move. "They want me to get a job slaving away for the man. I'd rather help my local hometown ho."

I snorted, and my mother clapped. "Praise be, little Don Draper. Praise be."

"Wait," Jericho cut in. "I'm not sure how I feel about you watching the videos I'm in. You're basically my little sister."

"I'm not your sister," Ru said. "And you're going to act like I haven't seen you naked a hundred times?"

"That's when we were kids," Jericho cut in. "You haven't seen me naked since my balls dropped."

"I'm sure your balls still look the same," Ru cut in, her eyes narrowed. "Besides, do you really think I came to the meeting without having done my research? I've already seen your videos, dumbass." Ru put her hands on her hips and stuck out her tongue, like she'd been doing it her entire life. Judging by his grumpy expression, I'd say she had.

My mother laughed. "She's got you there, Jer."

"Yeah, you're right, Penny." He rubbed his hands over his face and threw more bread in the egg mixture now that it appeared Castor and Ru might be joining us.

"You'd really do this?" I was so confused. *Why* were these people helping me? I barely knew them. I barely knew Jericho.

"Yeah," she said. "Wait, are you considering hiring me?"

"Yeah."

"What?" Jer called from the kitchen. "Really? Aris is gonna fucking kill me."

"No one is going to tell him, right?" Ru looked at Castor, who narrowed his eyes before he nodded. "RIGHT?" Ru called to Jericho.

"Yeah, yeah." He sighed and sat next to Castor. "Can you keep your mouth shut around Crow?"

"I'll make sure he does," Ru said.

Jericho shook his head. "That doesn't make me feel better."

Maybe not, but I liked Ru. I trusted her when she said she could help me. Between her and Jericho, we could do this if we played our cards right.

I caught my mother's eye in the living room and she smiled wider, still proud of me despite the nature of my work. It reminded me this would be over soon. I'd be gone. I'd pull my website down. I'd move on. Would these people still want me after I didn't have any income to offer? What would I do then?

I pretended not to care, refusing to let thoughts like that ruin the present. I'd deal with them when the time came. I just had to enjoy what little I had left.

18

JERICHO

Everything about the run was off from the jump. I'd left Alba's house with jitters in my gut, but I told myself that was because of the wild fucking scene Alba and I had shot the night before and not because of what I was about to do in the name of the MC.

I still had crop marks across my ass, and every time I moved, I thought of her. Every time my cut rubbed around where she'd dug her nails into my shoulders, I thought of her. Our sex was primal and passionate and fucking amazing.

"You all right, brother?" Hollywood asked, putting his hands on my shoulders to give me a shake.

I flicked my cigarette to the ground and nodded. "Yeah, man. You all right?"

"Freshly hydrated, caffeinated, and masturbated." Then he clapped the side of my face and winked. I shoved him away and gave him a fake punch to the gut.

"Fuck off," I said.

He laughed and circled around to his bike, swinging one giant leg over it. "You ready to do this?"

I nodded and sat on my Harley. "Let's ride."

It only took an hour to get to the drop, our pack of brothers twenty minutes behind us. We were supposed to set off the alarms, draw the guards out, and lead them away so our guys could swoop in for the kill. Crow had a truck and the rest of the club as an armed escort. While Hollywood and I distracted these cocksuckers, the crew would take the shipment and haul ass back to our turf.

All was going well until I saw more guys than we'd expected. More cars meant more witnesses.

"There's at least fifteen here," I whispered to Hollywood.

"You don't think you can lose them?"

"All of them might not chase me."

"You want me to call it in?" Hollywood glanced from me to the guys on the dock, where they directed the crane as it dropped a container onto the ground.

I swallowed and weighed the risk. Odds were, half of them followed me. Maybe three or four turned back after ten minutes, leaving three to fight off once I met up with Trojan and the guys. I could handle those odds.

"Nah," I said, kicking my bike to life. "Stick to the plan."

I drove closer, pulling up outside the locked gate a few feet away from where they unloaded the shipment right next to their parked cars. I revved my engine to draw their attention.

"Hey, you motherfuckers." I held up my gun, shooting out the window to the Mercedes closest to me. Next came the Molotov cocktail, a Caputi specialty. The bottle shattered against the seat, lighting the whole car on fire, and when I went to shoot at the gas tank, it exploded in a massive ball of flames. I rode by, gave them the finger, and took off as fast as I could.

Shouts and curses echoed behind me, and if I knew anything about these idiots, they'd chase first and wonder if it was a trap later. When I chanced a glance over my shoulder, I had at least three cars on my tail.

Three!

That's more than half the fucking crew. They'd just left the shipment?

Fuck. I didn't know who was stupider, them or me. Because if I got caught, this was it. I was fucking done. They'd pull all my limbs off my body before they killed me. I'd pray for death days before it would happen.

I could not get caught.

My heart pounded as I kicked it into the next gear, hauling ass over the backcountry roads. The roars of the engines behind me got closer, and a shot echoed out through the night air, a snapping tree at my right drawing my attention for a millisecond.

They're shooting at me.

Shit. Shit. Shit.

I went faster. Harder. Rubber to the asphalt. Pulse in my throat. Adrenaline coursed through my veins. My bike hugged the turns like she'd been made for it, and fuck yeah, she had. I'd built her for this.

Go, baby, go. Show them what we can do.

"Wooooo!" I shouted into the night as we went faster.

I couldn't make it too hard, so I slowed down to give them the temptation of shooting at me again. I swear to fucking God a bullet whizzed by my head. It missed me by a centimeter. I ducked lower and pushed the bike until she whined and screamed and begged for more.

God, it gave me a rush. All this power. This burst of life. Right between my legs.

"We know who you are, you Rose piece of shit," one of them snarled.

"We're coming for you," another one added.

I only laughed and gave them the finger.

"Get back here, you bastard!"

Slip had been specific. I had to make it to the rendezvous point by the deadline. That gave me no room to second guess what might have happened back at the docks. I had to trust that they could handle it, no matter what it was. I kept going.

Like I'd predicted, fifteen minutes into the chase, the car at the back turned around. A few minutes closer to Rose territory, the second one headed back. By the time I was there, it was just me and the Merc on my ass.

I pulled up to the spot where Trojan, Bear, and Saint came out of the shadows, guns drawn and shooting at the Merc's tires. The car spun out, coming to a hard stop against a tree on the side of the road. My guys swarmed it. I parked my bike and climbed off, grabbing my nine to join the battle.

Trojan fired at the driver as he held up a gun, nailing him in the chest. Saint hit the guy getting out of the passenger seat. And the guy in the back? Bear yanked him out of his seat and put him on his knees in front of us.

The dude smiled, his teeth bloody and his nose broken. His suit was now covered in mud and blood, and by the time we were done with him, probably his piss and shit, too.

"You stupid, dumb motherfuckers," he murmured, glancing between us.

"You're the one on your knees, you piece of Caputi shit." Bear held his pistol at the dude's temple.

The Caputi laughed, spitting blood at my feet and wiping his hands back through his shiny hair. "How many of your stupid, mangy shitheads did you bring out tonight? All of them, I hope."

My eyebrows furrowed, uneasiness slithering into my stomach. Why the hell would he say that? Unless—

My phone buzzed in my pocket, and I was even more confused when I saw Selene's name.

She knew not to call unless it was important.

"Hey," I said. "What's—"

"They're here," Selene said, in between deep pants. Like she was huffing it through a workout. "Caputi drew you out to the docks so his bastards could sneak on our property."

"What?" My stomach dropped. "What the fuck are you talking about?"

"The security alarms tripped at the garage. I came out to see what it was. There's five of them."

What the fuck?

All the tumblers fell together in my mind. The garage. Alba's house. It sat on Aris's property, SR property. Deep in those woods, we had a few big-ass storage sheds where we housed some of the MC's ammunition and dirty cash. This *had* been a trap, but not for the Caputis. This had been a trap for us. *We* were the fucking idiots here.

"Selene," I said. "Go back to the clubhouse. Right the fuck now."

"What's wrong?" Bear narrowed his eyes.

"This was a decoy. Caputi's after the shed." I raced over to my bike and hopped back on, kicking it to life. "Selene, get to the clubhouse."

Trojan shouted on the phone to one of our brothers up by the dock. "How many down?" A pause. "Is it bad?" Another pause.

"Selene, listen to me—" The line went dead, and I shoved my phone into my pocket. "Fuck. They're after the shed. Selene's tracking them. I've gotta get to her."

Trojan shook his head. "Thor says the container was empty, but there was a shootout. Two of Caputi's men down. Three Roses. Hollywood took a hit in the shoulder. They're packing up and clearing out."

"Tell them about the shed." I ran my hands through my hair. "I'm heading there now."

"Shit." Trojan nodded and looked back down at his phone.

"Go. Take Saint with you," Bear said, his voice falling into his cool demeanor. He reminded me of his father: commanding and practical, the voice of reason in the panic going through my head. "Be careful. If you're not sure, get Selene and get out of there. Losing some guns and cash is nothing compared to two brothers and my cousin. You understand?"

I nodded.

"Got it," Saint said, then looked at me. "C'mon, KC."

I whipped my bike around and headed home.

IT TOOK ENTIRELY TOO long to get there. Dread lined my stomach the entire way, and for all the power my bike had, it wasn't nearly fast enough when my sister's life was on the line. We didn't want them to know we were coming, so when we arrived, we parked on an access road that no one except SR knew about.

I cut off my engine and pulled out my gun, stalking through the woods behind the garage. Thank fucking fuck Selene and I had turned on "Find My Phone" for each other years ago, just in case this type of shit happened. If the Caputis had her, they hadn't done shit to her phone yet because I was still getting a signal a few hundred yards north.

Moving as soundlessly as possible, I rushed through the underbrush, my eyes wide and desperate, looking for the fuckers who did this.

But it had taken us nearly twenty minutes to get here. They could be long fucking gone by now. If Selene had been discovered? Fuck, I didn't even want to think about what could be happening to her.

Burning hot rage rolled through my gut, and I picked up my pace. *Selene, where the fuck are you?*

My hands shook as the panic set in. I didn't know what I'd do if I lost her. She was my last link to my family, my *blood* family. We'd come into this world together. She was my first friend, my best friend. I'd burn down the entire fucking world to get my vengeance if they hurt her.

"Where are they, slut?" A shout in the wind came from my right. I turned in that direction, held my gun higher, and took another few steps. The moonlight trickled in through the trees, giving me enough light to step over a body with its head blown off.

One of Caputi's men.

Which meant Selene had gotten him before they caught her.

"I told you." She sounded miserable, like they'd already beaten the fuck out of her. "I don't know, and if I did, I wouldn't tell you."

I damn near launched myself forward, but a huge hand on my shoulder stopped me. I scowled as Saint held up his index finger, gesturing for me to be quiet. He stepped ahead of me and looked around, giving me three fingers this time.

Three guys.

And Selene.

Fuck, my sister was tough, but this was outrageous. We took another silent step forward. And another. She was on her knees in front of them. Two guys held her arms out to either side and another held her own rifle to her forehead. They all wore suits and shiny shoes, even out here in the fucking sticks, which explained the difference between us better than anything else ever could. I recognized the one with the rifle as Julian Caputi, Benito's nearest and dearest nephew. His underboss.

The fucking heir apparent came here to do this himself?

Damn, we should feel honored.

Except I was about to blow his motherfucking head off. He should have taken her and left. Instead, I'd make sure he never stepped foot off this property again.

I moved toward them, holding my gun higher.

"That's all right, bitch," Julian said. "I don't mind fucking it right out of your ass. When I'm done with you, Stinky's gonna have a turn." He leaned in close. "Wanna guess why we call him Stinky?"

The two other guys laughed, and rage boiled through me. Saint held on to my shoulder, keeping me from doing anything stupid. I squeezed the trigger, itching for a reason to pull it tighter. I aimed at Julian, waiting for the right moment when he wouldn't be so close to Selene.

The last thing I wanted was for him to squeeze in reflex and kill her anyway.

Selene chuckled darkly, the sound breaking through the blood in her throat. "You're such a fucking stupid piece of shit. You have no idea what you've done, do you?"

Julian tilted his head to the side, considering her. I took one last step, bringing me within shooting distance. A twig cracked under my foot and all four heads turned in my direction.

"You hear that?" Julian said.

Selene didn't wait for any more confirmation. She used the surprise to yank her arms down, grab her rifle, and shove the butt into Julian's face, breaking his nose so hard that I heard it crack from where I stood. I leapt into action, firing at his head and watching his brains explode out the other side as he dropped to the ground.

Pop!

Pop!

Pop!

Gunshots echoed in the night air. Saint took the shithead on the other side of my sister, and I shot the guy closest to me. Before he could collapse, I had Selene in my arms, yanking her away from the fray.

Bright hot fire exploded up my spine and down my legs, and my knees buckled under my weight.

"Fuck." I curled in on my torso, grabbing at my stomach, and my fingers came away wet and sticky.

What the hell is that smell?

Metal in the air...

Blood.

My blood.

"Shit, Jer." Selene knelt next to me. She looked terrible. One eye was swollen, black and purple and red everywhere. But her tone is what scared me. "They got you."

"Fuck." We were out in the woods in the middle of nowhere, and I'd been fucking *shot?*

A groan got my attention and I snapped my head up to find Saint writhing on the ground, trying and failing to get up. I nodded to him, gesturing Selene to go while I checked out my own wound.

If I'd been standing two inches to the left, it would have nailed me right in the center of my stomach. As it was, the bullet had grazed my ribs. I'd had burns at the shop worse than this. I pushed myself to my feet, swallowing back the pain, and got to Saint.

"Okay, okay," Selene said, trying to calm his waving arms. "Let me see it." She pulled the fabric of his jeans away, muttering to herself about his femoral artery before flipping the limb to the other side. "It came out."

"Shit," Saint said. "Is that a good thing?"

"Maybe," Selene said. "Maybe not."

I grabbed at my belt, yanking the metal so I could slip it through the loops. I handed it to her and she wrapped it around his upper thigh, twisting it so tight he growled and shouted, "Fucking ow!"

"Listen, you big baby. You're losing a lot of blood. If we don't get you some place where I can close this up fast, you're gonna be fucked."

"What do we do?" He groaned.

I looked around. I knew where we were in relation to Rose Garage and Alba's house. The garage would be a quicker walk, but rougher terrain downhill. Alba's house, on the other hand, would be a few minutes due west, but mostly level ground. She had medical supplies. Morphine. A warm table and a sterile environment. The garage was a fucking pigsty.

Saint was a big dude. Carrying him would be a fucking challenge, especially because I was also injured. Selene looked like she couldn't see out of one eye. We were a Goddamned mess.

"Can you walk?" I knelt next to Saint and lifted him with my arm under his back, yanking him to his feet. "I've got a plan." Pain split me in two as I stood, but I pushed through it, knowing if I didn't, he might die right here in the middle of fucking nowhere.

He limped along, and Selene held the other side of him. The walk took three hundred fucking years. I'd aged centuries by the time we got there. But I got him there. Somehow. Some fucking way.

I stood in front of Alba's porch with my brother's blood dripping down my legs and knocked, praying I didn't scare the shit out of her.

19

ALBA

Banging on the door woke me up. It was late, just after two a.m., and I stuffed my glasses on my face while I trudged upstairs to answer. Frustration rankled down my spine.

Who the hell was knocking this late?

"Who is it?" my mother croaked out.

"I don't know, Mom." I checked through the peephole. Jericho held up Saint, and a badly beaten Selene leaned against the doorjamb. I quickly unlocked the entry and swung it open.

"What's going on?"

"Sorry," Jericho said. "I don't have my keys."

"Come in," I said. "What's happened?"

Jericho carried the big man through the house, his legs practically dragging on the carpet.

"Put him on the table." I clicked on the lights and grabbed the centerpiece, placing it on the desk by the window. Jer stretched his brother out over the top of it, and Saint groaned, clutching his leg.

"What can I do?" I asked.

"Do you have any clean towels? Medical supplies?" Selene wiped at the back of her bloody nose with her forearm. "Gauze, stitching, anything?"

"Jesus, you came to the right place," Mom piped up.

"Yes," I answered, turning toward the hallway that led toward the bathroom.

I didn't know what had happened or why, but Jericho needed my help. So I'd help him. My hands shook as I riffled through the closet.

Gauze, stitching, tape, antibiotics. I tossed it all in a plastic bag, hoping it would help. Mom had been sick for a while. She'd accumulated a lot of random items over the years. I came back into the dining room with my haul.

"What color's the blood?" Selene sifted through the supplies until she found what she needed.

"Red." Jericho poked at different parts, making Saint shout and launch off the table.

"But not black?"

"No," Jericho said.

Selene nodded and sniffed again. "You got lucky, Saint. If you nicked something important, you'd have bled out by now."

"It feels like fucking hell, Sel." Saint's voice sounded strained, and he winced while Jericho put more pressure on the wound.

"Doc's on his way, all right?" Jericho said. "Don't you fucking die on me."

"If I was gonna die," Saint said, "you think I'd be hanging on to look at your sorry fucking mug?"

Jericho laughed, and honestly, it made me feel better to hear the exchange. His face was pale, his eyes bloodshot, and his arms covered to his elbows in blood. It terrified me, and not only because of the horror.

My front door opened again and three enormous men walked through, the sound of shit-kickers echoing off my mother's hardwood. She sat up straighter, widening her eyes at the sight. I took a step back, clearing the way for the one with the patch that read *Doc.*

"Jesus fucking Christ, Saint," he said. "You've done a hell of a job making my night fucking perfect."

"Wouldn't be a raid if I didn't end up on your table, would it?"

Saint laughed in a soft whimper while two of his other brothers came to help Doc patch him up.

"I want to do an ultrasound." Doc leaned over Saint and poked at the wound in his thigh. "Can we get him to Rusty's?"

"I brought my pickup," a tall, bald guy said. *Slip.* The road captain.

"Good." He did some more examining before turning to Jericho. "You did the right thing, bringing him here. Any more jostling, and this could have been worse."

"How bad is it?" Slip crossed his arms over his chest. All of them were big with tattoos and auras that warned people to stay the fuck away.

"Difficult to say," Doc said.

"We'll get him to Rusty's and then take him to the clubhouse," Slip said. Then he looked at Selene and Jericho. "You two should stay here, just in case you were compromised."

"Compromised?" Selene glanced between Slip and Doc. "How?"

"I had a tail," Jericho said.

"We don't know if you were followed. But if you were, I don't like leaving civilians unprotected." Slip nodded. "I assume it's cool if Jer and Selene crash here for a few days?"

"Absolutely," Mom cut in. "Both are welcome as long as they want."

"Thank you," Slip said. "I'll send someone over to clean up the place tomorrow. I apologize for disrupting your evening."

"Please," Mom said, trying to wave him off. "I hope everyone's okay."

"Same." I wrapped my arms around my body. "I'm happy we could help."

"Mind if I use your bathroom?" Selene asked.

"Of course not." I grimaced at her busted lip and black eye. "That looks pretty bad. Let's get you cleaned up."

She nodded, and I led her down the hallway, closing the door behind us when we got inside.

"You all right?" She sat on my toilet while I dug through the bag for what remained of the peroxide and bandages.

"Me?" I raised my eyebrows, deciding on gauze and witch hazel for the bruising. "I'm fine. It's you I'm worried about. Do you think you have a concussion?"

She snorted out a laugh. "That fucker woulda needed to hit me harder than that."

I poured some liquid on a piece of gauze and dabbed at a deep cut on her forehead. She hissed and winced before jerking away, but I held her chin still in my hand and she darted her one good blue eye to me.

A few moments of silence passed between us while I patched her back together.

"This one might need stitches." I teased an area over her eyebrow, and she grimaced. It was deep and bleeding all over the place.

"Shit." She stood and looked in the mirror. "Nah. You got any butterflies?"

I dug through the bag, miraculously finding some. "I don't know how old they are."

"It's fine." She peeled them open so she could grab them with the tweezers, placing them like a fucking badass. "How much longer?"

At first, I didn't know what she meant, but then she nodded toward my mom in the living room.

"Not much. Weeks. Hours." I shrugged. "Some days she's better than others."

Selene nodded. "I did a rotation in the oncology ward."

"Really?"

She went back to closing herself up. "Before I dropped out."

"Why?"

She sighed before pulling the last stitch into place. "Life. Gemma went missing and Thor needed help at the garage and Jer..."

"Jer?"

Selene cleared her throat and turned to face me, leaning back against the sink. "Jer was fucked up over Nikki for a long time."

Oh.

Were Selene and Nikki friends? If so, winning her over might be difficult. That was... if I intended to be here long-term, which I hadn't decided yet.

"They weren't good together." Selene tilted her head to the side, raking her one good eye over me. "She didn't bring him to life like you."

"It's still new," I said. "And it's not..." I cleared my throat. "It's not really anything."

"Sure." She didn't sound convinced.

I waited a moment, remembering we still hadn't kissed or confessed our love or anything like that, despite whatever my stupid heart might be feeling. "What happened tonight?"

She took a deep breath. "Some assholes trespassed on my land. I shot one. The other three thought they could have their way with me." Selene shut her eye. "Guess it was stupid to go storming off on my own."

"You shot one?" I raised an eyebrow, dabbing at another area. "Jesus. You're awesome."

She laughed and shook her head, her messy brown hair caked with blood and mud and grass. I reached out to pick a piece off her, tossing it in the garbage.

"I'm an idiot." She sighed and shook her head. "They woulda killed me if Jericho hadn't shown up."

"Well, they didn't."

She almost had all the blood off her face when a loud voice boomed through the small house.

"Where is she? Where's Selene?"

"Fuck." Selene widened her eyes, meeting mine in panic. She gripped my forearm, digging her nails into my skin. Booted footsteps thundered down the hallway, drawing closer.

"Who is that?"

The handle to the bathroom door rattled.

"Selene?" said the loud voice on the other side, followed by three hard knocks on the door. "Open up."

"It's Thor," Selene said.

"Your uncle?" I went to open it, but she grabbed my wrist to stop me.

"He's not my uncle." She sighed. "Go away, Thor!"

"I need to see you." He sounded desperate and angry, like maybe she was his girlfriend or lover instead of his missing wife's niece. "Sel. Open the fucking door."

"I'm fine." She scowled, and even though half her face was purple and one eye had swollen shut, there was frustration in her expression, loud and clear. "I don't need your help."

"Selene, I swear to fucking God." Thor pounded harder and jiggled the handle again. "Open this fucking door, or I'll kick it down."

"You absolutely will not." My jaw dropped, and I balked at Selene. "What's going on?"

"If he sees me like this, he'll go fucking berserk."

"What?" My eyebrows furrowed as I tried to understand. "Why?"

"Just..." She shook her head and nodded toward the door. "Never mind. It's stupid. Can you tell him to wait outside? I'll come out when I'm ready."

"Are you sure?" I was skeptical. "You don't need help—"

"This isn't the first time I've patched myself up. Trust me."

I didn't like the look in her eye when she said that, but I didn't push.

"Thank you." Selene grabbed my hand and gave it a tender squeeze. "For what it's worth, whatever is between you and Jericho... it ain't nothing."

My cheeks burned, and I pushed my glasses higher on my face, giving her a small smile before opening the door to a six-feet-four Viking decked out in leather. His light-brown hair hung loose around his shoulders to the middle of his chest, and he stared down at me with his bright gray eyes. Tattoos lined his arms and neck, disappearing under his shirt and cut.

"Excuse me." I squeezed out the door, trying to shut it behind me. He put his hand out to stop it, grabbing the wood over my head. "She asked for you to wait outside."

"Yeah. No fucking way that's happening." He pushed it open, yanking it out of my hand. "Sel—Jesus Christ." His features dropped when he saw her, and I decided their business was none of mine.

Thor stepped inside the bathroom and shut the door behind him, and when I heard him speak softly to her behind the barrier, I went down the hallway to check on Jericho. He sat on the couch, clutching one side and laughing at something my mother said. She smiled when I came into the room, raising an eyebrow at my moonbeam.

"He needs some patching up, too," she said.

"It's nothing." He waved her off, but there was fresh blood on his fingertips, so I took a few steps closer and held a hand out to him.

"Let's go. I've got some more stuff downstairs."

He pursed his lips but let me tug him to his feet. Together, we hobbled down the steps to the other bathroom.

HE SAT shirtless on my toilet while I knelt on the floor between his knees, dabbing at the wound on his ribs with gauze. He winced and straightened, putting his hands on my shoulders to steady himself.

"You might need stitches," I said.

"Nah," he said. "Doc said I didn't. Just tape it closed, and I'll be good."

I placed one of the butterfly enclosures Doc had given him, tugging it into place across his wound. Good thing I didn't get wheezy at the sight of blood, or this would have gone in an entirely different direction. My initial shock had now faded away, leaving in its place a simmering rage at how close he'd come to danger.

It could have been him on my dining room table tonight. Two inches to the left, and it would have been.

Maybe he sensed that in my squared jaw or my hardened stare because he chuckled softly and said, "Guess my cam guy days are done for a while, huh?"

I blinked and snapped my gaze up to him. "You made me a deal. You better be prepared to stick to it."

"Ouch." He smiled and tilted his head to the side, his eyes softening. "You drive a hard bargain."

"Oh, rest assured. I am not one to be fucked with."

Something wild went through his eyes. "Oh yeah?"

"Yeah." I tried to sound more threatening, but I doubted I came off as anything more than a fussy cub pawing at a big, bad lion. Just to prove my point, I poked his wound a bit too hard, and he let out a small groan and flinched. "I'm smart and I listen to enough podcasts to know that if there's no body, there's no crime." Another sharp tug. "Get yourself in danger like this again, and I'll kill you myself." He tightened his hands on my shoulders, digging his fingertips into my skin. "They'll never find you."

"Yes, ma'am." His lips pulled into that devious grin, the one that said he had nothing but bad thoughts flitting through his head.

Done with his bandages, I stood to yank off my gloves and toss them in the trash. He grabbed my hips before I could take a step back, holding me in place. His forehead fell to the spot just over my heart.

"Thank you," he murmured, pressing a kiss to my sternum. "Thank you."

The tender moment nearly broke me, and my eyes burned with tears that I immediately blinked back. "Stand up. Let me get your pants off so I can clean you up."

He pursed his lips but did as I said, narrowing his eyes as I helped him to his feet. I unbuttoned his bloody jeans and shoved them down to his ankles. Then I led him into the shower and he sat on the bench. I got the water going, adjusting it so it didn't spray directly on him. I didn't want the bandages to come off, but I had to get some of this blood off him. Then I took off my own clothes and joined him, setting my glasses on the counter.

I went slow, sudsing the washcloth with soap, running it over his tattooed forearms, and scrubbing away Saint's blood. Selene's blood. His blood.

What a horrible fucking night.

I'd only known him two weeks, but they seemed like centuries when time was so precious. I didn't know how I'd go on once this was done between us. I cared about him, but I didn't know if love was reason enough to stay.

"Hey." He ran his hands up my ribcage, guiding me between his spread knees. When I stood in front of him, he took the washcloth and ran it over my stomach, up my chest to my breasts, and down my arms.

Washing me.

Caring for me.

"It's okay to be scared," he said. "I won't let anyone hurt you."

"I don't want anyone to hurt *you*." I swallowed down my terror.

"No one's gonna hurt me," he said. "Not if I can help it."

"You almost died tonight."

He shook his head. "But I didn't. Still got a little luck on my side."

"That luck's gonna run out one day." I raised an eyebrow.

"I'm sorry I scared you." He gave me a devil's grin as he ran soapy circles over my hip and down one thigh, closer to my clit. He teased the contact, running along the inside of my leg while he pressed his lips against my stomach. A small kiss. And then another. My pussy throbbed.

My heart raced.

My knees almost turned to jelly, and if I didn't have my hands on his shoulders to hold me up, I might have fainted right there in the misty hot shower.

"I'll make it up to you." Another kiss to my hipbone. Another lower. And another, the gentle swipe of his tongue against my sensitive skin making me shake. My clit pulsed, desperate for his attention, which he teased again by dragging the cloth up the other leg, grazing the edge of my pussy with his fingertips before coasting them down again. "Want me to make it up to you?"

"God, yes."

He chuckled. "So eager."

Had I said that out loud?

Whatever. Didn't matter.

I hadn't made it a secret how much I wanted him. He wanted me, too.

"Can I kiss it better?" He looked up at me with those big blue eyes and all the air pushed out of my lungs. I nodded. He grinned. Then he licked me and lifted one of my legs over his shoulder. He had to slouch to get the angle right, and I was on the ball of my other foot, but God, I didn't care. He worked me, sucking at my nub while he dug his fingers into my hip. Tugging me closer. He teased my entrance with his other hand, and when I bucked against him, he took that as invitation and pushed inside me.

I moaned and curled into him while he lapped at me harder, tunneling my fingers through his hair to hold him where I wanted him. My climax hit me hard and I shook, my legs finally giving out on me. But he held me up, somehow still strong despite his injury. He worked me through it, and once I'd come back to reality, I needed to fuck him. I needed him inside me in the worst way.

But he was hurt and I didn't want to make it any worse. I licked my lips and put my leg back on the ground, taking a step back and raising an eyebrow in question.

"My turn to kiss it better?" My knees protested against the tile floor when I dropped to the ground, but I ignored them, hoping I had bruises to show for it in the morning. I put my hands on his thighs and he leaned back against the wall, running his hand over my face to brush the wet hair back.

"Listen to me," he said. "No one will hurt you if I'm around to stop it. Understand?"

I stared into his soul, and the whole world stopped. Sure, I had been afraid that someone, whoever was following him, would come to hurt me. But my real fear, the one that had me shaking, was that he'd be taken away from me. That he'd be gone and soon my mom would be gone and in the end, I'd be alone.

I couldn't lose him.

I just *couldn't*.

"I love you." It came out before I could stop it. There I was, on the ground in front of him, tile digging into my knees, my elbows on his thighs, and his cock inches from my willing mouth, professing a love that had no right to be reciprocated.

For one heartbreaking moment, he froze. He didn't say anything. He didn't do anything. I thought I'd made a mistake.

I thought I'd crossed a line.

We'd only known each other for two weeks.

Two weeks!

And now I'm claiming to love him?

Jesus, Alba.

Did I even know what love—

He crashed his lips against mine so hard that it startled me. I melted into him. God, how amazing they felt on mine, and I almost couldn't believe it was happening. His tongue wrestled with me, demanding dominance over my mouth, a request I instantly gave into.

What hit me most was the emotion behind the touch. Every brush of his lips told me he loved me. Every agonized nibble reciprocated the desperation between us. My heart exploded. My veins pumped with adrenaline.

"I know." He murmured against my mouth. "I know, I know, I know."

Forgoing the blow job, I climbed into his lap, my knees on either side of his hips, and I slung my arm around his neck. I slowly impaled myself on him. All the way down. All of him. So, so slowly.

He gasped, his forehead pressed to mine. He dug one hand into my hip and clamped the other around my thigh.

I kissed him again and again, invading his mouth with my tongue.

"I love you, sunshine," he groaned, rocking into me and holding me tight against him. "It's stupid. I know it's stupid. But I love you. I love you so fucking much that it scares me."

"God, me too. Me too."

Now that it was out there, now that I knew, it freed me. An enormous weight lifted off my chest, and I couldn't contain my happiness.

Jericho had come out of nowhere. Savage and brutal, with a heart of fucking gold where it counted. Yeah, some fucked-up stuff had happened to him, and nights like tonight proved he had to do what he had to do sometimes. But there was a dark part of me, and I didn't know how big a part at the time saw a similarity.

The sounds he made rattled through me, and knowing I could do that to such a powerful man, to bring him to the brink like this, shattered what little restraint I had.

I came, using him for my pleasure and the way I wanted, and when he hit his climax, euphoria took over behind his eyes. There'd be no leaving him when the time came—either I'd stay or he'd come with me. Now that I had him, I could never *un*have him.

And I wasn't sure that was a problem anymore.

20

JERICHO

The next morning, I woke up wrapped around her, having sought her out even in my unconsciousness, not satisfied until we were connected from chest to toes. Kissing her neck and shoulders, I slipped inside her, still half-asleep. She moaned and curled into me, opening her legs for easier access. We intertwined our fingers while I took her, this time not on camera. This time just for us.

Alba's confession had rocked me. Once it was out there, I couldn't keep my feelings a secret anymore. Perhaps the fear of losing me had drawn it out of her, but I'd known for days what this was. Maybe since I met her, when she came storming back into the party with her hands in fists and those cute glasses perched on the end of her nose.

How'd I get so fucking lucky?

How'd *we* get so fucking lucky?

The downside slid into my brain and stuck there like a splinter. She had to be a part of the life now, whether she liked it or not. She'd have to be my old lady. She'd have to marry me—

Whooaaa... pump the brakes, my rational side said. I had only known her for *two weeks.*

I didn't care. I wanted all the good shit that would come with it—

my ring on her finger, her name inked on my skin, her on the back of my bike forever.

God, it got me so hard, and I understood then what my parents had that Thor and Gemma never did. This bond. This connection. This burn down the world for one person inferno in my gut.

For Alba, there was nothing I wouldn't do.

For Alba, I'd move fucking mountains.

After we both came, we showered and headed upstairs, where we stumbled upon Selene huddled close to Penny's head, whispering in hushed tones. They stopped when we shut the door behind us.

"Glad to see you two got acquainted," Alba said.

Penny smiled and Selene stood, but I froze when I got a good look at her. One eye had swollen shut. Her cheek and nose were badly bruised. If that Caputi son of a bitch wasn't already dead, I'd blow his head off again.

"Coffee's in the pot." Selene returned her attention to Penny. My phone buzzed in my pocket, and I pulled it out to see *Prez* on the ID.

"Hey." I excused myself outside, taking several steps away from the house so they didn't overhear. I checked my surroundings. Nothing but trees and wildlife. No strange vehicles. No uneasy feelings in my gut. We were alone. For now.

"Hey," Crow said, his voice gruffer than usual, indicating the hard night he'd had. "How you doing?"

"Fine," I said. "How's Saint? How's everyone else?"

"They'll live," he said. "We got lucky. No one is dead on our side."

Relief flooded my chest.

"We clean up?" I meant the bodies of the underboss and the other two idiots I'd dropped near the shed.

"Yeah," he said. "Last night. Pig shit by now."

"What next?"

"I'm sending a crew to you. They should be there soon," he said.

"Got it," I added.

There was a small pause before he said, "How well do you know Alba and her mother?"

"Well enough," I said. "She won't run her mouth."

He cleared his throat. "That's not what I'm afraid of."

Then what? "It's serious, me and her. Should I be worried?"

"Jee-sus Christ," he said. "You better be prepared to stand by those words."

What the hell was he talking about? "What's going on?"

"It's not my story to tell." He grunted a noise that sounded like frustration. "Just... keep an eye on her, yeah? For *her* safety."

Anxiety squeezed my chest. I was already doing that, but what wasn't he saying? I figured I'd learn sooner or later, so I didn't push it. "Ten-four."

"And KC? Nice work," he added. "You made the run, and you saved your sister's life. Even killed a few Caputi cocksuckers while you were at it. Your old man woulda been proud."

I couldn't help the swell of shame in my chest.

Would he?

I'd killed three people on the run, a few more before them. I'd beaten the hell out of anyone and everything in my way. I'd lived a hard life, a life he'd dragged me into and burdened me with. He'd been a lawyer once upon a time. And then his journey had taken a turn and he ended up here. Where he died.

"Thanks," I said, unsure if I meant it. "I'll see you in a bit."

I hung up in time for Selene to walk up next to me.

"How are you feeling?" I nodded to her face.

"It's not so bad." She shrugged and shoved her hands into her back pockets. "Hey, listen..." She cleared her throat. "I'm gonna stay with Alba for a while."

I narrowed my gaze, remembering Thor storming into the house last night, stalking down the hallway to the bathroom, and banging on the door until she opened up. Just another thing in a long list of weird and fucked up between them.

"You know what you're doing there?" I asked, subject matter implied.

She cleared her throat and ran her hands back through her hair, linking them behind her neck. "No." It was quiet and whispered, like she hated admitting it to herself, and worse yet, to me. Then she nodded back toward the house. "What about you?"

I cleared my throat and scrubbed my face. "I think I love her."

"I know," she said. "You're an idiot. But I know."

"Am I being stupid?"

She snorted and nudged me, this time more playfully. "Of course you're being stupid. But that's nothing new."

"You're the brains. I'm the brawn." An old mantra, something we used to say when we were kids. It still held true today.

"Always and forever." She gave me a hug and pulled back, staring up at me to say, "They're in this now, you know? Penny and Alba?"

I sighed. "Yeah, I know."

"You killing Julian Caputi not a mile from here? That's gonna lead them straight up the street."

My stomach rolled, tension coasting through me. "I know."

"There's what? Five other houses on this road, max? It won't take them long to track down the girl sleeping with a Rose and putting it online."

My jaw dropped as I whipped my attention to her. "How do you know about that?"

She laughed. "Ru's my best friend, silly. Plus, you asked me about it the day after you met her, remember?"

I scratched at the back of my head. How many more people knew about my side hustle? "We don't show our faces, and I wear a shirt to cover my tattoos. Castor fixed the security and ran it through some VPN shit out in Russia."

Selene narrowed her eyes at me. "Didn't you say you had a tail a few days ago?"

I nodded. "And a week ago at the run out west."

"You think they're with the Caputis?"

"Don't know." But I saw where she was going with this. It didn't matter what Castor did. It didn't matter what I did. If the Caputis had been following me for a week, they already knew where Alba lived. My big question was... how did they know about the shed? Why were they in the woods in the first place? "I already talked to Alba about staying here until things die down. She might leave after her mom passes."

"And go where?"

I shrugged. "Wherever she can't feel it."

Selene laughed out a sad noise and shook her head. "Well, we know all about that, don't we?"

She'd spent the better part of high school running away from it all, from Gemma and me and our fucked-up family. Thor usually tracked her down and dragged her ass back, much to her dismay.

"Want me to talk to her?"

I shook my head and pursed my lips. "She's gonna do what she's gonna do. No sense trying to stop her."

"You're still being an idiot."

The sounds of motorcycles echoing up the street brought my head up. Aris led the pack. Behind him were four prospects, here to clean up all the Saint left over in the dining room.

Aris didn't say anything when he finally parked. Just hopped off the bike and stormed inside like his ass was on fire.

ALBA

om looked rough this morning. The midnight interruption had taken its toll despite her insistence that she had enjoyed the adrenaline. Now, I stood at the window next to her, watching Jericho and his sister out front while Mom texted on her phone, her weak fingers barely keeping up.

She let out a frustrated groan and threw her head back.

"What's wrong with you?" I narrowed my eyes.

She turned toward me, and a tear rolled down her cheek.

"Remember how I didn't judge you for the way you made money?" She grabbed my hand, her fingers so cold and bony, bare ghosts of what they used to be. "Remember how much I've always loved and supported you?"

"Yeah," I said. "What's gotten into you?"

She let out a slow breath, and the sound of motorcycles echoed up the street like thunder, a warning I should have heeded. I should have found somewhere to hide. I should have rushed into the woods and prayed the fairies swept me away. But instead, I stared at her with this stupid, confused look on my face.

And when the front door burst open, a big gray-haired man

wearing a Steel Roses cut and shit-kickers rushed in, coming to a stop at the end of the bed.

His cut read Aris - Vice President.

"Ash," my mother said.

Ash.

The name hit me like a punch to the gut.

My father's name was Ash. It was one of the few things she'd ever told me about him. That and he'd once loved her too much. Things had ended so badly that she'd never told me anything else about him, and she never wanted to.

But here he was. And so was I.

"Penny," he said. And then those blue eyes fell on me, and I read the expression on his features. *My* features. My nose and my eyes and my forehead on *his* face. "Alba."

I didn't know what to say. My eyes burned, and I squared my jaw, yanking my hand away from my mother as recognition slugged me hard in the stomach. This man had fucked my mother some twenty-three years ago and left her. And now that she was knocking at death's door, he wanted to play his hand in the regret game.

He could fuck right off.

For my entire life, I practiced the way I'd make him feel like shit when I met him. I'd stick my finger in his face and yell at him for every missed spelling bee, dance recital, and movie night. I'd shame him for a whole life he didn't get to have with me. I'd remind him *I* was a gift *he* didn't get, and I fucking knew it.

But when the time came, I just stood there, knees locked and eyes wide.

"Is this what I think it is?" I asked, my voice shaking. "Is he..." I cleared my throat, trying not to sob. "Is he who I think he is?"

"I wanted to tell you, honey." Mom reached for me again. "Please believe me. It was never the right moment."

"My entire life, he's been down the street?" I couldn't believe this. All that time I'd spent at Rose Garage, I'd never met Aris personally before, but now that I knew who he was to the Roses, he must have been there. He must have seen my mom. He must have seen me. "Did you know?"

He cleared his throat and rubbed a hand over his mouth. "It's complicated."

I nodded, eyes stinging. "So complicated that it took twenty-two years for either of you to say something?"

While they struggled to put their story into words, my brain sprinted through the implications of this. I was the daughter of the SRMC's vice president. I had a whole other family out there.

Ru.

Ru is my sister.

My sister!

My heart pounded in my head. My vision swam. My lips trembled. Any second, I'd start crying right here in front of them. I wanted to be mad. I wanted to rage.

My mother finally let out a long sigh. "My father is Benito Caputi."

Every thought in my brain came to a stop.

"My real name is Alessandra Caputi. I wasn't supposed to fall in love with a Rose."

Standing by the door, Selene gasped.

"Fuck," Jericho murmured. Evidently he had put together something I was struggling to understand.

"I thought your parents were dead." I could barely form the words, my voice shook so hard.

She cleared her throat and nodded. "Dead to me. I've only ever told you they were dead to me. But I guess the opposite is true. I'm dead to them."

And that? Well, that shocked the shit out of me.

My knees turned to jelly, and I sank onto the couch next to the front window, struggling to process this new information.

"Your grandfather doesn't know about you," she said. "And if he ever found out..." There was an awkward silence in the room.

"I'm sorry we couldn't tell you." Aris took a step forward, his hands in his pockets, but his apology only pissed me off.

He's sorry?

Twenty-two years and he's *sorry?*

He had another daughter, an entire different life while we struggled and I fucked a stranger on the internet for money. My shock and denial slid into anger, and I pushed to my feet, my hands clenched and terrible things on the tip of my tongue.

"Alba." My mother's weak voice made me snap my focus to her. "Please say you'll forgive me. Maybe not today. Maybe not even before I'm gone. But someday. It's the only thing I've been keeping from you, baby. I swear."

"If it's any consolation"—Aris put his hands on the edge of her bed with a familiarity that bugged me—"I've done everything I could to protect you from afar."

"Like what?" I asked, my tone venomous.

"We live on his land," Mom said. "He bought you that car you drive around. He wanted to be here, but he couldn't."

The house up the street from the garage.

The car when I turned sixteen that I'd never been sure how Mom afforded. That I took such good care of because I didn't know if I'd ever be able to have anything else like it. I had to drive it until the wheels fell off.

All these random memories started to make sense.

"He did whatever I'd let him do," Mom said, giving him a wink. Then she coughed and struggled to breathe, taking long, deep gasps for air. "Benito can never find out I survived. He can never find out about you." She squeezed my hand. "Please say you'll forgive me."

I wanted to be happy for my mother. She'd longed for this man for decades. She'd never dated anyone else. She'd never moved on. And after all this time, he *still* looked at her like he might break her, but damn anyone else who tried. I knew what she meant when she said Jericho looked at me that way.

It was in me to storm off and punish her for her lies. And if I had time to make things right, I might have done that. But the sight of her frail body on that bed took the fight out of me.

I'd have years to be mad at her for this, and maybe it made me a coward because I didn't want to fight with her about it now. I didn't care. It wasn't the time to get angry over her regrets.

Wasn't it enough that she'd spent half her life regretting it?

"I forgive you, Mom," I said.

Her eyes lit up. "Really?"

I nodded. "Of course. Whatever you did, you must have had your reasons." I meant it. I truly did. There was nothing I knew more strongly than how much my mother loved me. If she thought she was protecting me by keeping Aris and the Caputi family from me, then I had to believe that.

"I love you," I told her.

"Oh, Alba," she said. But then her eyes rolled back in her eyes and she gasped for air, her arm falling limp and heavy from my hand.

"Mom?" Panic rushed through me, and Selene came to the other side of the bed, checking the machines and my mother's vitals. She put the oxygen mask over Mom's nose and mouth, but that did nothing to calm the alarms next to the bed.

"I'll call the hospice nurse," I said, going for my phone. But as I dialed the number, I knew it was a fruitless effort. Mom had a notarized DNR. Even if the nurse came, she would do nothing. This was how Mom wanted to go—at home, surrounded by the people who loved her.

"Alba, I think this is it," Selene said. "Her heart is giving out."

"No." I grabbed Mom's shoulders. Tears streamed down my cheeks, burning my eyes so I couldn't see. "Mom! No! Please don't go. I'm not ready. Mom!"

This couldn't be happening. *Not yet.*

I didn't know how to do anything on my own. I couldn't live without her.

God! I'd been so fucking stupid. I'd spent the last two weeks fucking around with Jericho and she was dying! *Dying!*

"I love you," I said, because I didn't want the last words she heard from me to be I'm not ready. "I love you." I said it again and again, over and over, so she'd carry it with her wherever she was headed. So she'd have it with her until we found each other again.

I DIDN'T KNOW whether she'd heard me or if this would have happened anyway, but she didn't immediately slip away. Once the mask was on her face, her heart kept pumping, but she never regained consciousness.

"I doubt she will," Martha said, taking my mother's pulse and checking the IV. "It won't be long now." She hung around for an hour or so, but there was nothing more she could do, so she left, telling me to call back when it happened.

I sat on the couch next to the hospital bed, Jericho next to me with Selene and Aris on the opposite side. Ignoring him took effort. He was tall and hulking and objectively handsome. I could see what my mother had liked about him. Why she had loved him all these years.

Jericho intertwined his fingers with mine.

"Were you her mystery date these last two weeks?"

He nodded. "We used to sneak away to meet up every so often. When she stopped calling, I got worried. A few months went by, and I found out she'd gotten sick. She wouldn't let me come over for another couple after that."

That sounded like her. Prideful. Unwilling to let the man of her dreams see her at her weakest.

"Damn stubborn woman." He leaned forward and grabbed her hand with a propriety that took decades to build. So easy and carefree. I didn't need a paternity test to know he was my father. But did I want to be his daughter?

Twenty-two years, and I wasn't sure.

I might never be sure.

"How did you two meet?"

"At a Halloween party," he said. "We both had masks on, so I didn't know it was her and she didn't know it was me. I'd always say it was love at first sight, but your mom says she didn't love me until she knew who I was... who I really was." He stopped to smile, perhaps remembering the younger version of my mother he'd met that night.

"It was off and on for a while. We couldn't tell anyone, obviously. I was raised in the MC. My father was VP before me. And your mom?" He sighed and shook his head. "She hated her old man. God, she hated him. And maybe that's what made her give me a shot. She wanted out of her life, and I was too eager to rescue her from it."

I sympathized with that version of Mom, and the more he talked, the more it all made sense. My mom had always been wild and care-free, unconcerned with any rules that didn't fit into her moral code. No wonder she had met a biker knight and rode off into the sunset on his mighty metal steed.

"I'm thankful she did." Aris rubbed at the back of his head and sighed, a thousand-year stare in his eyes. He was in a memory with her, not here. Not anymore. "I met Ruthie's mother during one of our off times. She got pregnant, so I ended it with Penny. But that didn't mean I stopped loving her. Or you."

I swallowed back my anger. I had a lot of choice words for him about claiming to love me. Giving us a house. Giving me a car. It meant nothing in the grand scheme of things. But I supposed it was all he could do. Shelter us. Provide for me through her when he couldn't do it in person.

"I'm too close to the Roses," he continued. "When your mom ran from Benito, she ran from it all. The entire life. Her entire family. Staying in Madison, staying on *our* turf, it's what kept you both safe from that motherfucker all this time."

A sliver of foreboding snaked down my spine, making me shiver. My grandfather was the boss of the Caputi family, one of the most powerful crime syndicates in the country and the sworn enemy of my father, the VP of the Steel Roses. My grandfather was responsible for the deaths of Jericho's parents, Crow's sister, and countless others. Likewise, how many of my grandfather's men had these two killed between them? Three from Jericho last night? Hundreds more before them?

This blood feud had been going on for over forty years, Benito the only one still alive from the start of it. My mother and Jericho's parents perpetuated what had already been there, adding more to the spilled blood. An endless crimson river flowed between the families.

Guilt settled in my gut like rotten cement. If I didn't exist, Jericho would have his parents. If I didn't exist, his Aunt Gemma would still be around, and Crow's old lady would still be here. All this violence, all because of me and my mother and this complicated asshole sitting in front of me.

I hated that most of all.

"What about Ru?" I said, my heart remembering I had a sister. "Does she know about me?"

He nodded. "She does."

"For how long?" Had she known about me this entire time and didn't tell me? Had she known when she was standing here a few days ago, proposing a business opportunity?

"I told her yesterday," he said. "She's about as pissed at me as you are." He smiled. "But she doesn't blame you. She seems to like you a lot."

Well, good. Because I liked her, too.

Wow. Ru is my sister. My actual sister.

"What happens now?"

He shrugged. "You can do what you want. You know the truth. May it set you free."

"Are you planning to stick around? Play dad?"

He tilted his head to the side and made a face I'd only ever seen before in the mirror. "Is that what you want?"

"No," I said.

"Then no."

"So... why are you here?" It was a selfish question born out of my resentment. He loved her. What other reason could there be?

"I just wanna say goodbye to my old friend."

I took a deep breath and swallowed back a sob.

"Veep," came a voice from the dining room. The prospects had been in there for the better part of an hour, pretending not to overhear us as they tried to get blood out of the hardwood. "It won't come off the table."

Jericho got up to help them, but after some hushed conversation I couldn't hear, he turned toward me and shrugged.

"It's not coming out." He crossed his arms over his chest. "What do you wanna do?"

"Trash it," Aris and I said at the same time.

"I'll get you a replacement," Aris added.

"Don't bother," I said. "I'm not staying here much longer."

I said the words because I'd been saying them for months, but when Jericho winced and straightened, shame snaked through my chest. Not two days ago, we had moved in together. I'd told him I loved him last night. My mother had given permission for him to stay here as long as he wanted. I planned to do the same.

But my heart was broken, and I couldn't make any promises about anything. At that moment, I wanted desperately to run away from all of this. To pretend my mother wasn't on her last breaths. To pretend she was happy and healthy and in love with Aris, even if she couldn't have him the way she wanted. I wanted it to go away.

Just. Go. Away.

"Where are you headed?" Aris asked.

"Anywhere." The word came out as exhausted as I was, and even though it was only two in the afternoon, I was about to crash out on this couch with a blanket and fall asleep holding my mother's hand. Aris flicked his eyes to Jericho, who didn't say anything despite the stiffness in his body.

Hours passed like decades, and finally, Aris stood and stretched his arms.

"Jericho and I need to get back to the clubhouse." He nodded toward the door. "Crow's called a meeting about last night."

Jericho nodded and leaned over to give me a kiss. "Are you okay?"

I shook my head. I didn't know if I'd ever be okay again. "But Selene's here." Besides, I was so tired that I could barely keep my eyes open. I'd probably sleep the whole time he was gone.

"I'll come back tonight?" He phrased it like a question, giving me permission to deny him. But I needed his support, now more than ever.

"Okay," I said.

"Okay." He grinned, kissed me, and walked toward the front door, leaving me with my sperm donor.

"I'd like to come back over, too," Aris said, shoving his hands in his pockets. "If that would be okay."

I envisioned shoving him out of my house, slamming the door in his face, and telling him this was what he got for twenty-two years of fucking nothing. But that didn't solve anything, and I'd only feel guilty about it later.

"Where's Ru?" Didn't she care her father was here instead of with her?

He shrugged and frowned. "Probably at home. Maybe at the club-house. She's a grown woman. She does what she wants."

"She doesn't mind you being here?"

Aris shook his head. "No, Ru is"—he cleared his throat—"understanding." Then he ran a hand through the back of his hair. "She'd like to come with me. I told her no, at first. I didn't know how you'd react to all this."

I certainly didn't want more people over. This was already too much. But Ru had been nice to me, and I liked her. Maybe it wouldn't be so bad to rip off the Band-Aid between us.

"Think about it." Then he turned to head out, closing the door behind him.

I watched them from the porch as they rode off. But once they were gone, I let out a deep sigh. It wasn't because of Jericho. It was because of Aris.

All of this was too much too soon.

Saint and my mother, and now him and Ru.

I couldn't wrap my head around it, and until I did, I couldn't figure out how to act. Was I mad at him? Yes, although I understood his reasons. Did I want him in my life? Yes, although I was angry at him for being away for most of it. Was I angry with my mom? Yes, although I forgave her. It was confusing and complicated and... I needed a nap.

When I went inside, Selene had turned on the television and crashed out on the other couch.

"Is there anything important you've got to do today?" I sat on the sofa opposite her, the one closest to the window.

She shrugged. "I got my ass handed to me last night." She looked at me. "Figured I'd hang here if that's okay. I promise not to bother you if you don't want me to."

I took a deep breath, appreciating Selene on a whole new level. I didn't want anyone here; I didn't want anyone to see me and my mom like this. But I also didn't want to be alone. Like with her brother, I felt safe with Selene. I'd known her a week, but my gut told me I could trust her.

"Yeah, that's fine," I said. "Stay as long as you want."

"Do you mean that?"

I nodded. "Yeah. I don't mind you being here."

"Thank you."

I paused before asking. It was none of my business, but I sensed maybe she wanted to talk about it. "Everything okay with you and Thor?"

The long, drawn-out sigh from across the room made me look up. "I can't be around him right now. I don't..." She cleared her throat and sighed again. "I don't trust myself around him when he's like this."

I narrowed my eyes. "What do you mean?"

"He makes me so angry." She shook her head. "Which only makes him angry, and then there's this explosive thing between us and..." She widened her eyes and pursed her lips. "It's not right. He's my uncle."

I tilted my head from side to side, considering. "But he's not your uncle. You said that last night. Not really."

"Not by blood," she said. "But when I ran off as a teenager, he's the one who brought me back. When I brought home scumbags in high school, he's the one who chased them off. When I fucked up, he's the one who fixed it."

"Sounds like he's got it bad for you, too." I shrugged. "From an outsider's perspective."

"Nothing's happened between us, to be clear." A tear leaked out, and she wiped it away, looking back up at the television. "He's just overprotective. They all are. Jericho, too."

That got my attention.

"So be careful," she added. "The Roses are alpha fucking assholes, and once you're in, you can't get out." She made a sad, laughing noise. "You think you're leaving once this is over? That you can take off in that Honda and disappear? Think again."

What the hell is that supposed to mean?

"You've got my brother by the heartstrings. You run, he chases. And that's how this story ends, *sunshine*." She crossed her arms over her chest. "They're possessive, territorial monsters. They'll worship you. They'll kill for you." She paused, seemingly lost in her thoughts for a second, before shaking her head and coming back to reality. "It's a whole different level of devotion."

I knew what she meant. It already vibrated in my bones. What I had with Jericho was stronger than anything I'd known before. It scared me. Enough to make me back away from it.

"There is no running from them. Understand? He'll never stop looking for you."

"How do you know that?"

She laughed again, this time louder and more genuine. "Why the hell do you think I'm hiding out here? I can't go home. If I do, that admits submission. But I can't run away. That means I'm prey. So I'm stuck in limbo until I figure out what to do." Selene pursed her lips again, considering. "You, on the other hand, have nothing to lose. You'd be lucky to score my brother." She looked around. "From what I can tell, he's lucky to have you, too."

Fair enough.

Selene looked up at my mother. "I know things are about to get rough for you. But Jericho and I are familiar with rough. Especially Jer. He's..." Selene wiped at her eyes again. "He's the strongest person I know."

I nodded and held myself tighter.

22

———————

JERICHO

"I told these sons a' bitches I was fine." Hollywood groaned from the bed in the back of the clubhouse. I sat on the chair next to him, smoking a joint and smiling at his whines. "But Doc won't let me up until I'm off the pain meds."

"Doc's right," I said. "If you're in too much pain to move without them, you shouldn't be moving."

He narrowed his eyes and snatched the joint out of my hand, bringing it to his lips for a deep inhale. I looked across the room at Saint, lounging back on another bed, his thigh wrapped in gauze.

"How about you? Doc stitch you up?"

Saint gave me a thumbs-up, but he was still heavily medicated. "Oh, I'm fine, KC. Fucking fiiiinnnne."

I snickered at his drugged-up slur.

"How's your girl?" Hollywood cut in, handing the joint back to me.

I shook my head and sighed. "I don't know."

I truly didn't. Yesterday, we were moving in together. Today, she wanted to leave again. Which brought me to a fork in the road. If I wanted to keep her, I had to let her know. I had to tell her that she was in this now, like it or not. And the best way to protect her was to make her mine.

Maybe I should have been afraid of that. Maybe I should have been outright terrified of committing myself to someone so completely after only knowing them for a few weeks. But I felt this rightness with her in my gut, and nothing could change my mind. She was going through a shitty fucking time. First, her mom, and now Aris.

Jesus Christ. Aris.

That shit blew my mind. I could only imagine what was going through hers.

"I heard about her mom," Saint said. "Shame. She seems like a nice lady."

I nodded. "She is."

"Give Alba my best, yeah?"

"Yeah. Can you still walk and shit? Or are you gonna need someone to lug your big ass around now?"

He laughed. "Yeah, motherfucker. Those Caputi assholes can't take me down that easy."

It was good to see Saint back in his spirits. He'd scared the shit out of me yesterday. We weren't as close as me and Hollywood were, but he was my brother. My family. I loved him. A quiet knock at the door brought my head up, and I found Ru standing there, her curly brown hair in a messy bun on top of her head. Add a pair of glasses, and I'd see the resemblance to Alba. Ru's face was rounder and she had higher cheekbones, but the eyes and the nose were the same.

"Hey," she said, taking a few steps inside. She looked rough, like she'd been up all night helping the club. Knowing her, she likely had.

"Hey," I said.

"How's Alba?"

I gave her the same overview I'd given Saint and Hollywood. "How are you doing?"

"Ah." She waved me off. "I'm not surprised, honestly. I found out about Penny years ago. I should have guessed there was a child."

"You seem well adjusted."

She shook her head. "My dad's an asshole. That's nothing new."

I glanced at the bodies milling around behind her. Crow bounced between groups of people, checking in to make sure everyone was okay, giving them his strength as only the President could. Almost the whole club was here, just over forty people with their spouses. Some had even brought their kids. When one of us bled, we *all* did.

"How are you?" She nodded to my side. "Heard you got winged."

"Yeah, it's a scratch."

She laughed and clapped me on the shoulder. "'Tis but a flesh wound." Ru focused her attention on Saint, a wistfulness coming to her eyes before she went to his bedside. I knew they were fucking once upon a time, and judging by the adoration in his gaze, I'd say they still were together.

I said my goodbyes and headed to Crow.

"Hey, KC," he said, pulling me into a hug. "Good to see you, kid. Glad you made it out okay."

"Glad no one else is seriously hurt."

"We got lucky," Crow said. "Those motherfuckers are gonna pay for this."

I had a thousand questions about last night. How had we gotten the bad intel? How had they known where the shed was in the first place? What were we going to do next? But Crow clapped the side of my face and turned to Aris, whispering something about calling church to order.

"C'mon," he said, and I followed him to the meeting room in the back while Aris shouted behind me for everyone else to join us. I pulled out my phone and checked for messages from Selene or Alba. I didn't know if I should be relieved or worried there weren't any. I'd only been gone an hour, but it felt like fucking years.

Jesus, if I hated the separation now, what would I do when she left?

I didn't like that look in her eye earlier today, like she didn't care if it bothered me. Grief could make people say fucked-up stuff they didn't mean and do shit they wouldn't normally do.

Alba had likely thought she had more time with her mom, and

now that she faced the end, the anger over that loss might make her act out. It had for me. Sometimes I still acted out, missing my dad, my mom, Gemma. Perhaps missing a childhood that included them most of all. Lamenting that version of me that got to have the big family.

Watching my brothers file in filled me with a strange nostalgia. Yeah, my parents were gone, but I still had family. I still had *them,* and they still had me. Every one of these fuckers would lay their life on the line for me if I needed them to. I'd do the same for them.

Is that not family?

Alba thought she was alone, but I loved her. And because I loved her, all of them loved her. They'd protect her. They'd come for her if anything happened.

Is that not family?

Thor found me and smiled, coming to stand next to me. I didn't have a chance to say anything before Aris opened with, "Thank you all for coming."

Switch closed the meeting doors. Bodies crammed into the small space, the most members we'd had at church in a long time.

"By now, you've all heard what happened last night," Aris said. "The run that produced nothing but a gunfight. The near miss with my storage shed. The Caputis we killed and fed to the pigs. I won't lie and say things look good. Things are pretty fucking bleak. But we're all here. Most of us are healthy."

"All of us are healthy, Veep," Hollywood shouted from the back.

"Shut the fuck up, Hollywood," Doc said. "And sit your ass down before you pass out, you dumb son of a—" The laughter of the room drowned out their tussle, but Hollywood ultimately gave in.

"All right," Crow barked in that booming voice of his, silencing everyone again. "Let the man speak."

"I've been keeping something from you," Aris said. "So I must ask your forgiveness. It put the whole club at risk." His steel-blue eyes came to me specifically. "Some more than others."

Whispers and murmurs echoed around me, but I straightened and shifted my shoulders, ignoring the ache in my side.

"Twenty-five years ago, I fell in love with Penelope Wright. Some of you know this, but most of you don't. She's the daughter of Benito Caputi."

The room fell quiet. No one even fucking breathed.

"Alessandra Caputi. When she got pregnant, she came to the MC for help. We faked her death and set her up here with a new name and identity."

More hushed talking amongst the brothers, but Aris hung his gray head and sighed. "I've tried to protect us the best I can, but last night, we were blindsided. All of this blood, it's on me."

Shouts of "No!" and "Stop it, Veep!" came from the crowd.

"Ain't your fault!"

"Benito started this bloodshed."

"Last night, we lost more than our pride. Saint took a hit in the leg. Hollywood got clipped in the shoulder. We let them get the better of us. Not again." Aris let out a deep sigh. "Penny and I had a child. A daughter."

That shut everyone up. I couldn't believe he was telling them, telling us all.

Why?

Why risk it like this?

It could get back to the Caputis. There were people here I hadn't seen in ages. Years, even.

Unless...

That's what they wanted. They used the excuse of me fucking her to set up surveillance at the house. And now? They were shining the bat signal.

They think we have a rat.

It was the only explanation. How could they have known where the shed was? How could they have known we'd come after them last night? How could they have known everything?

I glanced around the room, my paranoia at an all-time high.

Who could it be? Who could it be?

Almost the entire club was in this very space. Odds were the snitch was right here, right now.

I put my hand on my nine. If I ever found out who it was...

"Her name is Alba Wright," Aris said, drawing my attention back to the present. "And Penny is on her deathbed. Cancer. Can you believe it? She survived her father only to be taken out by her own fucking body." Aris clutched the back of the chair, leaning over it. "I know I've got blood on my hands—Rose and Caputi alike—and I'm sorry."

No one said anything, but I read the room. It wasn't because we thought Aris owed us an apology. It was because there was no forgiveness to give. Loving Penny shouldn't have been a crime. Loving Penny shouldn't have caused the mayhem it did.

Crow stood and walked closer to Aris, putting a hand on his shoulder.

"Anyone wanna impeach him?"

Silence and then, "Move to exonerate," came from Thor next to me.

"Seconded," Slip said.

"Anyone against?"

Silence.

"I agree." Crow turned to Aris and opened his arms, pulling him in for a giant hug. "Love is love, brother. Benito started this fucking shit." Aris gave him a nod and a pat on the back. When they separated, Crow turned to the rest of us. "The blood is on *his* hands, and it's led us here to this. Last night, we wasted three of Caputi's men, Julian Caputi included. Won't be long now before they come looking for revenge."

Crow took a couple of steps forward, moving into the crowd and making himself one of us.

"And when they do"—he crossed his arms over his chest—"we'll be fucking ready this time. When they do, this fucking ends."

The MC went wild, shouts and hollers coming from all directions. I joined in, the first taste of anticipation on my tongue. For thirteen years, I'd been waiting for my chance to get even. For thirteen years, I'd lusted for Benito's blood. And now? I'd finally get it.

DEATH COULD BE A SHADY BITCH.

She could make a man feel powerful as fuck—when he leaned over someone who was trying to take his life with his hands around that fucker's windpipe, watching as death pulled their soul from their body. And knowing, deep down, he was on death's side that day was some overwhelming shit. Addictive, too.

But sometimes... death could make a man feel more helpless than ever. Like when he stood next to the woman he loved and held her sobbing body while her mother took her last breath, knowing there wasn't a damn thing he could do to stop death this time.

Well, that's the flip side. That power he felt in the killing? That was just borrowed strength. Death always came for what was hers in the end.

Always.

Penny passed peacefully in her sleep at eleven-thirty that night, with Alba holding one hand and Aris holding the other. The two people who had loved her the most in her life were there with her at her end.

After the morticians took her body to the funeral home, I carried Alba down to her room and put her in her bed, crawling in behind her. We had a long few days ahead of us, and not just because of Penny's death. She'd need her rest.

This would be hard, yes. But the shit with the Caputis would be hard, too.

"I can't believe she's gone," Alba said.

I kissed her shoulder, the side of her head, and anywhere else I could. "I know, sunshine."

"It hurts, Jer," she said. "It hurts so bad."

"I'm sorry." I kissed her ear, holding her tighter and wishing there was something I could do to take away her pain. "I'm so sorry this is happening."

"No, I'm the one who's sorry." She turned in my hold so she faced me. "I'm sorry my grandfather did that to your parents. I'm sorry about all—"

I shut her up with a kiss, cupping her face to hold her still. I didn't want to hear that shit. It wasn't her fault. None of it. She didn't know. How could she? She'd been lied to her entire life.

"If I could kill him for you," she whispered, "I would."

I laughed and kissed her again. "I know."

"I'm sorry for what I said earlier." She shook her head. "It's a habit to say I'm leaving."

"Do you still want to?"

"I don't know. Sometimes I dream about it. Just running off and disappearing. Especially now, knowing about my family." She gave me a half-hearted smile and wiped at her cheeks, brushing away tears. "But then, I think about leaving you. Leaving this. It's scary, but I do love you, Jericho."

The weight on my chest lifted. I believed her when she said it, the truth radiating from inside her. And that was the fundamental difference between her and Nikki. When Nikki told me she loved me, I questioned it the entire time we were together. But with Alba? Not a single fucking part of me thought she was lying.

"I love you, too."

"What if I did disappear?" She said the words low and murmured. "What if Benito could never find me or learn about me?"

I shook my head. "He might never know. She's lived as Penny Wright all these years. No one has put it together yet."

"But if he does... he'll come for me."

"He won't get you." I kissed her softly and sweetly. "I promise."

She tightened her hands around my wrists. "Why? Why does he want me so bad?"

"You're his granddaughter. His blood." But it was worse than that. "And you're half Rose."

"Rose. Caputi. These are stupid labels. I'm a human."

"Benito doesn't see it that way," I said. "There's too much history. Too much bad blood."

"Would giving me to him end this?" She glanced at me and bit her bottom lip. "If he finally found me, would it stop the war between you?"

I shook my head, firm when I said, "No fucking way. I don't know what you're thinking, but you knock that shit off right the fuck now. Remember what I told you the first night we spent together? It's about more than some stupid love affair. It always was. Benito killed my parents. He killed Crow's old lady and most of his family." I kissed her knuckles, hoping the tenderness would ease what I was about to say. "Benito has to die. That's the only way this ends."

"Won't someone else take his place?"

"Don't care," I said. "If they do, we'll stop them, too."

"Or maybe things will get worse." She sighed and rolled onto her back, staring up at the ceiling. "Do you think… if I talked to him… maybe…"

Alarm prickled down my spine. "Alba, don't you fucking dare."

She snapped her attention to me.

"He's dangerous," I said. "If he finds you, if he even suspects, he'll kill you. And it won't be a bullet to the head. It'll take days for you to die. Do you understand?"

She trembled and I pulled her closer, kissing her shoulder again.

"I'll protect you," I told her. "If you let me."

Please let me.

23

ALBA

The day of the memorial passed in seconds. It was small with barely ten people there. We huddled around the grave marker while Saint said some prayers from his crutches. I put her ashes in the concrete hole, wiping my eyes as I sat a copy of *Charlotte's Web* on the other side. She used to read that to me as a child, and it was one of my most cherished memories of her.

Aris put a sunflower in next, and I tried not to let that affect me.

Mom's favorite flower.

He knew that.

Then we left her there and headed to my house for the wake. Mom wouldn't have wanted anything fancy, and I didn't have the energy for much else. Aris threw some burgers on the grill and Selene made a salad. Jericho held my hand while the medical equipment company packed her bed and the machines into their box truck.

And just like that... the house felt empty. Despite all the people there. Despite the fact it hadn't been this occupied in years. I wanted to curl up in the basement and never leave again.

"C'mon," Jer said, nodding out back. "You should eat something."

My stomach knotted. I hadn't eaten much in a few days; I'd been too anxious and depressed. But I sensed that if I didn't agree, he'd find some dastardly way to coerce me, so I complied. I swallowed down the burger and chips, but tasted none of it. I smiled at the MC members who stopped by to pay their respects, but it didn't feel genuine. I forced my way through the formalities because the wake wasn't really about me or my mom. It was about all of them. It was about making them feel better being around us during our grief.

I lost it when Ru showed up.

Tears streamed down my face, and I threw my arms around her to pull her into a hug. I didn't know why. Perhaps it was the straw that broke my back. Now that I knew who she was, I saw the resemblance clear as day.

My sister.

I had a fucking sister.

I'd been raised without any family. I had my mom, and that was it. I'd thought my father was gone. I'd thought my grandparents had died. No cousins. No aunts or uncles. Just Mom. But, as a normal, functioning human, it was natural to want to see myself in others and feel a familial bond with someone else. Humans were pack animals, after all.

To see *myself* in her? It was like a missing puzzle piece I'd never known I yearned for.

She hugged me back, whispering, "I'm so sorry," over and over again.

"It's not your fault," I said. "I'm happy you came."

Ru pulled away and wiped at her eyes, cupping my cheek. "How are you holding up?"

Not well.

We chatted for a bit, but someone called me away to decide what to do with the leftovers, and she'd gotten distracted by her dad... *our* dad... before I could come back. Now wasn't the right time to talk to her, anyway. I wanted to heal first and take some time to process before we put all the cards out on the table.

"Hey, kid," a deep voice said from behind me.

Crow.

I hadn't officially met him, and I loathed the fact it had to be today of all days. But time stopped for no one, so when he asked, "Is there somewhere we could talk?" I agreed and took him back to my mother's old bedroom, closing the door slightly but not shutting it completely.

Crow was tall, well over six feet, and had long, dark hair down to his waist. Covered in tattoos, he scared the shit out of me with his alpha vibe, even though I knew he was a softy deep down inside, like Jericho and all of those dominant assholes out there.

"I know you got no reason to trust me," Crow said. "I know you got no reason to believe what I'm about to say, but I gotta say it."

I cleared my throat and blinked back tears, sensing where this was going.

"I knew your momma when all this was going down. She was a brave lady. Smart." Crow crossed his arms over his chest. "Real ride-or-die woman. I knew Aris loved her the moment I saw them together, and it sucks she left us before her time."

My clothes suffocated me, and I glanced at the door, desperate to get out of this conversation. I didn't want to rehash this. I just wanted to move on with my life.

"But Aris is a good guy, yeah? One of the best. He's saved my life more times than I can count."

I furrowed my eyebrows. The fucking audacity of this guy to make a pledge for his VP while I was still mourning my mother.

"All I'm saying is... give him a chance. He's mourning her, too. Not the same as you. But he loved her."

I ran my hands over my face and sighed. "Thanks for the advice. Anything else?"

"That wasn't what I wanted to talk about."

"Okay?"

"KC tell you about Benito?"

I nodded.

"So you know why you gotta stay outta sight, right?"

I whipped my attention to him. Where was this conversation going?

"If I were you, I'd be thinking some stupid things right now. Like maybe this all started 'cause of me. Like maybe I could finish it."

My heart pounded, and I fisted my hands. How could he have known that? Did Jer tell him? Not that I thought I could do much. Who was I compared to the Caputi crime mob? But my mind was all over the place.

"In this life," he continued, "there's no half-assed one foot in, one foot out. Now, I know you didn't get much choice, but I gotta ask... You're not planning to run off half-cocked and disappear on me, are you?"

Still, I said nothing, refusing to incriminate myself. I considered his calm, collected stature and his rough around the edges appearance. He had a scar across his eyebrow, cutting down his cheek to the corner of his mouth. Crow had been through some shit and lived to tell the tale.

This. This is why he's their leader.

"Right." He nodded. "That's what Aris told me. And that shit's not gonna fly with me. Or KC."

I crossed my arms over my chest, spilling out the same garbage I'd rehearsed for so long. "There's nothing left for me here—"

"Maybe so, before you started fucking a Rose. But now? The Caputis saw you with KC, and the minute they catch wind of who Penelope Wright was, they're gonna come straight for you."

That's what I was afraid of. Sure, I had a gun and knew how to shoot it. But I was one girl against an army of mafia motherfuckers who wanted me dead. Running off and getting away from it all was the best thing for me.

"That's the look I'm talking about." Crow mirrored my stance, folding his massive arms over his chest. "I see those wheels turning, and I'm warning you to pump the fucking brakes." He took a step closer. "What do you think happens to KC if you run and the Caputis find you because he wasn't there to protect you? What do you think happens to Aris or Ru?"

"I've only known them two weeks."

"More than enough time to find a family, I'd say. You think you got nothing left for you here? I'd say there's nothing for you out there."

"Isn't that up to me to decide?"

He smirked. "Just like your mother."

"I'm not offended by that."

"It wasn't meant to offend you. That's a compliment. She was smart, too. But she knew when it was time to lay low." He took another step toward me. "So, I'm telling ya now. Lay. Low. Benito is coming, and the safest place for you is on our territory, surrounded by the motherfuckers who kept your mom safe all these years."

My jaw trembled, the thought of all she'd sacrificed for me, because of me, nearly bringing me to sobs again. What would she want? What would she say?

"Benito can never find out I survived. He can never find out about you."

She wouldn't want me to go off half-crazed into danger. She wouldn't want me thinking about tracking him down or luring him out. She'd want me to be safe. Otherwise, everything she'd ever done for me would have been in vain.

"Okay," I finally said, swallowing down the bitterness that welled in my throat. "I'll lay low."

"I'm gonna need you to swear it to me." Crow raised an eyebrow. "I know your mother was a woman of her word, so I am going to trust you are, too."

Goddamn it.

Way to lay it on thick.

"Fine." I forced the words out, even though I wasn't sure I meant them. "I swear. I'm not going to disappear. I'm not going to do anything stupid."

He nodded. "In exchange for your loyalty, I'll provide around-the-clock protection until this blows over. You might not always see us, but from now on, a Rose will always be close by."

It didn't make me happier, but the thought of constant protection did make me feel safer. "Thanks, Crow."

He turned toward the door, but stopped before leaving. "You're the best damn thing to happen to that boy. You know that, right?"

He meant KC. He meant this rare, once-in-a-lifetime love that had blossomed between us. I felt it in my molecules, so I nodded. He didn't have to say anything else for me to understand what he meant. KC was the best damn thing to happen to me, too.

ABOUT TWO WEEKS LATER, Selene packed what she had at my house and went back to Thor's place. I didn't know if they'd made up or if she'd gotten tired of my weeping, but once she was gone, it was just Jer and me.

Thor had given him time off work, but now he had to go back. We had to appear as normal as possible, like a mafia princess turned protected MC secret hadn't just died.

Life moved on, but I had a different perspective now.

Like Crow and Jericho, I blamed Benito for all of it. If he hadn't run her out of town, maybe things would have been different. If he hadn't sent someone to raid the SR property, Saint wouldn't have gotten shot. It wouldn't have landed on my doorstep. *Maybe* Mom would still be alive and I'd have gotten another few days, a week, a month.

In any case, the longer Mom was ashes, the more bitter I grew.

I'd given Crow my word I wouldn't do anything stupid like running off, but I still had an obligation to keep myself and the people around me safe, right?

I kept seeing Saint on my dining room table and picturing Jericho in his place. Perhaps a bullet to the gut or a slug to the head. If Benito was after me, Jericho would be safer as far away as possible. If it would end this, Benito could have me. If it meant no one else had to run or die for this stupid blood feud, then bring it on.

I loved Jericho, and I wouldn't have him wrapped up in it.

Which meant he had to go.

"We need to talk." We sat at the new dining room table Aris had brought over a few days ago, coffee steaming between us and a plate of bagels in front of me.

"Uh-oh." He narrowed his blue eyes. "What's that look?"

I bit my bottom lip, nervous. He wouldn't like it, and after all we'd been through together, it would feel like a slap in the face. But it was the only way to end this, the only way I saw.

"I need some space," I said.

"Space." He tilted his chin up at me, rubbing a hand over his mouth. "What kind of space?"

"I think you should go home for a few days."

Silence. He blinked, perhaps taking a moment to make sure he'd heard me right. "Are you breaking up with me?"

"We don't have anything to break up. We never put a label on this. We're barely friends. And I don't need the money anymore, so there's nothing left for us as coworkers."

Fucking. Ouch. It hurt *me* to say it. I could only imagine how it must have felt to hear it.

He snorted out a sardonic laugh through his nose. "Wow."

I didn't expect that response. "I mean, c'mon, Jericho. We've known each other, what? A month?"

"You tell all your coworkers you love them?"

I cleared my throat and choked back a sob. "Please don't make this difficult for me. I'm going through a lot."

"I'm trying to be here for you," he said, "to support you."

"I don't want your support," I said. "I want you to go."

"Goddamn it, Alba." He banged his hands on the table and stood, leaning over it like he hoped to intimidate me with his height and build. When I didn't back down, he said, "Don't fucking do this."

"I've already done it," I said. "I called Aris earlier. He's sending some prospects to watch me until it's safe."

"Prospects?" His jaw hung open. "You'd rather have random fucking prospects here than me?"

I licked my lips, refusing to say something that wasn't true. I wanted him to leave, but I didn't want to hurt him. "I'm asking for some room to gather my thoughts, Jericho. Please."

The frustration in his eyes broke, and he squared his jaw, hanging his head between his shoulders with resolution. "How long do you need?"

"I don't know," I said. "I'll call you when I'm ready to see you again."

He sighed, ran a hand over the back of his head, and went down to the basement. I heard him packing up his stuff, and when he came upstairs, he paused to stand in front of me in his jeans and cut, looking just as beautiful as the first night I'd met him.

Except he was really fucking pissed.

"What's going on?" he said. "This isn't like you."

"How the fuck would you know?" I threw it in his face. Out of everyone *alive* on this Earth, Jericho probably knew me the best. But I aimed to hurt, not to speak reason. "It's only been a month. You have no idea who I am."

"Maybe so." Jericho's eyes nailed me to the spot, that brilliant mind at work behind them. "But you wouldn't throw me out on your worst day. You're doing this because you're up to something."

I swallowed down the truth, keeping it from tumbling over my lips.

"When I find out what it is, I'm gonna take it out on your ass." He took a step closer to me. "I told you at the beginning, I don't do this on-again, off-again bullshit." One more step brought him next to me, and he kicked my chair out from under the table in one quick motion, turning me so I faced him. He put his hands on the wooden arms, leaning down to be level with me.

I wanted to kiss him, even now in the middle of trying to break up with him.

I still wanted him.

I'd always want him.

"So tell me, Alba," he said. "What the fuck are you up to?"

"I'm not up to anything." Not technically a lie.

He moved closer, bringing his face millimeters from mine, and my heart pounded. Could he see through me? Could he see how badly I wanted to protect him? He shot out a hand and wrapped it around my throat, his palm right up against my pulse and his thumb under my jaw, wrapped around my windpipe. I stiffened, my back straight against the chair.

"Your heart is racing," he said. "You're nervous."

"You're making me nervous," I said. "You're scaring me."

His teeth brushed my ear when he hissed out, "Why?"

"Because you're angry."

"Angry." He leaned back so he could look down at me. In that moment, I'd never felt so small, so utterly helpless against whatever he planned to do to me. "You think I'm angry?"

"No? What would you call it?"

"Fucking furious." He yanked me up and turned me around, bending me over the dining room table so fast that I didn't understand what had happened until I had the cool wood under my face, my hands spread out on either side. I tried to push myself up, but he slammed me back down again, and I winced against the jolt of pain that erupted across the front of my body.

He stood behind me, his cock pressed into my ass and his hand on the back of my neck, pinning me in place. He leaned his hard body over me, his chest to my spine and his mouth next to my ear. "You wanna know what I think?"

I shivered as a response, giving him all the ammunition he needed to keep going.

"I think you're pushing me away because you're scared. I think you're trying to get rid of me because you think it'll keep me safe."

I swallowed, my pulse throbbing. In my clit. In my hands and feet. In the space where his cock slid in between my ass cheeks. Every part of me was so aware of every part of him.

"Is that what you're doing?"

Was I so easy to read?

I couldn't lie, not to him, so I didn't answer. I balled my hands into fists, and again, I tried to push myself up, to struggle against his weight. But he held me tighter.

"Oh yeah. Keep fighting it."

I growled, *actually fucking growled,* and tried to claw at his face to get him off me, but he grabbed my wrists and pinned them above my head, which stretched him out on top of me completely. He kicked my legs open and moved his free hand to my shorts, digging his fingertips under the waistband.

"You remember your safe word?" He yanked my jeans down to my ankles.

"Of fucking course," I said, the word *crimson* on the tip of my tongue. "But if you try to fuck me, Jericho, I'll bite your Goddamn dick off."

He laughed out a dark, sick noise. "If I don't fuck you, you'll never learn your lesson."

"Yeah?" I sounded like an animal, like a caged wild beast that had reached my breaking point. I'd lash out at anything that came too close. "What lesson is that?"

He speared his fingers into me, and I arched off the table, my ass pressing back against his hand, wanting his touch even though I was supposed to be repulsed by it.

"You're fucking mine," he said. "You need space? Fine. Take it. But if you break up with me, you better have a good Goddamn reason." He bit my shoulder hard. Agony radiated down that whole side of my body, amplifying what he was doing between my legs.

"I can't break up with you if we were never together." It was mean. I knew that. But I was saying whatever I could to get him to leave. If he wasn't here, if he was with his brothers, he'd be safe. They'd protect him. I couldn't. "We're just friends, Jericho. Just friends."

The word squeezed a trigger between us, and I pulled it. I remembered how passionate he'd been at the clubhouse on our first date, when I'd told Hollywood that's all we were. We may not have made it official, but Jericho and I had *never* been friends. This had been lust, love, and hormones from the beginning.

He stood and wrapped my arms behind my back so they were pinned above my ass. He held them there with one big hand, snarling, "Say it again."

This was fucked up, so fucking fucked up, but I stood by it. I had to keep up the charade, or he would never leave.

"We're coworkers," I said. "Friends."

The sound hit me before the feeling did. A fleshy *slap* echoed off the walls, and then agony surged up my spine. He'd spanked me.

Hard.

Harder than he'd ever done when we'd had sex. This was... kind of fucking hot, even though it pissed me off. Maybe even hotter than it should be because of how it enraged me. I moaned and sank into the feeling, arching into him and urging him on.

"Say it."

"We're friends, Jericho. That's all."

Another spank, this time harder. I hissed and winced.

"One more time." He tightened his hold on my wrists, his cock digging into my hip. I wanted him to fuck me in the worst way. "Just so we're clear."

"We're friends."

His slap hit my pussy this time, and I howled, even when he massaged the skin afterward and he sank his fingers into me again. Pumping me once. Twice.

"Please," I cried, pushing up on my tiptoes to get closer to him. I wanted his big dick inside me. I wanted him to prove I was his, to remind me again and again until I never forgot it.

"Please what?" He bit my neck. My ear. My jaw. Marking me. Making me break out in gooseflesh.

"Please fuck me," I moaned. "I want you so bad."

"Yeah? You're wet as fuck for me right now. My good fucking girl, getting so ready. So willing."

I moaned, rolling my pelvis against him.

"Which makes you a fucking liar." He ripped his fingers out of me, the absence of him more painful than his earlier spanking. He twisted his hand in my hair and yanked me up, my arms still pinned behind my back. "We're more than friends and you fucking know it."

He shoved his fingers in my mouth, the ones that had been inside my body, and I tasted the evidence of how badly I ached for him.

"Tell me you love me."

His middle and index finger pressed on my tongue, so I mumbled the words around his grip. "I wub 'ou."

"Now, there's the first honest thing you've said all morning."

He moved away, leaving me cold and empty and trembling. He laughed and picked up his bag while I struggled to right myself, scrambling for my shorts to pull them up again, wiping the tears from my eyes and the spit from my chin.

"You rented your old room to me. I already gave you the money for this month, so I'm not leaving." He palmed his dick and adjusted it in his pants while I shook from the adrenaline fading in my bloodstream. "You don't wanna see me? You wanna clear your head? Fine. I'll stay out of your way. But I'm not fucking going anywhere. You don't like that? Tough shit."

He stalked down the hallway to the room, pausing to say, "I fought for Nikki for twelve fucking years, and I didn't even love her. Imagine what I'll do for you," before slamming the door closed behind him.

I collapsed on the chair and let the tears come.

24

———

JERICHO

She didn't mean it.

Or at least... I thought she didn't mean it.

When I showed up at the garage later that morning for work, Thor pushed out from under a beat-up sedan and wiped grease off his hands. "You look like shit."

I ran my hands over my face and shook my head. "I need more time off."

Thor's eyebrows rose. "We can't afford that."

"Then you fuckers need to up the number of people watching her."

Thor balked and crossed his arms over his chest. "Watch your fucking tone, son."

"I'm not your son." The girl of my dreams didn't want me around, and that itched like a son of a bitch. Even if I knew why she was doing it. Even if I might do the same thing to her if I were in her shoes.

He pushed to his feet, nearly the same height as me. "You're right. You're not my son. You're my Goddamn brother, and as my brother, I'm going to ignore that fucking look."

I nearly snarled when I said, "I love her, Thor. I can't lose her."

He nodded, gesturing to the office in the back. I walked past the break room and found Selene shoving her things into a locker. She turned when she realized it was me, slamming the door shut. "What's going on?"

"We're not doing enough to keep her safe," I said.

"We're doing what we can," Thor cut in. "In case you haven't noticed, we've got eyes on her twenty-four seven. If Benito comes knocking, we'll know the minute he does."

I couldn't believe I had to ask it. I couldn't believe I even thought it. "Was this Crow's idea? Did he tell her to end it with me so he could use her as bait?"

Thor's grey expression turned stormy, like he was two seconds from knocking my damn lights out. In hindsight, an accusation like that woulda deserved it.

"What happened?" Selene grabbed my face, forcing me to look at her like she used to do when we were kids and my temper had hit its fucking peak. "Look at me. What happened?"

I stared at my sister, willing her to help me calm down.

I told them about Alba. I told them what she said, what I thought she planned to do.

"She's got that look in her eye," I said. "Like she's gonna take off in the middle of the night, maybe throw herself at him to prevent the rest of us from getting hurt."

"Thor?" Selene glanced at our uncle, who pursed his lips and straightened his shoulders.

"Crow wouldn't put her at risk like that. He told her to stay fucking put," Thor said. "If she's got plans of her own, she hasn't shared them with the rest of the class."

I took a deep breath and let it out slowly through my nose, admitting he was right.

"But"—Thor looked between the two of us—"if Benito was going to make a move, now would be the time."

The expression in his eye said he had a gut feeling about something, and I probably wouldn't like it.

"What are you thinking?"

He cleared his throat, going to the radio so he could turn it up all the way. Then he stepped closer, leaning down so only Selene and I could hear him.

"You know we have a leak."

I nodded.

"Aris announced who she was two weeks ago."

Again, I nodded. I'd called it at the time.

"This on top of what happened out by the shed?" Thor shook his head. "Benito's going to be pissed. He hasn't retaliated yet, but he's going to. When he does, it'll be emotional."

"Emotional," I repeated. "You mean he'll fuck up."

"His only daughter survived all those years ago? He's got a granddaughter he doesn't know about? Yeah, I'd say that would make a man emotional. Maybe reckless." He shrugged. "If he does, aren't you glad we're watching her?"

Yeah, and who was watching them?

I didn't like this shit, not one fucking bit. The whole thing made me twitchy, but what was I going to do to stop it?

"I'd feel better if I was in the house all day." I lit a cigarette and offered one to Thor.

He took it and lit it. "If you need the time off, take it. I'll get Bear to cover your shifts if I have to." Thor exhaled before clapping me on the shoulder. "She's only trying to protect you, so give her some grace."

And I'd gotten pissed. So pissed, I left both of us with blue balls and said nothing to her when I went to work. I inhaled deep on the cigarette and sighed, running a hand over my head.

I dug my thumbs into my eyes, hoping the pressure would alleviate the headache I had building there. "I'm in love with her, Thor. I'm gonna ask her to marry me."

Selene gasped, and Thor laughed, tightening his grip on my shoulder. "I'm happy for you, brother. But listen, you ever come into my shop again accusing me of anything having to do with harming you or your girl? I'll fucking gut you myself." He gave me one last clap on the cheek before turning to head for the garage. "For now, you've got a fucking engine to drop in a Tacoma."

I looked at Selene, our unspoken communication sparking to life.

"She's safe, brother," her eyes said.

"She's not. And you know it."

I remembered my mother, my father, and both of my aunts. When would it stop? When would I stop being terrified of losing people?

"I wouldn't trade her life to end this." I knew it in my heart.

"That's not what anyone is saying." She leaned closer. "Thor's right. We're watching her. You're watching her—"

"Thor couldn't keep his own old lady safe," I snapped. "Just because you're fucking him doesn't mean he's bulletproof."

Selene reared back like I'd slapped her, and as soon as the words were out, I felt like shit for saying them. Yeah, most siblings fought like they hated each other. But Selene and I had agreed when we were children that *me and her* were always on the same team. It was us against the world until we died. In a world where family kept dropping like fucking flies, we swore to live for each other. I had her back, and she had mine. So this was crossing a line. I knew it. But I was in a fucking mood.

"I'm sorry—"

She didn't let me finish. She grabbed her paperwork and left the office, slamming the door behind her.

"Great," I murmured, rubbing my hand over my eyes. "Fucking great."

I debated with myself for the rest of the day. I should have tucked my tail between my legs and gone back to Alba's house to apologize. Fuck, Benito could be headed to her right this fucking second.

I trusted my club. Correction: I trusted a vital few members of my club. Crow knew what he was doing. Neither he nor Aris would risk her life, not even to end this war with Benito. But that didn't mean we were without our faults. We didn't know who the leak was or why they'd done it. Until we did, we couldn't be sure who to trust.

That scared me.

No place was fucking safe anymore.

25

ALBA

I made a mistake after Jericho left for work, but I wouldn't realize it until well after I'd made it.

I showered and tried not to cry as I went over the documents the estate lawyer had sent me. Turned out, Mom had a lot of secrets. I flipped through the bank statements, my veins burning with the fury of all she'd kept from me.

Aris had given us the house, so there was no mortgage. I thought I'd been paying into an account set to auto bill, but Mom had been taking it and saving it. I had over thirty thousand in one account and another hundred and fifty thousand in another. She had multiple life insurance policies that I didn't know about, on top of stocks and bonds and... Jesus Christ. I had more than enough to set myself up for life.

Mom had set me up for life.

I'd been camming to make ends meet, and she'd been hoarding money away like a squirrel. The whole thing infuriated me, and there was no one to be angry with but myself.

A knock at my door caused me to look up.

When I went to the entry, I recognized Ru through the peephole, so I put in the code for the alarm, swinging the entry open so she could step inside. I shut it, turned the deadbolt, and put my arms around her when she hugged me.

"Hey." She gave me a warm smile. "I know I'm early."

We had plans to do lunch in about an hour, but I didn't mind her company, so I waved her into the dining room. We had a lot to talk about.

"Please. No worries." I put the documents back into a pile and sat it at the other end of the table. "How are you?"

She shrugged. "Okay. How are you?"

I sighed. "I've been better."

"No doubt." She glanced at where my mother's hospital bed used to be and back to me. "You wanna talk about it?"

"God no." I headed to the kitchen, pulling out the things I'd planned to make for lunch. Sandwiches. Chips. Finger foods. "What'd you bring me?"

She held up the binders and sat them on the table. "My complete business plan, including rebranding, expansion, and—"

"Expansion?" I raised my eyebrows.

"Yeah," she said. "You could produce. You've got the setup." She gestured to my whole house. "You could get at least... three or four other cam girls in here. Maybe a few couples."

I laughed. "Wait... what? Who the hell is going to do that?"

"I would." She shrugged. "If I didn't have to show my face."

"Really?"

"Yeah, it beats slinging beers to assholes at the strip club." Ru put her hands in her back pockets. "I'm just saying. You're not thinking big enough." She got this dreamy, wistful look in her eye. "When I hear Aurora Dawn, I picture beautiful biker babes owning their own sexualities and making their own money. I see a place for strong, powerful women to work for someone who won't take advantage of them." Then she settled those blue eyes on me again. "You give them the platform. They give you a cut. It's a good business model."

She held the binder out for me to take.

"Check it out. Let me know what you think."

I flipped through the first few pages. "You don't think this is weird, do you?" I cleared my throat, shifting anxiously on my feet. "Now that we're sisters?"

She shrugged and crossed her arms over her chest. "I could be mad at you, I guess. I could resent you. Maybe you could resent me. But where does that lead us?"

I liked Ru. A lot. She had an old soul for such a young age.

"I'd rather get to know you. I always wanted a sister."

I smiled. "Yeah, me too."

"Then it's settled. You'll be my sister, I'll be yours, and that's it." She pushed upright when I held out her plate, taking it into the dining room. "I'll find us a different editor. Someone I trust. Nowhere near as good as me, of course. But almost as good."

Which made me laugh. The conversation flowed easily between us, and I appreciated having her there. We had a lot in common despite not having grown up together, and when she laughed, I heard echoes of my own in the pattern.

We'd just gotten to the point of cleaning up when a loud *pop* echoed from the woods behind the house. I launched out of my seat.

"Was that a gunshot?" I went for the nine Jericho had stashed next to the fridge, switching off the safety and checking it was loaded the way he'd shown me. Ru, likewise, had drawn a pistol from her purse, holding it out in front of her.

Trojan burst through my front door, and I nearly shot him in the head, seeing the SR cut at the last second and lowering my gun.

"It's him." He nodded toward the back of the house, hustling us to go first.

"Fuck!" Ru scrambled around the table, grabbing my arm to lead me along with her.

As soon as she opened the back door, we froze.

Standing on the step with a rifle in his hands and a smirk on his face was a taller, older version of my mother. Darker eyes. Grayer hair. But undoubtedly related to her.

Benito.

"Greetings," he said. God, he looked the part. He had on an

expensive suit with shiny black loafers, his hair slicked back, and a bodyguard on either side of him.

I held up my gun to shoot him, but one of his henchmen aimed at Trojan and fired. I ducked, my entire world going dark with the deafening shot. My eardrums burst. Gunpowder burned my cheeks and my shoulders. Something warm and sticky hit my back.

I had to run. I had to get out of here, but my feet wouldn't respond to my brain. *Move,* it shouted. *Move! Go!* But all I did was pick at the slime in my hair, widening my eyes when my fingers came back bloody.

Trojan!

No!

There was no time. Ru yanked me to my feet, and I took two steps before strong arms wrapped around my torso like a vice grip and a hood blackened the world.

I kicked, my heart pounding blood to all my extremities. I thrashed my arms. I scratched and clawed, making it as difficult as possible for them to take me.

Ru's scream cut through my terror.

"Stop it. Leave her alone!" I squirmed harder. "It's me you want. Let her go!"

"If I only wanted you, Alba," Benito snarled, "I would only take you."

Horror coated my veins. He wanted *both* of Aris's children, and he'd killed four Roses to do it. My heart broke for Trojan, who was surely dead based on the amount of blood I'd seen. I refocused on the present, struggling and yanking at my blindfold.

Then cold, bony hands gripped my upper arm.

"Listen to me, you little Rose bitch. If you don't stop fighting, I'm gonna bend your sister over and shoot her head off in front of you. You want that?"

I sobbed and sagged into his hold, giving into his threat.

"That's what you think, motherfuc—" Ru started to say, but then a grunt and a muffled *son of a bitch* told me they'd hit her to shut her up.

"Put them in the truck," Benito said.

The guys who had ahold of me weren't gentle. They lifted me into the back of a vehicle, and I banged my shins on the metal bummer, making me hiss as I tumbled forward. My hands were tied behind my back, so I caught my fall with my face. My nose busted, and splintering fire ricocheted through my skull and down my spine. I felt it in my toes.

"Goddamn it!" I rolled over and sucked back blood, spitting it out into the mask. "I broke my nose."

"Shit, are you okay?" Ru said.

"Shut the fuck up!" someone shouted from the front.

The truck started, and we jerked backward.

Oh, God.

We were being taken, actually fucking taken. We were so fucking screwed.

My sister moved next to me, shifting her weight so we were shoulder to shoulder. My face throbbed and warm, sticky blood dribbled down over my mouth and chin, onto my chest. A lot of it. I tasted it in my mouth and my throat and stomach, nearly making me gag.

"Listen," Ru whispered, so low I could barely hear her. "Whatever they do. Whatever they say. Don't tell them anything, you understand? I'm not going to talk to save you. Don't do it for me."

That only amped up my panic. This was going to be terrible.

"The Roses will come for us."

"What if they don't know where to look? What if—"

"There's no way our father will let that happen. There's no way KC would let that happen."

I wanted to believe her. I *had* to believe her. Because if I didn't, I'd sink into a blind hole of hopelessness. That helped no one.

But it was only a few seconds later I realized my mistake, my one fatal error.

I'd never reset the alarm after Ru arrived.

No one even knew we were in trouble.

26

———

JERICHO

I watched the white van turn off Mount Zion Lane, and something dropped in my gut. I'd been sitting outside the shop, smoking a cigarette and thinking about what I was gonna say to Alba when I went home.

I'd tell her I knew she was scared and trying to protect me, but if we were in this together, then we had to stay together. I'd make her come for the next two hours to prove I meant it. Then I'd take it out on her ass for stressing me the fuck out.

The van made the left at the corner and kept on driving, my focus zeroing in on the dented back fender. I shifted my gaze to the NC tags. What was that piece of shit was doing so far away from home?

The dent and the NC tags were the only reason I noticed it. If it weren't for those two things, it might have driven by without any further thought.

But I *did* notice it, and I stood to take a few steps closer.

There were only five people who lived on this street. I didn't know all of them, but I'd never seen that van before. Call it a lover's intuition, but something seemed... *off.*

I scrambled to dig my phone out of my pants, but I didn't have any alerts telling me something was wrong at the Wright house. I didn't want to admit to myself that I stalked Alba, but fuck it, who's pretending at this point? Yeah, I opened the security app on my phone just to check in on the video feeds and make sure everything was okay.

The first thing I saw was the back door wide open and a pair of boots sticking out.

Trojan.

"Shit!" I sprinted back into the shop, surprising Thor and Selene. Bear slouched in one of the corners, but he bolted upright at my presence. "They took her! They fucking took her!"

"What?" Selene stood, but Thor looked down at my phone and reached for his own, dialing someone and holding it up to his ear.

"Crow," he said. "Check the feeds. They got Alba."

"I saw a white van drive by." I grabbed my keys out of my pocket and sprinted toward my bike. "It was them. Go up to the house. I'll see if I can track them."

"Wait, Jericho!" Bear shouted, trailing after me, but I was off before he could stop me. I didn't know how I knew, but I did. My girl was in that van. I had to stop it. I had to.

I turned left at the corner and sped up the two-lane road, slowing to glance down side streets as I went.

I didn't see them. My phone buzzed in my pocket. I ignored it. I had to keep looking for her. I had to keep tracking her.

They couldn't have gone far, right?

Where are you? Where are you?

A bike pulled up alongside me, and Bear gave me a signal to pull over. Grimacing, I stopped and ripped off my helmet.

"What?"

"Castor hacked her phone weeks ago, man," he said. "After you said you had a tail. We're tracking her."

"How do you know she has it with her?"

"It's moving. Come back to the clubhouse." Bear grabbed my shoulders, looking me in the eye. "Crow's regrouping, and everyone's heading out to follow it."

Rage swelled up inside me. If that motherfucker hurt so much as a hair on her head, I'd rip his insides out through his mouth.

"KC." Bear clapped the side of my face, almost a slap to bring me back to reality. "We're gonna get her, okay? I swear it to you."

I went with him, hating myself the whole time. Besides, what the fuck did I think I was going to do if I caught up to the van? If there were enough of them to get the drop on Trojan and the guys at the house, then there were enough to take my dumb ass out with little effort.

When we got back to the club, I was so pissed that I couldn't fucking see straight. I marched inside, my boots echoing off the walls like drums.

"Crow!" I found him in the back, leaning over our meeting table, the sigil of a metal rose with a blade through it gleaming at me. "Where is she? Where'd they take her?"

"Calm down." Crow stood. "It's not just her. They took Ru, too."

"Trojan's on the way to the hospital," Slip added. "It's not looking good. He was barely alive when they got there."

My heart dropped into my stomach, and I glanced at Aris, who paced the back of the room with his hands on his head. Likewise, Saint sat on the couch, bouncing his good knee and chain-smoking cigarettes. I didn't know him to be a smoker, but he and Ru had started a secret romance last Christmas, and he looked just as twitchy as me or Aris. Worse because he couldn't tell anyone about it.

Switch and Castor sat over by the computers, while Slip, Picasso, and Doc talked around the table. Bear sat next to Saint, leaning over an iPad while he planned our next steps. Wheels, Hollister, and a few others mingled by the bar. I looked for Hollywood, but I figured he was in the hospital with his brother and Marissa, Trojan's old lady.

"Fuck." My heart raced in my chest and I balled my hands into fists. I didn't know what I'd do if I lost her. It was the first real taste of fear I'd had in ages, since I was a child. "What's the plan? What are we doing?"

"Switch is tracking her." Thor pointed to the corner where a group of brothers stood around the computer monitors. "We're calling everyone in. We're storming the castle."

"We can't wait that long," I said. "Every second we waste, that motherfucker has a chance to hurt her."

"She's his granddaughter," Thor said.

"If he cared about that, he wouldn't have taken her."

"This is about me," Aris cut in, dropping his hands to his sides in defeat. "The fucker wants me. Just give me to him."

"Not happening, brother," Crow said.

"You knew she was in danger." I struggled to keep my cool, venom racing in my veins like acid. I burned with my fury for her. "You promised she wouldn't get hurt."

"They hacked our security setup," Switch cut in. "I didn't see this coming. It's impossible."

"What do you mean?" Thor stood up and turned to face our IT guru.

"It's like they got in from here." Switch looked around, flipped pages over on his desk, and bent under the thing to look around.

"What do you mean?" Crow said.

Switch turned back to face us, putting a finger over his mouth like he meant we should be quiet.

"Bug," he mouthed, standing to walk around.

"Jesus Christ." Thor rubbed his hands over his face.

How could this have happened?

How could we have been so fucking blind?

We scoured the place, coming up with two. We dumped them in water and cranked the music, rendering any other bug useless.

"The software they used to hack us was installed *here*." Switch pointed around. "As in, right here."

Someone, maybe even someone in this very room, had planted two bugs and installed malware on our servers that granted the enemy access to everything. And because of that, my girl had been taken.

I glanced around, meeting everyone's eyes and wondering who *wasn't* here.

These were the first responders, right? The first into a crisis. My trusted inner circle.

Could one of them be the villain? I didn't fucking know, but when I found out who it was, I planned to kill him slowly. Over days. Weeks.

"Get to work figuring out who did this," Crow said. Then he looked at me. "We'll get her back, kid. I swear it to you."

I wanted to believe him. I wanted to think he wouldn't fucking disappoint me. He was my uncle, after all.

One of the prospects walked into the room. "The PD is ringing the gate. What do you want me to do?"

"Shit!" Crow stormed over to the window, looking out and running his hands through his hair. "What the fuck do they want?" Slip and Picasso walked out front, Crow following close behind them.

Aris shook his head and kept pacing, muttering, "We don't have time for this shit."

But I went with them out front, crossing my arms over my chest and determined not to let these assholes stop us from going to get my girl. Crow put his hand up halfway there to stall me.

"Wait here," he said. "If shit goes south, get as many of them out as you can."

I nodded, and Bear stood beside me to put a hand on my shoulder. "I've got your back, brother."

"Every fucking second we wait is another—" I started, but Crow's booming voice stopped me.

"To what do I owe this fucking pleasure on a Friday afternoon?" Crow crossed his arms over his chest. Slip and Picasso flanked him. Picasso stood like he was apathetic about the whole thing, probably because he was, and Slip leaned against the gate in case shit got shady.

Two officers stood on the other side of the barred metal enclosure, one a petite black woman with sunshine-yellow eyes, the other a tall white guy with brown hair. "Randall Montgomery?"

Crow snorted out a laugh. "I haven't gone by that name in a long time."

"I'm Detective Jordan," the woman said. "This is Detective Green. We need to ask you a few questions."

"About?"

Green shook his head and rolled his eyes, but Jordan remained unfazed. "Two weeks ago, there was a shootout on the Holabird Docks. Three members of the Caputi family were killed. One of their vehicles was set on fire. You know anything about that?"

Crow shrugged and shook his head. "Why would I?"

Green laughed. "Don't play fucking stupid, Montgomery. We know the Roses and the Caputi family have a history."

Jordan held up a finger, and Green closed his mouth. "Would you be willing to come down to the station to put that on record?"

"You got an arrest warrant?" Slip said.

Jordan looked at him but didn't say anything, which meant no. They didn't have fucking shit.

"Oh, c'mon, detective." Crow threw his head back and laughed, clapping jovially. "You know better than that. You don't have a warrant? It's been nice talking to you." Crow turned to head back inside, but Jordan put her hands on her hips.

"You make this hard on me, I'll make it hard on you."

Crow paused, his spine stiffening before he turned back around on his heels, his eyes narrowed. "Is that a threat or an invitation, detective?"

She shrugged and pursed her lips, moving her eyes behind us to the bodies spilling out of the clubhouse. All forty or fifty of them. "Got a full house today, huh?" She shifted her attention back to Crow. "Planning something fun?"

"Yeah." He nodded. "A cookout to celebrate National Fuck the Police Day. Want a hotdog?"

Her lip twitched like she wanted to smile but couldn't without losing face. "Don't go anywhere, Montgomery. I'll be back."

"Can't wait."

The two pigs went back to their shitty patrol car and climbed inside, but Jordan's eyes never left Crow. My uncle and brothers walked back to the clubhouse, the gate closing behind them, but he turned to the crowd and shook his head. "You go on without me."

"If they got eyes on you, they got eyes on all of us," Slip said.

"Fuck." Aris ran his hands over his head and took a deep breath. "If we ride in heavy, we go packing heat."

"How are we going to do this?" Wheels asked.

"I've got an idea." Thor took a deep breath and looked between us. He'd been a Navy SEAL once upon a time, so if anyone had any experience with covert ops, it was this motherfucker. "Give me five guys. I'll go get them tonight."

Crow took a deep breath and put a hand on his shoulder. "Okay, brother. Let's hear your plan."

27

ALBA

I'd never been hit before. Not like this. Not with a blinding hatred that ran so deep, there could be no scrubbing it out.

I sat in the corner of a cold, dank basement, the sound of dripping water slowly making me lose my mind, a single hanging light overhead swinging every so often as the AC kicked on.

When I first got here, they'd taken turns beating the hell out of me. Beating me in front of Ru. Beating Ru in front of me. They'd searched us and taken our phones, smashing them to pieces in front of us.

I'd been terrified they planned to rape us. There were over twenty of them here. But when they shoved us down the rickety wooden stairs, bloody and bruised but otherwise intact, I shivered with the notion that they meant to keep us here for a while.

I rubbed my fingers together for circulation, my hands still tied behind my back and my feet tied together in front of me. We'd gotten all the way here before they ruined the only chance we had of being found, and I just prayed the Roses figured out we were gone before then.

God, please let them come before I die.

I remembered the last thing I said to Jericho—we were friends, nothing more, and I didn't want him around, that I needed space.

All fucking lies.

Sitting there in that basement, I wanted nothing more than his arms around me, his scent in my nose, and the feel of his hard body against my soft curves. If I got out of this alive, I'd never talk about leaving again. I'd marry him tomorrow and be his old lady for real. I just prayed I had the chance.

Mom, if there is an afterlife, please help me. Please look out for me.

Mom, I miss you. I love you.

They kept us down there for who knows how long, with a few of their henchmen watching us to make sure we didn't try to escape. Their eyes glowed in the dark like monsters lurking in the shadows, and any second, I feared they'd strike.

There weren't any windows. There wasn't any way to get outside. I had no idea what day it was or how long we'd been captured. It felt like centuries, like I'd been down here since the dawn of time, each ticking second a full millennium.

Suddenly, the door at the top of the stairs opened and multiple sets of shoes echoed off the concrete walls. I scooted closer to Ru, touching her from shoulder to hip and kneecap since we couldn't use our hands.

A man wearing an expensive suit and shiny loafers descended the stairs first, a cigar in between his fingers and his gray hair styled back from his face. Three other guys followed him, each as decadently dressed. Collectively, their outfits were worth more than everything I owned. God, how at odds they seemed with our surroundings. We were obviously in some backwoods cabin out in the middle of nowhere.

Benito loomed over us, taking a long draw on his cigar as one eyebrow shot halfway up his forehead. The light he was standing under cast him in sinister shadows, making him seem even more majestic and malevolent.

"So." He tilted his head to one side as he ran his piercing gaze over the length of us, cowering in his dungeon. "Picked myself two little Roses. Now what's an old man to do?" The big dickheads behind him laughed, and Benito looked at me. "Your boyfriend killed three of my men and my nephew, Julian."

"They were trespassing on Rose property. They deserved it," I sneered.

One of his thugs backhanded me quicker than I could blink, and the jolt of pain radiated down my spine. I'd already been smashed to bits, so this added to my injuries. I didn't know how I'd be standing when this was all over.

"Keep your fucking hands off her," Ru piped up.

The thug smacked her, too.

Fury rolled through me, and if I wasn't sure they'd kill me, I'd lunge at this fucker's face. I'd gouge his eyes out. And once the SR got here, I'd do just that. Genetic ties or not, I didn't see any of myself in him. Even though he looked like my mother, I didn't see any of her, either. Mom's eyes had always been loving and gentle. This man was soulless. Evil. He'd lost his empathy long ago.

"What do you want from us?" I sputtered, tensing my muscles so he didn't see me shake.

"You? Nothing." He shook his head and inhaled on his cigar again. The smell made me want to puke. "Now, your daddy on the other hand..." He shook his head. "It didn't have to be this way, you know. I didn't have any arguments with Aris or Crow, not like I did with Piston. But when I handled him, they both took that personally." Benito shrugged. "That's not my fault. They should have let it go. But desperate times, am I right?" The mob boss let out a sigh. "They went after my family, took my only daughter from me. Then they took my sister's son, and I can't let that stand." He paused to let out a dark, twisted chuckle. "I'm just gonna keep going until no one can remember a single fucking one of you."

He'd meant to be terrifying, and a little shiver of fear coasted into my gut. But Ru shook her head and laughed in a frightening dark tone.

"You think that's funny?"

"You know how fucking sick in the head you gotta be to do this to your own flesh and blood?" She chuckled harder, perhaps smearing it in his face.

Benito shook his head, a sad, forlorn expression flickering behind his eyes. "She's not my flesh and blood. As soon as her whore mother fucked that Rose piece of shit, she wasn't mine anymore. My daughter died a long time ago." He looked at me. "Your blood's as filthy as your sister's. I mean that."

My blood. As if my genetics defined me. As if I had any control over who had brought me into this world. If that alone wasn't enough to infuriate me, hearing him call my mother a whore made my blood sizzle.

I swore to myself right then and there, before this was over, I would watch the life bleed from his eyes. Like a rabid dog, I would hunt him down to save the world from his mania.

Movement toward the back of the room brought my gaze over Benito's shoulder, and I recognized the guy hiding by the stairs.

Pie.

Nikki's new husband. The guy who had choked her and convinced her to blame Jericho.

The fucking traitor.

Imagining what the Roses would do to him made me laugh, sounding eerily similar to Ru's.

"They're gonna feed your own cock to you," Ru said, nodding to Pie. "You know that, right?"

"I'm gonna kill your daddy in front of you," Pie spat back. "You know that, right?"

"Now, there's no need to be impolite," Benito said. "We only have to decide which piece to cut off first. I'm in the business of sending messages, you understand."

"You said you wouldn't hurt her," Pie interrupted. "You said this was about Aris, not the girls."

"You'll shut your mouth before I shut it for you." Benito sneered over his shoulder. "You seem to have forgotten my last name is Caputi. What's yours again? Judas?"

Benito's thugs laughed and Pie shut his mouth, darting his eyes between me and Ru, a fleeting look of sympathy in his features.

Benito decided to honor whatever arrangement he'd made with Pie because he shook his head and turned to head back through the crowd, pausing when he passed the proverbial Brutus. "Since you're so attached to them, you stay down here to guard them." Benito held up his cigar, pointing it just under Pie's eye. "And don't let me catch you sleeping. If I do, *I'll* cut off your cock and feed it to you."

Benito turned and walked back upstairs, leaving Pie to stand there with his arms crossed over his body.

"What did Aris ever do to you?" Ru shook her head. "What did *I* ever do to you to deserve this?"

"It ain't about deserving," he said.

Ru snorted out an incredulous laugh through her nose. "Jesus Christ. It's about money. Isn't it?"

Pie shifted uncomfortably.

"How much?" She shook her head, the words coming out louder when she said them again. "Look at me, you fucking coward. How much did it take to sell us out?"

"Two fifty," he murmured.

"A measly two hundred and fifty K." She made a disgusted noise low in her throat. "You're pathetic."

"They're gonna kill her, okay?" He pushed off the wall. "Nikki. The baby. I owed them a ton of money."

"How?" Ru clenched her jaw. "How'd you get in so deep?"

He shook his head and sighed. "Doesn't matter anymore. They said they'd cut the baby out of her if I didn't do it." Pie rubbed a hand over his bald scalp. "So I did it. I don't feel bad." His voice got louder. "Don't make me feel bad."

"What about Nikki?" I asked.

Ru narrowed her gaze. "Does she know what you're up to? Does she know you sold me out to the Caputis?"

His spine stiffened, giving both of us our answer.

No, Nikki didn't know. If she did, would she condone it?

"That's what I thought." She let out a long, slow sigh. "You'll be lucky to make it out of this alive, Pie. If Crow doesn't kill you, Nikki's going to."

He shook his head. "Nikki'll do what she's told. She always has. This is the best thing for both of us. For our baby."

"No." My sister pursed her lips. "The best thing would have been for you to go to Crow with your problems. Now? Nikki's gonna face the streets. The club's never gonna believe that she didn't know what you were up to. And that baby?" She made a dark and demented noise. "She might drown it herself to save it the shame of being related to you."

I gasped. Pie froze, stalked forward, and hit her hard in the face.

She laughed and spit blood at him. It landed on his cheek and slid down to his chest, and he hit her again and again, hard enough to make her fall over on her side, unable to right herself.

"Stay down, you dumb fucking cunt."

"Don't fucking touch her again," I said.

"Oh, you want some, too?"

I squared my jaw at him, prepared to take a hit if he was going to dish it out, but he didn't. He chuckled and turned to switch off the light, leaving Ru and me in the pitch dark. The sound of his boots on the stairs echoed as he climbed them and shut the door behind him.

Once again, we were alone, cold, and unable to see.

28

JERICHO

We waited until the house went dark and the sounds inside died down. This time of night? Those fuckers were probably passed out, especially given the day they'd had. Doc, Thor, and Saint stood to one side of me just beyond the tree line, their eyes on the house and their hands folded in front of them. Bear and Aris stood on the other.

I'd done everything I could to convince both Saint and Aris to stay behind. Saint had been in a boot up until a week ago, and Aris's eyes had gone pitch black when his girls had been taken. I didn't trust him to stay levelheaded once we got inside. But who the fuck was I to tell him no? There was no one who could keep me from coming to save Alba, to make sure she was okay.

Once we had a location, Castor hacked into their security system and looped the feed, meaning we'd get in and out with no one seeing us.

Anticipation rocked around my stomach like bad sushi, and my nerves were so fucking shot that I thought I might explode. I took deep breaths to calm myself and keep from rushing into the fucking house prematurely. I didn't want to ruin Thor's plan, and of the two of us, he was the one thinking like a rational person.

I wanted blood.

I wanted Benito's head on a fucking spike.

I wanted to wipe out every fucking one of them.

Thor tapped me on the shoulder and nodded, pointing his finger toward the house twice to indicate it was time. He crouched and walked forward, sticking to the shadows at the edge of the property until we got to the house. Two Caputi men sat on the steps in front of the back door, smoking cigarettes and bullshitting. They didn't see us yet.

Thor held his gun up over the plants, aiming for the one on the left, and shooting twice.

The bullets whizzed through the silencer, downing both of them with quiet precision. We took the steps two at a time, carefully avoiding the carcasses and the rapidly growing pools of blood on either side. We slipped inside the back door, thankfully unlocked.

Three guys slept on the couch in the living room. I raised my gun and fired. Three guys dead on the couch in the living room.

I didn't care. The cold blind rage burning inside me had created a monster dead set on one thing and one thing only: finding my girl.

She better be alive.

Or so fucking help me.

The urge to stalk through the house and kill everyone inside boiled through my blood, and if I had more time, I would have done it. But my goal was to find Alba and Ru and get them out.

Thor, Aris, and Doc? They were the assassination squad. They were the ones who got to silently stalk through the house and take out anyone in our way. I counted twenty earlier in the night, including the mob boss and *Pie,* the fucking prick.

Speak of the Goddamned devil.

When I turned the corner into the kitchen, there he was, sound asleep on the ground in front of a door I assumed led to the basement. I padded softly toward him and squatted, taking the tip of my nine and pressing it to his lips. He woke with a start, his wide eyes meeting mine with panic at first, followed by recognition, and finally hatred.

"I ought to pull the trigger," I whispered. "But that would be too easy a death for you." Before he could scream, I hit him in the temple, knocking his Goddamned lights out. Bear grabbed his body and threw him over his shoulder, fireman style. Castor waited just on the other side of the woods with the truck, and Bear would get him there before he woke up and sounded the alarm. Saint followed me into the basement.

I clicked on my flashlight, waving it around the room. Catching the sight in the corner, my heart damn near ripped out of my chest.

Ru and Alba huddled together on the concrete floor, leaning up against each other. Their faces bruised and bloody and—

Fuck, I'd kill that son of a bitch with my bare hands.

"Alba," I murmured as I knelt. She cracked open her blue eyes and startled, pushing away from me and shaking Ru awake. I held my hands up and recoiled an inch, letting her adjust before I got any closer. "Alba, it's me. It's Jericho."

"Jericho?" Her voice croaked, and I couldn't stand it any longer. I reached for her face, running a hand along her battered cheek.

"It's me, sunshine."

"Is this a dream?"

"No." I shook my head. "No, it's me."

She leaned into my arms, sobbing, broken from the whole experience. Ru leapt at Saint, kissing him and muttering words about never leaving him again.

As much as I wanted to spend the rest of my fucking life soothing her, we didn't have time. Soon, someone was going to realize we were here, and we were vastly outnumbered. Our rescue mission could turn into a suicide mission real fucking quick.

I grabbed my knife from my boot and cut the bindings on her wrists and ankles, massaging her hands with my mine when she struggled to move her fingers. They were cold and pale, and if we'd taken any fucking longer, she might have lost them. After a few moments, I helped her to her feet and scooped her into my arms, carrying her up the stairs and back through the house.

But... the best laid plans of mice and men and all that shit.

We made it to the back door in time for a squad of cars to pull up in the lot behind the house. Black Range Rovers and Bentleys as far as the eye could see.

I shook my head and snorted at the fucking flashiness. Leave it to the mob to be prima fucking donnas, bringing diamond-encrusted guns to a knife fight.

"Shit," Thor muttered, backing into the kitchen. "Okay, time for plan B."

"What's plan B?" Saint asked, hitching Ru higher in his arms. For someone who'd been shot in the leg less than a month ago, he was holding onto her surprisingly well. Of course, you'd have to fucking kill me to pry Alba out of my arms, so I could imagine how he felt.

Thor pulled out his phone and sent a text. "We need backup."

"Backup?" Aris raised an eyebrow. "What backup?"

Benito and his men got out of their cars, coming closer. "Come out, come out, with your hands held high." Some of his men laughed. "We know you're in there."

As soon as he cleared the headlights, something soured in my stomach. Not only were we surrounded by at least thirty guys, but they'd also found our getaway car. Four of Benito's men held Castor and Bear with their arms behind their back, shoving them to their knees in front of him.

"Now, tell me. Why would Crow send two of his boys to do a man's job? Hmm?" Benito raised his cigar to his mouth and took a deep inhale, the rings on his fingers glistening as they caught in the light. "Is it because he's a coward? Is it because he won't face me himself?"

Benito held out his right hand, and one of his men put a gun into it. He bit the cigar between his teeth before pointing it at Castor. My heart raced. I took slow, deep breaths, trying to keep my shit focused and centered.

"Tell you what." Benito pursed his lips and tilted his head to the side. "I'll trade you one of Crow's little shits for two of Aris's. Now, I know what you're thinking. That's not a fair trade." Benito shrugged. "You killed my nephew. You killed my legacy. And now, I gotta kill Crow's."

"Wait!" I shouted, shoving Alba into Thor's arms and going for my nine in the holster under my arm.

"KC, what are you doing?" Thor said.

"KC, stop." Saint shook his head. "Don't do this."

"Jer, no. Please." Alba dropped her legs to the ground, refusing Thor's help.

"I'm not gonna watch him kill my cousin." I was out the door before they could stop me, holding my hands up. "You want the guy who killed Julian? That's me."

Saint growled behind me. "You stupid son of a—" Then he joined me on the porch. "And me."

Benito laughed, the headlights beaming me right in the face and making it hard to see anything else.

"There he is. The Killer Cock himself. Put your guns down." Saint and I did, bending to put them on the porch. I figured my life was over. I figured they would shoot me in the head right there, but at least the guys would get my girl out safely. At least Castor and Bear would live. "Come over here."

Saint and I walked down the wooden steps together, our boots thudding almost as loudly as my heart. I might not have had a plan when I gave myself up, but the closer I got to Benito, the more one started to form in my mind. I met Bear's pissed-off gaze, the one that chastised me for giving myself up.

Whatever, you fucking prick.

Like I was gonna let him die?

I still had my hunting knife in my boot, and if I could get close enough to Benito, I could ram it in his throat before any of these fuckers could get me. They might fill me with bullet holes after, but I'd end this. Once and for all.

What a way to go. One fucking blaze of glory.

"Release them," I said, standing in front of my cousins now. "They weren't there that night."

Benito tilted his head to either side, considering. "They're Roses. They're guilty by association."

Then a couple of things happened so fast, it took my brain a few seconds to catch up.

First, a pop echoed from the tree line, and one of Benito's men to my right dropped to the ground. This caused the other Caputi fuckers to turn in that direction, taking their attention off me and my brothers. I went for my knife.

I had it in my hand just as Benito turned back to face me.

Another pop rang out, this one nailing another Caputi in the head, blood splattering me in the face.

I tightened my grip around the hilt, and all the rage and fury I'd ever harbored for this fucking shithead barreled out of my chest.

I thought of my father.

I thought of my mother.

I thought of Aunt Gemma and Crow's old lady, Holly. I thought of Alba and Ru and the bad fucking blood between us.

Enough.

I sank the blade into Benito's carotid, and he dug his hands into my shoulders, trying to shove me away. But I gripped the back of his neck and plunged the knife deeper. The blade scraped against muscle and tissue until eventually I hit the thud of hard bone.

I didn't stop.

Chaos erupted after that.

Most of the Caputi men ducked into their cars and hauled ass outta there. Some tried to peel me off their boss, but Saint, Bear, and Castor picked up their own weapons and fired back. Thor and Aris ran out of the house, Slip close behind them, supporting Alba and Ru as they came toward me.

My focus went to watching the life bleed from this asshole.

I was a bad man. I'd told Alba that from the start.

Benito wasn't the first man I'd killed, and he likely wouldn't be the last. I wasn't a violent person by nature. But I recognized all humans were animals, and the worst ones needed to be put down. I wasn't afraid of doing it.

Especially a fucking scumbag like Benito Caputi.

He'd been rampaging through this town for too long.

Enough now.

Enough.

He sputtered out a bloody last breath, and the light drained from his pale gray eyes.

IN THE END, Selene saved us all. She'd been Thor's backup plan, arriving without any of us knowing it and setting up in the trees just in case things went south. Which they had. He'd been teaching her how to shoot since she was a child, and she could hit a squirrel in the eye from three hundred yards away. She distracted Caputi's men long enough for me to take down the main boss. Once he was gone, the rest of those mafia pricks tucked tail and abandoned ship.

But just because Benito was dead didn't mean the war was over. Some other Caputi fucker would rise up in his place. I'd only created a void, a power grab. However, it gave us some breathing room.

While the Caputi family bickered amongst themselves about who would be the next head of their crime ring, we healed.

And we dealt out justice.

Rumor was that when Doc joined us, Crow and Aris had wanted to nickname him Butcher, on account of how skilled he was with a set of knives. They'd gone with Doc because he generally used those skills for good. When we were hurt or fucked up from whatever bull-shit we'd gotten into, Doc put us back together again.

But tonight?

I understood Doc's dark alter ego.

Doc was short for Doctor Jekyll, because Mr. Hyde was a fucking monster.

I saw it with my own eyes—the change in him, the darkness that took over his mind and his soul when he set to working on someone.

"What's the plan, Pie?" He cut off another slice of flesh and tossed it in the fire, the smell of cooking meat nearly making me vomit. It reminded me of pork roast, and that both churned my stomach and revoltingly reminded me of the last time I'd eaten, far too long ago.

Pie screamed and writhed on the table, yanking at the restraints and blubbering like a fucking baby. The little stupid shit.

"Were you just going to fuck us forever?" Doc sliced into him again, and Pie's body went slack, shock taking over and knocking him out again. Doc sighed and shook his head, grabbing some water to splash on Pie's sweaty face. He startled awake, glancing around between me, Doc, and the few other brothers who had come to see justice dealt. "Did you think I'd let you sleep that easy?" Doc whistled and shook his head. "You must be one stupid fuck. It's like you don't know me at all."

"Please," Pie said. "Please, I'll tell you anything. Anything."

"Aw, I'm almost offended." Doc shook his head, a furrow on his eyebrows, a fake pout on his lips. "I worked so hard to make a name for myself in this club." He dug his knife into Pie's armpit, dragging the blade over the skin and peeling back another bit. I grimaced, almost feeling sorry for him. "And now you're saying I didn't do a good job." He leaned in, his eyes absolutely terrifying when he said, "Guess I'll have to start doing better now." Another long strip tore away from Pie's body, and he screamed.

"Okay, okay," he said. "I'll tell you. Benito, he just wanted Aris and Crow. That's it."

"What makes you think I don't know that?" Doc shook his head. "I wanna know what *your* plan was. Why'd you betray us? Your own brothers, you piece of shit."

I wanted to stay and watch the rest of it. Doc was an artist with a blade and motivation, but I had a shaken-up girl to tend to, and I didn't want her ever thinking I wouldn't be there for her again. It had been a long fucking day, and I needed to curl up next to her in the worst way, if only to reassure myself she was okay and safely back with me, mostly unharmed.

I left the barn and walked across the property, my hands in my pockets and memories of plunging that knife into Benito's throat going through my mind. My brothers had taken out nearly fifteen of those assholes, more after Selene started shooting from the trees.

Quick. Lethal. Efficient. That was Thor's style, and I couldn't fault it.

This fight was far from over, unfortunately. All of us knew it.

I got on my bike and drove the short twenty minutes down to the hospital, where the rest had gathered as we waited to hear news about Trojan. After rescuing Alba and Ru, Aris had insisted they be checked out, and Doc had other things to do with his time.

Last I heard, Trojan had been taken back for surgery. Now, we sat around in dank chairs and waited for news. Nikki had shown up a few hours ago, insisting she didn't know Pie was betraying us. Alba and Ru tried to vouch for her, saying Pie had told them the same in Benito's basement, but none of us believed her.

Least of all me.

Nikki could spin a web of fucking lies if she wanted. I knew that better than anyone, so when Crow ordered her back to her house and to *stay fucking put*, she went with no argument.

Things were fucking awful when I entered the waiting room this time. Hollywood sat with his face in his hands and his elbows on his knees, shaking his head back and forth. Crow held him under an arm, whispering something low in his ear. Aris and Selene sat next to Marissa, Trojan's old lady, who wept in my sister's arms.

"No, no, no," Marissa whimpered, sobs racking her body.

"What's wrong? What happened?" I looked to Fingers, who shook her head and sighed.

"Trojan died a few minutes ago. He never made it out of surgery."

My heart fell into my gut, and I dragged my ass over to Hollywood, squatting in front of him so I could grab his hands and press my forehead to his.

"I'm here, brother," I told him. "I'm here, and I share this fucking pain with you."

"He's gone," Hollywood groaned, his red-rimmed eyes full of tears streaking down his cheeks. "He's gone."

I sat next to him, holding him through this as best I could. I should have gone to find Alba, but my brother needed me, and I thought she might understand.

When she emerged a few minutes later, she hunkered down next to me, wrapping an arm over Hollywood's shoulder to pull him into a hug and resting his head under her chin. She'd been patched up, the cuts on her face stitched and her broken nose reset and splinted. Despite it all, she was still the most radiant person I'd ever seen. My heart beat for her and her alone.

Hollywood nodded and held her closer. Between the few people in that waiting room, we processed it as a family, knowing we had each other.

A few hours later, we all went back to the clubhouse.

Thor returned to announce Pie was now fertilizing the back forty, and Crow personally saw to Marissa and Hollywood in his paternal way—loving them, hugging them, and making sure they knew he was there as the proverbial patriarch of this fucking madhouse.

Alba and I went to the back room where I'd fucked her senseless a week ago. I showered and she joined me, if only so she could cling to me and hold me the entire time.

"Thank you for coming for me."

The broken tone of her voice almost shattered what remained of my heart. "I'll always come for you. I mean that."

"I'm sorry I said we were only friends." She wiped at her cheeks and pressed her forehead into my sternum. "It wasn't true."

I cupped her cheek and tilted her face up, careful not to push anywhere that might hurt her. Looking down at her battered features made me want to kill Pie and Benito all over again.

"I know," I said, leaning down to press a gentle kiss on her lips. The top one was busted and she'd bitten the bottom one when someone punched her. Still, she kissed me back, pushing up on her toes to get more of me, all of me. I let her have it. And then I dried her off, put her in one of my old T-shirts, and led her to the bed, insisting she take the space closest to the wall.

"From now on, I sleep in between you and the door. Got it?"

She laughed. The urge to argue went through her eyes, but she didn't. She just gave me another kiss, rolled onto her side, and relaxed into the mattress. I curled my body around hers, wrapped my arms over her waist, and tucked her in close, damned determined to never let her go again.

29

ALBA

SIX WEEKS LATER

I would never look the same again. Even though the doctors in the ER fixed my nose. Even though they'd stitched up my cuts and gave me ointment for the scars. Something about my face had changed. Something in the set of my jaw and the sway of my shoulders when I walked.

My eyes had been forced open, and all the anger toward Aris had been snatched away. I understood why he'd stayed out of my life. I kinda secretly wished he had continued to, but that ship had long since sailed.

"I wish I could tell you so many things," I said to the headstone, brushing the stray piece of grass off my mother's name. "I wish I could tell you I didn't have to forgive you. That I would have done the same thing if I were you." I shook my head, wiping away the tears. "That I would have done worse." That I probably still would do worse.

In the weeks since the abduction, I'd started therapy. I'd come to grips with the nightmares and the PTSD and the sounds of my own grandfather threatening to kill me. Sometimes it plagued me, but I was working on making my peace with it. That's all I could ask of myself.

"What would you do, Mom?" I pursed my lips, glancing down at the picture on my phone, the blurry shot of Leo Caputi, one of Benito's nephews and the new Caputi boss, hanging on Nikki at a storage facility on the other side of DC. He had his arm over her shoulder, leaning down to kiss her. She carried a baby. Pie's baby, I assumed. Had Leo taken it in as his? I wasn't sure I cared. Switch found footage of her sneaking into the club when no one else was there and fucking with the computers.

After the botched attempt to get to Aris through me and Ru, the Caputis had retreated and gone home one crime boss short. I didn't know how many my rescue cohort had killed that night in that house, and I didn't want to know.

It would only make me more pissed. It would only twist this vengeance tighter around my heart. I tried to imagine myself standing over Nikki's sleeping form, a gun in my hand and my finger on the trigger. She deserved it.

"Would you hunt her down? Would you hunt him down to save what he might do to me... to Jericho?"

A wind picked up, rustling the trees around me and carrying a light birdsong with it.

"Is that you?"

The wind blew harder, lifting my hair and swirling it around me. I closed my eyes and smiled softly, picturing my mother brushing it behind my ear the way she used to.

"I thought you were light and love and forgiveness."

A crow landed on her headstone, startling me. But I didn't move. It bounced forward, its black beak pecking at the granite. It squawked. Once. Twice. And despite it all, I laughed. I had to.

Yeah, Mom was light and love and forgiveness... until it came to me. And then she was a momma tiger protecting her cub. If she'd been alive and well enough, she would have already done it. Nikki and the Caputi men would no longer be an issue.

But... was I a killer? I believed I had it in me to defend myself, but to seek out violence? To go to her, knowing what I would do, to plan it and execute the both of them like rabid dogs?

After everything she'd done, she was still human.

"Hey, Sunshine," came the voice behind me, and I turned to find Selene with a bundle of sunflowers in her hand. She sat them next to mine and held out her palm, yanking me to my feet when I took it. Ru walked up on the other side, setting her own flowers down.

After Mom died and I'd been taken, Alba retreated deep down inside my mind. I didn't know if she died, or if maybe Benito had killed her when he beat the hell out of her. But I didn't feel like her anymore. She'd been a librarian. A D&D playing nerd. The kind of girl who wore a cardigan and knee-length tweed skirt to a party. She'd been bold enough to invite a stranger back to her house and film him fucking her to put it on the internet.

Today, I couldn't picture myself ever being that girl again.

I would have changed my name to Aurora Dawn, but she still had a life online, hopefully an even bigger and more popular one as soon as I enacted Ru's plan. I had the top site on OnlyFans. My feed had more subscribers than the next three channels under me combined. I'd never have to worry about money again.

So who was I?

Wright wasn't a real last name. Caputi made me want to puke. Washington didn't suit me either, and Aris didn't want to force that on me if I didn't want it.

For right now, I was going by Sunshine. It was the name KC had given me, the name he'd inked into his skin under his collarbone shortly after we went official. I kissed it every day of my life.

Of course, I had a delicate KC on the inside of my wrist, which he couldn't stop licking or biting anytime he fucked me.

Things between us were good.

"What'd you decide?" Selene raised an eyebrow, thinning her lips while she waited for my answer.

"She deserves it," I said.

"She does," Ru agreed.

"But there's been enough death for a while." I thought of Nikki's baby. I thought of what it would go through, growing up not knowing its biological father. I couldn't take its mother from it, too. But Nikki and me? We had unfinished business. And one day, the women of the Steel Roses MC would come for her.

Just not today.

Today, we laid to rest one of our own. We'd finally healed enough to put Trojan in the ground, and since we were already in the cemetery, I'd thought a visit to Mom was in order. Selene grabbed one hand and Ru grabbed the other, and with them on either side, we went back to the ceremony. I took my place next to Jericho, who wrapped an arm over my shoulder and pulled me in for a kiss.

The MC didn't do funerals like everyone else. Sure, there was the placing of the ashes in the headstone. Trojan had been religious, so Saint said a few words about God calling his chosen warrior home.

But when we got back to the clubhouse, some of the old ladies had already fired up the grill, the smell of cooking hamburgers hitting me in the face as soon as I'd arrived.

After a brother fell, the MC partied until they couldn't feel the pain anymore. They locked the gates and drank to their lost soldier the entire night.

Hollywood drank the hardest, as was his right. Mom had died almost three months ago, but the pain felt as real as if it had happened yesterday, so I understood. Bear and Castor kept up, urging him on, reminiscing about the first time they'd met Trojan. Slip, Picasso, and Thor lit the fire pit, and Crow made his rounds through the crowd, the father figure checking on everyone.

"I want to make a toast," he finally said, bringing everyone's attention to him. "First and foremost, to our beloved Trojan. He lived life to the fullest, and he went down fighting. When I met him, he wasn't nothing but a fucked-up soldier with a little brother to feed. We took him in. We gave him a home. And he repaid that with his life. A true fucking brother." Crow held up a shot and shouted, "May we see him at the end," before slinging it back.

I drank to that, tears burning my eyes when I thought about how much this club had sacrificed for me. How much more they'd have to go.

"May we see him at the end!" everyone chanted.

"Next, to our brother, KC." Crow pointed at him, standing by the pool table.

Everyone whooped and hollered, and Bear clapped him on the back.

"Who stabbed Benito Caputi in the neck so fucking deep that it severed his spine."

"I said I'd cut that fucker's head off. I'm a man of my word." Jericho laughed and clapped when everyone whooped again.

"Finally, to Thor and Selene, for getting our people out of there. And taking some fucking Caputis with them!"

Everyone shouted and clapped again, and I toasted to them, too. If it wasn't for Selene, we all would have died. If it wasn't for Thor's plans B, C, and D, we definitely would have died.

"All right, you fuckers," Crow said, winding down his speech. "Have a good time. Celebrate life the way Trojan woulda wanted. Drink like you're dying and fuck like you just got outta jail!"

After that, someone put on the radio, and once AC/DC blared into the night, Ru grabbed a few of her friends. She pulled them into the center of the parking lot to dance, everyone getting drunker with each song.

I sat at the bar and watched the revelry go on around me. Jericho played pool with Pollox, occasionally shooting me a wink to let me know he still had his eye on me. After I'd been kidnapped, it took me three weeks to convince him to let me out of his sight. And even then, it was only so I could go to the grocery store with Slip and Thor to get more beans to make chili.

"How you holding up?" Aris sat down next to me, tipping a beer over his mouth and downing a deep gulp. Since Mom died, I'd decided to give him a shot. If she loved him so much, there must have been something to love. After experiencing Benito myself, I understood their discretion. It still fucked me up, I still brought it up in therapy. I was only human, after all. And so was he. And so was my mom.

"Not feeling much like celebrating, to be honest." Trojan had died protecting me and Ru. If I hadn't needed protecting, if I hadn't been stupid enough not to reset the alarm, Trojan might still be here today. I bore the weight of that shame inside me, another thing my therapist told me I had to work on.

I do not own the actions of others. I do not own my mother's. I do not own Trojan's.

"I get that." Aris nodded. "Trojan would have understood, too."

"Do you believe in an afterlife, Aris?"

He shrugged and took another sip of beer. "Never thought much about it."

"But if you had to guess?"

He nodded, pulling one side of his mouth into a smile. "I hope so. I hope Trojan and Penny are here. That they know how much we miss them."

I blinked back tears and nodded, trailing my gaze across the space to find Saint and Ru talking in a dark corner alone. She had her arms wrapped around his waist and tears streaking down her cheeks. He looked heartbroken, but in that marble way of his that meant he was trying to hide it.

I'd been pretty fucking out of it in that basement, but I remembered the kiss she'd given him. I remembered the way he kissed her back and the panicked look in his eyes when he found her.

Ru and Saint had been together a few months, but after the abduction, they'd broken up. She wouldn't tell me why, but from the looks of it, things had gotten bad between them.

"I don't think I ever thanked you." Aris's voice got my attention, bringing me back to him. "For letting me be there. At the end."

I laughed. "Let you?" I raised an eyebrow. "Aris, she loved you. I saw it. Every day of my life, I saw it." I shook my head and sighed, wishing she had told me sooner, wishing so many things had been different. "I grew up thinking I didn't have a family. And now I've got the biggest, baddest family in Madison County." I said the words, knowing them to be true in my heart. Once upon a time, I'd planned to pack my shit and take off. My heart still hurt enough to do that. But the thought of leaving these people, of leaving Jericho? It ached almost as much.

I couldn't live knowing I wouldn't see my sister every day. I couldn't abandon Selene when I'd just started getting to know her, another sister I'd always wanted. And I couldn't leave the only parent I had left, not when I'd just found out about him.

See? Therapy. Progress. I was healing. One mindset shift at a time.

30

JERICHO

I followed my girl into the back room at the clubhouse. I'd had a few shots, so my inhibitions were low. I locked the door while she finished in the bathroom. When she came out, she froze, breaking into a smile when she realized it was me.

"Hiya, moonbeam." She came closer, wrapping her arms around my waist and pulling me in for a kiss. This girl unmade me, turning a grown man into fucking jelly. I had Sunshine tattooed on my collarbone, and she had KC on the inside of her wrist, but it wouldn't be enough.

"Hiya, sunshine." I kissed her again, slumping when she leaned her weight on me. I wasn't drunk, but I wouldn't say I was sober, either.

"How ya feeling?"

I shrugged, and she giggled, pushing up on her toes to bite my bottom lip and sending a jolt straight down to my balls. God, I fucking wanted her. I'd want her until the day I died.

Was three months too soon to propose to someone?

I didn't know, and holding her like this, her ass so fucking squeezable in my hands, I didn't care. Alba soothed an ache I didn't know was there, but it had been there my entire life.

"Sit down, Jericho."

I did, buckling on the bed and trying not to tremble from her using my real name. Almost no one called me Jericho anymore. Only her. Only like this. Her bottom lip was tucked between her teeth, and I reached out to run my thumb along the length of it. She opened, accepting my finger in her mouth and sucking on it. That felt too fucking good, and my cock throbbed. Once. Twice. Enough to urge me on.

"I fucking love you," I told her as she sank to the ground in between my legs.

Fuck yeah.

She grabbed my belt, the jingling metal like fucking music to my ears.

"How much have you had to drink?" She grinned while she unbuttoned my pants, sliding the zipper down.

I shrugged again, pursing my lips. "Three shots. I think."

Her eyes lit up. "Three... exactly?"

Oh, shit.

I'd told her she could put her finger in my ass after three shots. I'd told her she could do anything she wanted to me. And too fucking true, I'd agree to whatever had put that cute as fuck smile on her face.

We'd fucked since the bad shit went down, of course, but we hadn't filmed, and I definitely hadn't seen this playful side of her. To see it now gave me fucking hope. We were healing. We were moving on. Together.

"Yeah. Three exactly." I licked my lips, nudging my hips up to remind her she'd been on a mission only a few seconds ago. She pulled my cock out and licked the tip, the sight of her pretty pink tongue doing more to me than anyone else ever had. I fucking worshipped the ground she walked on, and when she slipped me all the way inside her and down her throat with no problem, I hissed in a gasp and moaned.

"You're too fucking good to me," I told her. "So fucking good."

She knew how to suck a cock, and after three months of doing it to mine exclusively, she could make me come in less than ten minutes, so it didn't surprise me when my balls started clenching in an embarrassingly short amount of time. She stood and climbed on top of me, positioning me at her entrance and holding my shoulder with the other hand while she impaled herself.

I put my hands on her thighs, sliding them under her dress and up to her hips, where I discovered she hadn't been wearing any panties.

"Jesus. This whole time?"

She shook her head and smiled, stuffing the lace panties in my mouth and forcing me back on the bed. I let out a muffled laugh because my girl was so fucking nasty. And I loved everything about her. She rode me hard, taking whatever she needed from me. I let her.

I fucked her as hard as she fucked me.

When she came, I grabbed her throat and yanked her to me so I could swallow down those moans. After she came back to reality, I thrust into her slowly, taking my time to work her back up to it. She smiled and pulled her panties out of my mouth so she could kiss me, spearing her tongue through my teeth and wrestling with mine. She tasted like me and beer and sex, and the intoxicating combination reached down inside, yanking out every bit of me that was male.

"Marry me, sunshine." The words came out without my conscious doing. Like my primal instinct had taken over and I needed to know I could have this forever. That I could have her forever.

"You're drunk." She laughed and shook her head, rocking back against me and rolling my dick inside her. I tightened my hands on her ass, helping her along.

"No, I'm not. I swear I'm not." I reached in my pocket for a box I'd bought a few weeks ago. After she'd almost died. After I'd almost died. I'd been waiting for the right time. Not like Trojan's memorial was the right time, but God Herself could not stop me once I had the ring in my hand, sliding it on her finger. "Marry me."

"Jesus, Jericho." She sat up straight and stared down at it.

"You said you're not a Wright. You're not a Washington. You're sure as shit not a Caputi." I pulled her back down, rubbing my nose against hers and holding her tight, refusing to let her go again. "You're a Montgomery. And you have been since the night I met you."

I looked between her eyes as I waited for her to say yes, my cock rubbing at the places inside that made her moan and wilt in my arms.

"Yes. This is fucking outrageous, but yes."

I smiled and bit her bottom lip between my teeth, letting it go with a laugh before flipping us so she was under me. I lay down on top of her, spearing my fingers through hers and holding them above her head. I kissed her scorpion tattoo, the one that had led me to her, and then I kissed her KC tattoo, the one that announced her as mine.

"Tell me you love me." She kissed me, biting my lips this time, hard enough to hurt and draw blood. But that urged me on.

"I love you."

She rolled her hips against me and dug her heels into my jeans, wanting me deeper inside her. I fucking drove myself home like I might find gold.

"Say it again."

"I love you." I kissed her. "I love you." I kissed her harder. "I love you."

When I came, her cunt clenched around me, and she rode the wave of euphoria with me. Nothing in this world compared to having her climax while I was inside her.

"Yes, yes, yes," I snarled. "Fucking yes."

I collapsed on top of her, my arms shaking and my legs like fucking jelly. Alba ran one hand through my hair and held up her ring on the other, looking at it again. But I grabbed her knuckles and kissed them, reminding myself one last time she was mine.

She'd said yes, and now? She couldn't fucking run anywhere I couldn't go.

31

ALBA

After KC proposed, the whole fucking club went wild. We waited a few days to say anything, but Hollywood sniffed it out. And once he knew, the rest of the club knew. Selene and Ru planned to throw us an engagement party later in the week, but I had a few personal things to deal with first.

Like my mother's house.

We'd had it cleaned since Trojan died there, but I still had to go pack everything up. KC insisted he could have the prospects do it, but I wanted to do it myself.

It seemed like closure.

But when we pulled up to the house, a black Range Rover sat out front, the windows tinted. Jericho and Saint went on high alert.

"You stay here," Jericho said to Ru and me, shutting the door of Saint's new truck behind him.

"Yeah, fucking right." I climbed out anyway, much to Jericho's chagrin. "If they're at my house, they're here to see me."

Saint pulled out his phone to text for backup, but when I walked up the front steps and opened the door, I froze at the sight on the other side.

Perhaps I expected Nikki or Leo Caputi.

But instead, I found an older woman with dark-brown hair and bright blue eyes. Eyes that looked like my mother's. A nose and cheeks that looked like my mother's.

This had to have been Gabriella Caputi, Benito's wife.

My grandmother.

She wore a pair of dark slacks and a white blouse, the heels on her feet too high for what I'd expect someone her age to wear. Jericho raised his gun, and Saint followed suit, but the men on either side of Gabriella raised theirs in response.

"Please." She shook her head. "Lower your weapons. I am not here for a fight."

"Then why are you here?" I took a step toward her.

"This is where my only child died." Her bottom lip quivered. "Can't a mother mourn her daughter?"

I raised an eyebrow. "Having your husband kidnap your granddaughter and hold her for ransom is a funny way to show your love."

Now it was Gabriella's turn to look skeptical. "No real harm would have come to you. I wouldn't have allowed it."

"Right." Saint reholstered his gun and took a step in front of Ru, blocking her with his body. "And I suppose she broke her own nose."

Gabriella looked at Saint and Jericho before returning her gaze to me.

She stiffened, adjusting her shoulders and regaining her composure. "We may fight like cats and dogs, the Caputis and the Roses, but we are not that different. We have family, loved ones. And in that family, we find our strength." She reached inside her purse to retrieve a flat, golden case. She opened it, pulled out a cigarette, and closed it. "But we also find our weakness." Gabriella lit her smoke and took a step toward us, making Jericho tense and push my body behind his. "Please. If I wanted to kill you, you'd already be dead."

She inhaled deep on the cigarette as she came another step closer, her long brown hair swaying toward her waist.

"I came to give you a warning, and it is this. If you cut off the head, three more will grow in its place." She looked between the four of us. "You took my daughter from me. You took my grandchild. You took my beloved nephew, and finally, my husband."

"Your husband killed countless Roses," I tried to say.

"Enough." Gabriella lifted her chin, peering down at us. "There is one thing that you and I understand well, my dear Alba. It is not the men who hold the true power. And soon? You will know what a mother's grief can do." We moved as she walked toward the front door, her men following behind her. "I'll be seeing you. All of you." She walked down the steps and climbed into her Range Rover when one of the men held the door open for her.

We may have hoped to end a war by killing Benito, but we'd only pissed off his widow.

And hell hath no fury like a mother scorned.

EPILOGUE
FOUR YEARS LATER

ALBA

I checked my watch for the fifth time, groaning as I poured tea into a to-go mug. I was running super fucking late. And Goddamn it, I had to pee again.

"Have I told you lately how fucking sexy you are like this?" Jericho's arms came around me from behind, rounding my belly, sinking his teeth into my earlobe. We'd been married going on three years now, but I'd been pregnant for at least a hundred.

Okay, it had only been eight and a half months, but I was so damn uncomfortable and ready to pop that it felt like a hundred.

"Only every fucking day." I turned in his hold, leaning over my massive baby bump to give my husband a kiss. He grinned against my mouth. "And night. And morning."

"Sunshine, I'm fixing to keep you pregnant for the next twenty years. Are you okay with that?"

I narrowed my gaze and laughed. "Who knew you had a breeding kink?"

He pretended to be confused. "Pretty sure you made me fill out a kink checklist before we started fucking."

"Hmm. I guess I'll have to pull that out again."

"Where do you think you're going?"

I huffed and rolled my eyes, slinging my purse over my shoulder and taking a sip of my herbal tea, wishing it was coffee. "I have to run by the studio."

"Oh no." Jericho wagged a finger at me. "No work. You promised."

"It's not work." I just needed to make sure things were going okay and Ru had a handle on it while I was out.

Jericho narrowed his eyes, unconvinced. "Then let me drive you."

"I can drive myself."

"I'm not having this argument with you." He shook his head and kissed my temple. "You promised me. While you're growing our baby, I care for you. That means taking you to your fucking studio so you can micromanage shit you left to your sister weeks ago."

I took a deep breath and let it out through my nose, reminding my pregnancy hormones I needed the father of my child and that punching his adorable, smug face was frowned upon by modern society. So I relented. "Fine. Chauffeur me around. I enjoy being pampered."

"That's what I like to hear."

He helped me into the new pickup truck we'd gotten, having traded in my old beat-up Honda. He still had his bike, of course. But we both wanted something bigger, something that drove like a tank. After selling my mom's place and buying our own closer to the MC, I'd bought a studio where we could expand Crimson. Ru and I had a vision of an ethical cam app, one catered to a sex-positive creator base. Some of the hang-arounds from the MC had joined in. Some of the guys, too.

We had fun. We made money. And we treated our employees like employees.

Health insurance. 401k. The whole fucking gambit.

I wanted to turn sex work into an empire, and with Ru's ambition and my eye for detail, we were already at an advantage. But being at home all day was torture. I couldn't stand not knowing what was going on, even if I had Jericho to entertain me.

When we got there, he helped me out of the truck and I waddled my way inside, greeting a few performers at the entry. Bodies bustled about, some sewing costumes, others messing around with camera equipment.

I heard Ru before I saw her. "Take those to bay one."

She turned the corner, saw me, and raised an eyebrow, her jaw ticking before she looked at Jericho. "You were supposed to keep her on the couch."

He put an arm over my shoulder and pulled me in for a kiss. "She's fucking stubborn."

"She'd have to be to put up with you." Ru softened and came closer, pulling me in for a hug before rubbing my belly. "How's my little nibling?"

"Nibling?" Jericho's brows furrowed.

"Yeah, since you're waiting to see if it's a boy or a girl. Right now, it's a nibling." A gender-neutral niece or nephew.

Jericho laughed, but caught sight of Saint a few feet away and went to catch up with him. I looked around at the warehouse turned bustling studio. We sectioned off areas for performers to have privacy while they worked. We gave them the equipment, the space, and the tech. They maintained their own client base and took home most of the cut. By trying to make everything as accessible for the performer to meet the client, we brought in more employees. And thus more clients.

Ru and I caught up some more, just in time for my child to start kicking at my bladder again, which sent me to the bathroom. And while I walked, I glanced around at everything I'd built with what my mom left me. I couldn't have done this without her.

Was she happy? Was she proud? Was she watching from the great beyond and guiding me in ways I'd never know about?

I'd like to think she was. And when I brought my little baby Montgomery into the world, I'd like to think she'd be proud of that, too.

I was happy, and I finally had a family where I felt at home.

And that was all she ever wanted for me in the end.

JERICHO

SUNSHINE SQUEEZED MY HAND, her sweaty hair stuck to her head and her nails digging into my hand.

"One more push," the doctor said, glancing up at us from between her legs. My girl had gone into labor early this morning, and now she was on the last leg of bringing our kid into the world. We'd purposely decided not to find out the sex. It didn't matter to us what it was, and the anticipation was half the fun.

"C'mon, you can do it." I kissed her and held her up, supporting her as she gave another good grunt.

"There we go." The doctor and her team pulled a bloody baby from between Alba's legs and placed it in her arms. "You've got a healthy, strong daughter." My little girl started wailing and shaking her tiny red fists, but as soon as Alba pushed her up on her chest, she quieted down. I scooted onto the bed next to my girls, my heart pounding behind my ribs.

I was so happy that I could fucking burst. I'd never known true love like this. Not in my entire life. She had Alba's big, blue eyes and my dark hair, the tiny patch on top of her head so fucking soft.

"Jesus, she's so fucking beautiful." Alba started crying, sobbing into my chest while she held our little girl. Our little Penny.

"Aw, why are you crying?" I ran a finger down the side of my daughter's face and watched her stare up at her momma with wonder.

Could an infant know what adoration was?

I thought so. Because it was the same look I got when I looked at Alba.

I kissed my girl again. Then I went to tell the rest of our family the news. Our nearest and dearest had gathered in the waiting room.

Selene was first out of her seat, followed by Ru and Aris.

"We have a girl! Penelope Montgomery has come screaming into the world at last!"

Crow shouted, "Wooooo!"

Aris leapt up, throwing his arms around me in a big hug. "I'm a granddad?"

"You're a granddad, old man." I clapped his shoulder and his eyes turned red, tears streaming down his cheeks. Selene hugged me, kissing each of my cheeks before going to Aris and doing the same. Thor pulled me into an embrace, followed by Crow, and then each one of them wanted to know when they could meet the little hell-raiser. I had to check with the doctors, but she seemed healthy enough. And they'd told us we could go home soon if all went well.

Four years ago, I'd hesitated to bring Alba into my world. But standing there in that room, so full of love and joy and family, I didn't know what I'd been so fucking afraid of. It led me to all of this.

Things got shitty.

Things would always get shitty.

But little Penny would have these rough motherfuckers looking out for her.

And anything that came for my girls would have to go through all of us first.

WANNA JOIN THE ROSES?

Thank you for reading! If you enjoyed this book, please consider leaving a review.

Get a **BONUS** epilogue from Jericho/Alba <u>and</u> the Steel Roses prequel, **THEY CALLED HIM SAINT,** when you sign up for my newsletter.

http://join.jenadoyle.com/roses

(No spam, only smut. I promise.)

Keep scrolling for a teaser of **SAVAGE SAINT,** out now wherever you read.

STEEL ROSES
2
MOTORCYCLE CLUB

In a life of secrets, sins,
and second chances,
where's the line between
savage and saint?

SAVAGE
SAINT

JENA DOYLE

BLURB

<u>Ru</u>

Loving Saint is the worst mistake I ever made. The secrets between us are explosive, and after a near-death experience, I won't be anyone's forbidden romance. He broke my heart like it was nothing and sent me packing to college.

Now that I'm home, my father needs my help at the MC's strip club. I'm the only one who knows how to run it like him, so it should be an easy job. Except the one person I can never tell anyone about, the one person who still holds my heart, is the manager.

Two weeks into the job, I learn there is a thin line between lust and forgiveness, and my clumsy ass keeps tripping over it.

<u>Saint</u>

Touching Ru is the worst mistake I ever made. Her skin is like velvet under my fingertips, and when she moans, it sounds like angels heralding me home to heaven. I love her more than anyone else in this world, but I fucked that up months ago.

Now that she's back, I need to keep my hands to myself. Her father is my best friend, and if he ever found out about all the depraved shit I've done to Ru, he'd kill me.

I don't deserve her. Never have, never will. Even if the temptation of our sin is greater than it ever was. Even if living without her turns me into a savage.

<u>Ru</u>

"What the hell?" I ran my hands through my hair and narrowed my eyes at the profit and loss statement from the last six months. Holy crap, there was a lot of red. Even though I was supposed to be bartending, the strip club owned by Steel Roses Motorcycle Club didn't have many customers tonight, so I'd spent the majority of my shift digging through reports.

Sales were dismal. The dancers had reduced their hours or quit altogether. My dad's best friend, Saint, had stepped up as general manager, but between the crumbling building and the lack of staff, he was overwhelmed. He worked here at the Beacon in addition to his MC responsibilities. Pretty soon, there wouldn't be a Beacon. No one knew how to run it like my dad, Aris—no one except me.

"This can't be right." I grimaced and went to the next page. The building had become costly to maintain, and Dad hadn't done anything to modernize it in years. No wonder Saint was having such a hard time.

"Hey, can I get a drink?" one of the regulars said.

"Last call was ten minutes ago, Rodney."

"C'mon, Ru!" He wagged his eyebrows. "Your old man never gave a shit."

"My old man's not here," I said. "And if you don't stop talking to me in that tone, I'm gonna bend you over my sink and scrub your mouth out like your momma shoulda done." He was an old-timer and had been coming here since I was in pigtails. I wasn't scared of his drunk ass.

Rodney slammed his hand on the bar and gave a loud guffaw before turning and walking toward the door, grabbing his belly as he stumbled away and hooted.

My dad and I didn't have a typical father-daughter relationship. My mom had split soon after I was born, and last I heard, she was doing fifteen to twenty for manslaughter. Because of this, I'd done a lot of my own raising. My dad called me an old soul, but I called it having to grow up before I was supposed to. Dad and I were more like a team. I cooked and cleaned before I was ten, and sometimes, I was pretty sure he forgot which one of us was the parent.

Last year, I learned he had a secret life I hadn't known about—a lover named Penny, a child named Alba, a whole other personality. There was so much to unpack that I could fund a therapist's salary for years. My dad had never dated anyone else after my mom, and once I'd met Penny, I understood. Dad had loved her since he met her. This past July, she died of cancer and his grief forced him to take a step back from running things at the Beacon. Hence the reason I'd started working here again as soon as I graduated from college and moved home permanently.

Aside from the decrepit building and failing finances, the enormous alpha asshole of a problem with this place was my new boss, Saint—the same sexy biker that called himself my dad's brother by oath, the one that had been at every Thanksgiving and Christmas since I was a teenager. Eighteen months ago, we'd secretly started an affair that lasted for a while after that. I had irrevocably fallen in love with him, and he had crushed my silly heart under his steel-toed boot.

"Hey you," came the familiar voice from my right.

"Hey." I locked eyes with Lore, the newest member of the Roses, and leaned over the bar to kiss him on the cheek. Originally a part of the New England chapter, he had transferred to Madison County two years ago when his security job brought him to the area. He was tall with dark hair and a matching beard, completely covered in tats... yeah, I had a type, even if it wasn't like that between Lore and me.

"You ready?" Lore nodded toward the door and grinned, winking as he tapped his tattooed knuckles on the bar.

"Almost," I said. Rodney was the last customer, and he'd taken my threat serious enough to waddle his way to the door a while ago. "Let me count down my till and take it upstairs." Saint had disappeared up there earlier, but at this time of night he'd probably hit the road. That was good, because if he saw the affection between Lore and me, he'd get pissed. I didn't have the energy to deal with him.

Lore smiled and nodded, shoving his hands in his pockets as he sat on a stool. I put the excess cash into a plastic bag and taped it closed before grabbing the till out of the register and walking to the front door so I could lock it on my way toward the stairs.

Last year had brought me more than heartache. I'd gotten abducted by the MC's enemy, Benito Caputi, and the rest of the Caputi crime family. I spent sixteen hours in a cold, dank basement, huddled against my sister, believing we were both going to die. Luckily, we survived (mostly) unscathed.

When I wanted to go back to Mount Vernon for my senior year at Thomas Washington University, it had taken nearly the entire club to convince my father to let me go. Dad eventually relented when I agreed to take a brother with me. Lore had patched in right around the same time, so being a brat, I'd chosen the brother who looked the most like Saint and knew the least about me.

I thought it would piss him off, that maybe he'd see a younger version of himself in Lore and come running back out of jealousy. Like a lot of things related to Saint, he'd disappointed me, and all these months later, I was still the stupid woman addicted to a man who'd never feel the same way.

Unrequited love was such bullshit.

Perhaps, in another life, it could have been more between Lore and me, but the precise reason I'd picked him turned into why we couldn't be more than friends. He reminded me *too* much of Saint, and if I ever thought about taking things further, that fact threw cold water on the whole thing. It was like being addicted to name-brand soda and only having the dollar store version as an option. It *sort of* tasted right, but something always smelled off.

When I got to the office on the second floor, I froze just inside the door. Saint leaned back against the desk, his long legs stretched out in front of him, his big arms crossed over his chest. He raised an eyebrow at my entrance and tilted his head to the side, running his heated dark eyes down the length of me, burning me where I stood.

I tried not to let my tremble show, tensing my muscles to keep from shaking.

"What's he doing here?" he growled.

"He's my friend." I swallowed, my throat dry and scratchy, and forced my legs to move toward the safe behind the desk.

Saint tracked me as I walked. "Hmm."

I'd known him long enough to understand the noises he made. This one said he didn't like that I was friends with Lore, and he had more questions.

"Hmm," I mocked, mine saying I didn't give a rat's ass what he liked. I punched in the combination on the safe and twisted open the door. My heart pounded so hard I heard it in my head, but I forced myself to focus on putting the money away.

"You two together?"

I debated how to react. The fire that surged in my chest wanted me to turn around and kick him in the shin. For the eight months we were hooking up, he'd had every opportunity to openly claim me. When I told him I wouldn't be his secret anymore, he broke it off like it meant nothing and sent me packing to college. *"Go have fun,"* he'd told me with that annoying apathetic look in his eyes. *"Go be twenty-two."* That was what made it hurt so much—as if the eight months I'd spent on my knees for him weren't enjoyable, like the time we'd had together was an insignificant blip on his radar. He didn't even fight to keep me. He'd had his chance, and he blew it.

I turned so I could look at him.

The glint in Saint's expression said he expected an answer. Once upon a time, we'd promised each other the truth, only ever the truth between us. Now, we'd smushed that all to hell. Perhaps he didn't deserve my wrath, but he certainly didn't deserve to know my secrets anymore.

"That's none of your business." I put the till next to the others and placed the deposit on top of the stacks of cash on the upper shelf. Then I closed the door and twisted the handle shut.

"Hmm." Another noncommittal sound. This one meant he'd picked up on the animosity in my voice and was now considering how he wanted to respond. When we were together, he would have wrapped his hand around my throat and pushed me to the ground, reminding me exactly what I could do with my attitude. Now, he only took a deep breath and let it out on a disappointed sigh. "Next time, tell him to leave the cut at home. It distracts the clientele."

I made a sad laughing noise and raised an eyebrow, taking a step toward the lockers. "There's no clientele. We haven't made money in six months."

He shot his hand out, wrapping his fingers around my wrist as I passed. The touch startled me, and I gasped before I could stop it.

"Careful," he murmured. "I'm patient, but I have my limits."

"Limits?" The brat inside me blinked awake at the threat. I had once lived to test his boundaries, breaking his rules and reveling in the punishment. Saint and I had a kink dynamic few others would understand, especially given the age difference between us. He gave me rules, I broke them, and both of us loved the punishment that came after that.

Even now that we were broken up, I couldn't help myself. I struggled in his hold, trying to yank away from him. "What are you gonna do, huh? Bend me over my daddy's desk and hold me down while you spank me?" I took a step closer, pleased when his jaw tightened and his lips turned into a thin line. I stuck my lower lip out, half taunting him, half pretending to pout. "Please, sir. I've been so bad."

That tipped the scales. He launched off the desk, snarling as he got in my face and seared me with his gaze, the pain and hunger of the months apart behind it. He didn't say anything, but he didn't have to. I understood what his growl meant. *Don't throw that in my face.*

A jolt of lust hit me between the legs, my cunt clenching. I stared right back, squeezing my thighs together in a pathetic attempt to soothe the pain, but even my lady parts admitted he had a point. I bared my teeth, jerking against his hold again. This time, he let me go with a tiny shove, and I stumbled back, taking a deep breath as I righted myself and brushed my hands over my corset top.

"Tell your boyfriend the next time he wears his cut in here, I'll rip it off and shove it up his ass." Saint straightened and circled around behind the desk, focusing his attention on some papers. I didn't say anything, just grabbed my purse from my locker and slammed it shut, stalking to the door and giving Saint my best "eat shit" look as I did.

How dare he?

Lore was more than just my friend and former bodyguard. He was technically Saint's brother by oath. Saint couldn't threaten whomever he wanted. I didn't give a shit who my dad had left in charge. I was so pissed and turned on and frustrated that if he *did* throw me over the desk and fuck me on it, I wouldn't have stopped him.

Fuck Saint. Fuck his gorgeous mouth and that incinerating stare. Fuck everything about him.

When I'd asked him to go public and tell my dad about us, he said it was too fucked-up, too depraved, Aris would never forgive him, blah, blah, blah. Those were his hang-ups, not mine, but it told me something about him. I didn't like what I'd learned. In the battle between my father and me, Saint would always choose him. I wouldn't be with someone who didn't put me first.

I saw the love my dad had for Penny, what Alba had with her fiancé, KC. I wanted that with a desperation that chafed. If Saint wouldn't give it to me, I'd find someone who would. Being abducted by Benito Caputi had put a lot of things into perspective and made me question my choices. I wouldn't be anyone's dirty little secret, not anymore. Life was too damn short.

"You ready?" I asked Lore when he stood.

"Yeah. Let's roll." He wrapped an arm over my shoulders, and I grabbed his fingers, a blatant display of familiarity between us.

Feast your eyes on that, you fucker.

"Oh, and Ru?" Saint's voice came from the doorway to the stairs, and I stopped, shooting a death glare in his direction. His predatory stare hit me in the gut, like he meant to circle me until I got weak enough for him to make an easy strike. "Clean the floors when you open tomorrow."

Fury surged in my veins, and I clamped my teeth together so hard that I thought I might break a molar. He'd given me a direct order in front of someone he believed I was fucking. As my sort-of boss, he had that right, but that wasn't the tone he'd used. No, that meant, *Get on your fucking knees.*

Read Savage Saint anywhere you get your books

ACKNOWLEDGMENTS

Dear Reader, thank you for picking up my motorcycle club story. I couldn't do this without your support. I appreciate every one of you.

There are a lot of people that helped me get here, most prominently my husband and best friend, who fed me and loved me while I locked myself away to create my stories. (You haven't known true partnership until you've emerged from a three day writing sprint, disheveled and disgusting, only to have your husband call you beautiful and say you "don't stink *that much.*")

To my life sisters, Sarah and Tori, thank you for being my tribe while we walk this twisted path together. I send a lot of love to my my alpha and beta readers, Leslie, Maggie, and Jen, thank you for your early input and support.

To Dr. C. You were the first person who ever made me cry over my work, but you were also the first person to encourage me to publish once it was ready. I suspect you'd cringe and roll your eyes if you knew what I'm writing now. Like I always said, the canon is bullshit.

Cheers!

ALSO BY JENA DOYLE

<u>MIDSUMMER</u>

We Wild Things (Novella)

Midsummer

Samhain

Solstice

Beltane

<u>STEEL ROSES MC</u>

They Called Him Saint (Novella)

Crimson Chaos

Savage Saint

Oleander Oaths

Mischief Mayhem

Ruthless Reign

<u>ROYAL BASTARDS MC: HELENA, MT</u>

Blood and Whiskey

Caves and Claws (Novella)

Blood and Magic

Heats and Holidays (Novella)

Blood and Trouble

<u>ROYAL HARLOTS MC: ASHEVILLE, NC</u>

Filthy Little Witch